Finding Starlight

SHANNON NIKOLE

Finding Starlight

Chase the light,
Whatever
And wherever
It may be
For you.
Chase it.

-Tyler Knott Gregson

Prologue

Ellawyn

Six months ago

I tiptoed toward my side of the bed and crouched down, lifting the side of the comforter that hung down over the mattress and carefully placing it on top of the bed. Holding my breath, desperate not to make any noise, I used my fingernails to pry up a piece of the floorboard.

My heartbeat radiated in my chest, beating faster and faster, ticking like a bomb ready to detonate at any given moment.

And there'd be no one to sort through the wreckage if that happened.

I pulled on the floorboard with all my might, wiggling it until it finally gave way. I slumped back onto the floor, gripping the piece of wood to my chest, and let out the breath I'd been holding. I carefully placed the floorboard next to me and shifted so I could reach inside the small space.

It only took a few seconds to find the envelope I'd kept hidden there for over a year. My secret hiding spot hadn't been discovered. The corners of my mouth tipped up as relief coursed through my veins.

Though, I'd have known if it were.

I opened the envelope, checking the contents inside as I heard a truck pull into the driveway. I abruptly sat up as the sound of a door being slammed radiated throughout the house.

Tick, tick, tick.

Panic laced my movements as I rushed to untie the laces of my right boot. I yanked it off as fast as I could while I listened to the heavy footsteps come up the steps.

He was early today. This could ruin everything.

I grabbed the floorboard that I'd removed and ducked my head underneath the bed, placing it down as softly as I could.

I jumped up and pushed the comforter back down where it belonged before sitting on the edge of the bed. After shoving the envelope inside my boot, I quickly placed my foot back inside, concealing my secret.

Just as the doorknob turned, I bent over and started tying the laces of my boots, hoping my heartbeat wasn't as loud as I thought.

I didn't turn when I heard him enter the room or when his footsteps thudded across the old wooden floor. It wasn't until he was directly in front of me that he addressed me.

"What are you doing?" he barked.

I swallowed, trying to remain calm as I finished tying my boot. When I met his gaze, the anger was palpable, his eyes narrowed in a heated glare.

I cleared my throat. "I was just cleaning up here and about to start lunch." I placed my hands on the edge of the bed before getting the courage to stand.

His nostrils flared before he shoved my shoulders, pushing me back down onto the bed. The pain from the contact pulsed through my shoulder blades as I tried to move. I closed my eyes, grateful to have landed on a soft bed . . . this time.

"You should have had lunch done by the time I got home," he shouted.

I winced, glancing at the clock on my nightstand and noting

the time. "You're home two hours earlier than normal. I couldn't have known."

He took a few steps back and crossed his arms over his chest as his lips curled in disgust. "Sounds like some bullshit excuse to me, Ellawyn." He started for the door and turned. "You don't fucking work. You could have called to see when I'd be home."

I had to bite my tongue to keep from reminding him that I didn't have a job because he wouldn't let me. He didn't trust me enough. I pushed myself up to a seated position and rubbed my shoulders one at a time. I didn't feel like arguing with him this time. I simply nodded and kept my gaze on the wall in front of me. "I'll be down in a minute, Joshua."

"Don't bother. I'm going back to work. See if you can manage getting to the grocery store on time this afternoon."

The door slammed closed, and my body shook at the intensity. A strangled breath escaped my lungs as I wrapped my arms around myself. Even my own touch was comforting—a reminder that I hadn't had a hug in so long.

I listened as his footsteps thundered down the steps.

It wasn't until I heard the car door slam shut that I sprang into action. I went to my closet and pulled out my favorite coat that my mother had given me, along with a beanie and gloves. I tossed the garments on the bed before I walked to my nightstand and removed the drawer from the track.

The contents dropped to the bed with a light thud as I dumped the drawer and took in what had fallen out: my birth certificate, social security card, phone chargers, hair ties, and other useless junk. I plucked up the social security card and birth certificate and placed them into the small section of my purse. I grabbed my wallet next and pulled out my bank and credit cards, then placed them into the bottom of the drawer, underneath all the useless items. The cards were useless to me; he monitored everything I purchased. Every penny spent, he questioned. He knew how much groceries ran weekly, and if I spent over the typical amount, he'd pounce on me, demanding the receipt. There had been no trust in even the miniscule things.

Lastly, I took my cell phone off the charger, powered it down, and placed it into the drawer. The cell phone didn't hold any amount of power either. It'd been a monitoring device that tracked my location at all times. The phone calls and texts had all been checked daily. The only contact in my phone was him.

I'd had no escape. I'd become a prisoner in my own life.

I took one last look around the bedroom I shared with Joshua. The walls were painted bright white, and everything else in the room matched. There wasn't anything warm about the space. No colorful, cozy blankets or throw pillows. Just white everywhere. And white showed everything—flaws and mistakes. *My flaws and mistakes.*

The room was as cold as a prison and Joshua as rough as a hardened criminal in a shared jail cell.

An escape was imminent.

I'd been planning my own disappearance for over a year. I'd found the perfect small town tucked away in Pennsylvania to start over in.

After today, Moon Harbor, Maine would be a distant memory.

And I'd become a ghost, haunted by my past.

CHAPTER 1
Ellawyn

"GOOD MORNING, ELLAWYN," Benji greeted me as soon as I walked through the door of his bookshop. "You're the one good thing I can count on each day." He pulled me into a quick hug before he reached around me to flip over the CLOSED sign that hung in the window.

About six months ago, I'd ended up leaving my hometown of Moon Harbor, Maine and relocating to Quimby Grove, Pennsylvania in a bit of a hurry. But Quimby Grove had become my saving grace, and along with the charming small town, came Benji's bookstore, Starlight Books.

I'd lucked out and stumbled upon the quaint bookstore on my first day in town and had instantly fell in love with it.

And I'd spent every single day there since.

There's something calming about hiding out in Starlight Books. In fact, this lovely treasure is exactly that—a hideout.

Benji, the owner, was a kind old man with graying hair and a huge heart who allowed me to encroach on his territory, and as a bonus, didn't ask questions of the young woman who stayed here all day and all night.

"Good morning, Benji," I answered as I approached the counter.

I pulled my wallet out of my tote bag, and my sketch pad and pencils went flying to the ground. I stifled a groan as I bent down to pick them up. "I'd like my usual, please."

Benji belly laughed as he watched me pick up what I'd dropped. "Are you ever going to order something different?"

Every day, like clockwork, I ordered the same thing—a vanilla latte and a blueberry lemon scone.

And every day he gave me a hard time.

"What can I say? I'm a creature of habit."

"You're a creature all right. You're in luck, though, I just finished making you your beloved beverage," Benji teased as he placed my latte and scone on the counter and shooed my hand away when I tried to hand him a ten-dollar bill.

I stood tall and stuck my tongue out at him while we laughed at each other.

Once he stepped away, I snuck the money into his tip jar and went over to my usual spot in the far corner of the store—the spot where I had a perfect view of the entrance.

Once settled, I gathered my supplies for the day—a notebook, a sketch pad, and pencils—and placed them on the table in front of me.

I took a moment and breathed in the comforting aromas of coffee, new books, and fresh pastries. As I listened to Benji while he worked behind the counter, humming to the radio, I felt at peace for the first time in a long time.

I sipped my latte and decided to dive headfirst into the project that had been haunting me for months on end—a mixed media piece based on a poem I wrote not too long ago.

Taking a deep breath, I let myself remember that time of my life. The pain rushed back in flashes as I was transported to the difficult time that tainted my past. Suddenly, I couldn't catch my breath.

My eyes stung with the threat of tears. I desperately tried to blink them away and force my attention back into my project, reminding myself that now wasn't the time to get emotional.

My hand worked on muscle memory as I picked up the pencil and placed it against my sketch pad. The long strokes of my lines covered the page as I worked to bring to life what had lingered within my heart for so long.

Hours must have passed while I'd gotten lost in the art, having zoned out and sketched until my hand cramped up. When I sat back and risked a glance down to where my sketch pad was resting on the table, I couldn't help the small gasp that escaped.

My finger carefully traced the outline of the broken girl that resided on the page and the attached strings that had begun to snap.

A puppeteer's doll, a real-life marionette.

I could see what my heart felt like during those months, and it wasn't a happy picture. I'd left everything that I loved, and once loved, back in Moon Harbor. I'd left my parents, who were everything to me. I'd left my favorite cousins, who were more like best friends than family. And I'd left my abusive ex-boyfriend.

Everyone from my life back home had been cut off. I couldn't risk having my ex-boyfriend find me. I had to do something to survive.

I had to run.

So, I'd planned and disappeared from my old life and hoped that I'd taken enough precautions to not be found. Despite giving up so much, I was incredibly lucky to be in Starlight Books in Quimby Grove. I was safe here.

And while Benji didn't know my story, I felt supported by him as well.

I cast a glance around the bookstore, wanting to check on Benji, and noticed he was in the middle of working the lunch rush. Benji was a one-man show here at Starlight Books. He did the prep work each morning, made the food throughout the day, ran the counter, bussed the tables, and closed the place down. I'd never seen anyone else work here throughout the six months I'd been around. It was a lot of work for one person, but even when

I'd offered to help, he'd declined and said that he thrived in the madness.

"Chaos is beauty" is what he'd always told me.

Placing my sketch pad down, I decided to take a break and let myself people watch instead.

The store was filled to the brim with customers today. Younger children sat with their parents on the couch by the window, eating cookies and laughing at the book their parents were reading them. Teenagers took over a few of the tables and sat arguing over whether movie adaptations were superior to books.

The book is always better.

I had to refrain from chiming in, and instead, kept surveying the store.

Next, were a handful of older couples enjoying coffee together and catching up during their lunch breaks. And a lot of lovey-dovey couples that seemed to be around my age that couldn't stop staring into each other's eyes or keep their hands off each other.

A pang of jealousy hit, and I immediately pushed the thought from my mind. I reminded myself that being single wasn't the end of the world. I'd rather be safe and alone than in a terrible relationship. In fact, I was perfectly content on my own.

"Ellie?" Benji appeared at my side.

I snapped myself out of my people-watching daze and turned to give Benji my attention. "Hey, Benji." I leaned forward to rest my forearms on the table, covering up my sketch. "How was the lunch rush?"

Benji shuffled to the chair across from mine and joined me. "It was good. Busy is always best in a business like mine." He chuckled. "Will you be around until closing tonight?"

I paused for a moment, my body stiffening as I considered my words. "Yeah, of course. Unless you're growing tired of me."

My mind instantly went into worst-case-scenario mode, worrying that my presence had become burdensome.

"Never, dear girl." Benji leaned over the table and snagged my notebook out from under my arms before I could stop him. "Oh,

Ellawyn..." He studied the sketch for a moment. "I'm so glad to see you working on your art. I'm quite proud of you." He nodded toward the sketchbook.

Heat crept up my cheeks with embarrassment. I'd never felt comfortable having attention centered around me in any capacity, but it always felt more vulnerable, rawer, whenever someone saw a piece of art I'd created.

Feeling unsure of how to respond to the compliment, I simply smiled at him. "Thanks." I pulled my sketch pad back toward me, placing it in my lap this time. "I appreciate that."

Benji stood and came to stand beside me, placing a hand on my shoulder. "I'd like to talk to you about something tonight after we close, okay?"

I nodded just before Benji squeezed my shoulder and went back to work.

He stepped up to the counter with a smile plastered on his face, greeting each customer as if they were a part of his family. I hadn't known Benji for long, but he had a way of pulling people in and making them feel cared for. He was like the grandfather I'd never had and the closest thing I had to family in this town.

If Benji wanted to talk this evening, then of course I'd talk with him. But it didn't mean that I wasn't worried about what he might say. We'd never really discussed things that went beyond surface level.

There were never deep conversations about my past or talks about his family. We didn't spend the evenings chatting away. He ran his business while I stayed to myself and either worked in my sketchbook, read books, or daydreamed.

Our friendship was basic, but there was an unspoken agreement that we were there for the other if needed.

I secretly thought Benji enjoyed me hanging around Starlight Books all day and that he considered me family, too.

At least I hoped he did.

☾

THE REST of the afternoon flew by. I went back to finishing my sketch that I'd started earlier in the morning, and by the end of the day, I was happy with what I'd sketched out. I planned to paint the piece in my studio at home as soon as I had the time.

When I first moved to Quimby Grove, I managed to stumble upon a two-bedroom apartment for rent a few blocks away from the bookstore. The master bedroom had been claimed as my own, and I used the second, slightly smaller, bedroom as an art studio.

It wasn't anything fancy, but it worked for me.

It was close enough for me to walk to and from the bookstore each day and anywhere else that I would need to go to within Quimby Grove.

The main part of the town had been dubbed "the Square." It was filled with small-town charm and an abundance of small businesses, such as The Quimby Grove Theatre, Remnant Hearts Bar, Illusion Wine Bar, multiple courthouses, various coffee shops and restaurants, and a lovely church with the most beautiful stained-glass windows I'd ever laid eyes on. There were also rage and axe-throwing rooms and a restaurant dedicated entirely to hot dogs. And then there was Starlight Books.

Quimby Grove Square was the heart of Quimby Grove.

It was full of the light, community, passion, art, and sense of familiarity that came with a small town where everyone knew each other.

People were even beginning to become familiar with me. I'd flown under the radar for the longest time, since I generally only ever went to Starlight Books and my apartment, but I was slowly becoming associated with the town as a more permanent fixture.

The thought of people knowing who I was and recognizing me made me uneasy. My focus since moving here had been to blend in and not draw too much attention to myself. But I couldn't help the warm feeling that often came with people caring for me and asking how I was. Even a smile on the street made me feel good.

Besides in the company of my family, the feeling was somewhat foreign to me.

And because of that, I did my best to cling to the feeling of people caring about me, and I held my breath that the safe world I'd created here didn't get ripped away from me.

I stood and stretched out my limbs after being confined to a chair all day. As I looked out toward the big windows of the bookstore, I was instantly drawn into the beauty of this life.

The street was lined with sparkling lights hanging between the streetlights and even wrapped around the awnings of most storefronts. The sunset tonight looked as if an artist had painted the most perfect cotton candy sky. The old school movie theatre across the street, with the lit-up marquee, beckoned to anyone who passed by.

A beautiful night for a beautiful town.

"Time to close up."

The sudden shock of Benji's voice caused me to practically jump out of my skin. My hand flew to my chest as I tried to slow my racing heart. "You scared me. I didn't hear you come up."

He laughed. "You're so easy to frighten." He jerked his head toward the area of the store with a few couches and a couple armchairs. "Let's sit."

Benji led the way toward the couches as I trailed behind. He chose the armchair while I sunk into the cushions of the comfiest couch I'd ever sat on.

"What's up?" I asked as I grabbed a throw pillow and set it on my lap.

Benji's facial expression changed before my eyes. Gone was the happy-go-lucky man from earlier today. Now, he looked worn down. Exhausted.

My heart ached as he let the mask slip free.

"I'm afraid I'm going to be taking a leave of absence in the near future." His gaze found mine. "I've been diagnosed with a brain tumor."

My hands stilled on the throw pillow, and my mouth dropped open as a small gasp escaped. How could Benji be sick? He was the hardest working, healthiest old man I'd ever known. A million questions raced to my mind. How long had he been sick? What would happen to him? To Starlight Books? He didn't seem sick at all. He was just mopping the floors, for crying out loud.

"Are..." I stammered. "Are you sure?"

He sighed. "I'm sure. I've seen multiple specialists for a second, and hell, a third opinion. I was so sure they'd gotten it wrong. I was certain they'd just made a terrible mistake." Benji's voice trembled as he spoke. "My extended leave of absence is meant to grant me the flexibility to look into treatment options and come up with a plan of attack."

Words couldn't come fast enough. I wasn't sure the right words even existed for this situation. I never would have expected this to happen to someone as kindhearted as Benji. But I guess what they say is true—bad things happen to good people, and situations like this don't discriminate.

I'm stunned by his confession but also thankful that he chose to confide in me.

"Within the next few days, my grandson, Beckett, will be arriving and will hopefully help with Starlight Books while I try to figure all of this out."

"I didn't realize you had a grandson." He'd never mentioned him before. I tried to refrain from asking my next question but couldn't help myself; I needed to know if Benji would have any real support. "It's none of my business, but how did he take the news?"

He gave me a sad smile. "I haven't told him yet. It's not something that should be done over the phone."

I nodded my understanding, clutching the pillow to my chest for comfort.

Benji continued. "I wanted to let you know because I want you to remain comfortable here. Nothing has to change." He leaned over the coffee table to take one of my hands. "I don't know a lot about you Ellie, but I know you must have gone through something terrible before you showed up in Quimby

Grove. You've found a safe place here at Starlight Books, and I want you to continue to have this safe space. Your routine is safe here, do you understand me?"

Tears formed in my eyes as I took in what he'd just told me. "How did you... How did you know that something happened to me? Why would you let me hang around here if you won't be around as much?"

With a squeeze to Benji's hand, I pulled away to snag a tissue from my bag to wipe up the tears that had fallen.

"Ellawyn, you hold on to this place as if it holds the key to your very being. You are family to me, and you are always welcome here whenever you want. Beckett will be told the exact same thing." Benji laughed to himself. "I think you two will have more in common than you'd imagine. He's about twenty-seven years old, and he may be a bit rough around the edges, but he's a good man. I promise you that."

"I hope you know that I consider you family as well. I'll do anything I can to help you."

Even as the words left my mouth, I knew it wasn't enough. My heart broke for Benji. If I could, I would take away all his worries along with his health concerns and make them my own. A man as good as Benji didn't deserve the hardships life had thrown at him.

No one did.

We both stood from our seats and met in the middle for a hug. "I've got to go lock up, and then we can head out for the evening, okay?"

"Okay."

He went to lock up while I sat back down on the couch. He wasn't acting like he was sick, was he? I guessed that was how some illnesses worked. Despite not showing any outward signs of despair, the distress and pain could still linger just beneath the surface. I couldn't see his struggle, but I knew it was there.

It was brewing within me, too. The threat of change lingered in the air, and I knew things would never be the same again.

CHAPTER 2
Beckett

A HAND LANDED on my shoulder. "Sir, if you could please put your seat in an upright position. We're about to make our descent into Harrisburg." The flight attendant flashed a seductive smile and winked.

"Sorry about that," I replied as I straightened my seat.

She frowned when I didn't respond to her flirtation, mumbled a thank-you, and stormed off with disappointment written all over her face.

After shoving my laptop back into its case, I slid the cover on the window up, and gazed down into the city of Harrisburg, Pennsylvania.

It'd been years since I'd set foot in Pennsylvania, and almost just as long since I'd seen my Pops. The last time we had seen each other was about two years ago for Christmas when he had come to visit me in Boston.

The separation hadn't been intentional.

Life had just sort of... happened.

And so had the drift that'd subsequently occurred.

There was no denying that I'd disappointed him with the lack of phone calls and visits within the last two years. So, when he had reached out last week and asked to meet, I'd decided to drop everything to come and visit for two weeks.

I glanced at my watch as I racked my brain, trying to remember how long the commute would be to town. I hoped we'd land in time for me to make it to Quimby Grove before Pop closed Starlight Books for the night.

I couldn't get there fast enough.

WHAT THE ACTUAL FUCK?

I stood at Gate C3 without another soul in sight. Even the people who were on my flight had disappeared into thin air, nowhere to be found.

Harrisburg International Airport was a ghost town. I'd never seen anything like it. Most of my airport experience had been at large cities where the airport had been bustling with activity.

This airport was the opposite.

The smell of antiseptic and lemon had taken over the airport corridors. The lights throughout the terminal were dim, and the metal security gates had been pulled down on the Auntie Anne's and Dunkin Donuts stores without an employee in sight.

I trekked my way to the baggage claim and found a handful of people with their faces glued to their phones while various suitcases passed them by on the carousel.

I rolled my eyes and walked over to my navy blue suitcase. I yanked it from the conveyer belt and noticed a rip in the seam.

Great, first use of the suitcase and it's ruined.

"Mr. Walden," called a familiar voice. "Nice to see you again, sir."

I turned to see my buddy Max closing the gap between us. "Cut that shit out, dude." I laughed and joined him as we made our way outside toward his truck. "I don't need you of all people calling me sir," I quipped.

He chuckled. "I know you have a driver back in Boston, so I'm just trying to make you feel like the royalty that you are." He swung open the back door of his truck.

I mocked his laugh and hit him on the back of the head before I tossed my ripped suitcase onto the backseat. "Hilarious. How about you make yourself useful? Get behind the wheel and get us the hell out of here."

Max is my oldest friend from Quimby Grove, and my best friend. Anytime I'd visited Pops, I'd always be hanging around with Max. We were practically inseparable growing up. He knew all about my life back in Boston—my company, Walden Advertising, my driver, my impossible-to-manage social calendar (ahem, women)—and he loved to rag on me about all of it.

We spent most of the ride catching up on Max's life since it had been so long since we had spoken.

Max owned Remnant Hearts Bar, which was located on the Square in Quimby Grove. Shortly after Max had graduated high school, his dad died and left him the bar. He had worked hard to restore it and had reopened it with a pub-like vibe under a new name.

"How long are you in town for?" Max asked.

"About two weeks. Pops wants to talk about something—not sure what it is—but I don't want to rush the trip."

He turned onto High Street and nodded.

I looked out my window as Quimby Grove Square came into view, and the memories rushed back. The sidewalks were filled with people milling around. Kids skipped by while they laughed, their parents following closely behind with smiles stretched wide. A teenager held open the door to an art gallery for an elderly couple, who appeared grateful for the random act of kindness. The lights on the marquee at the Quimby Grove Theatre lit up the street with its old-time charm.

The town still looked the same; it was almost as if I'd never left. It was good to be back.

"It's been too long, man." My chest tightened—a longing for a place I hadn't been in a while. The desire to be home. "I miss Pops. I miss hanging out with you." I laughed. "Hell, I even miss getting into trouble."

Max smiled. "We did get into trouble, didn't we?"

He pulled up outside of the bar and parked. "Welcome home." We both hopped out of the truck, and I grabbed my suitcase from the backseat and let the door slam shut. "Remnant Hearts once you're settled?"

"Absolutely." I pulled him in for a hug. "Thanks for the lift, dude."

He nodded. "Enjoy surprising Benji," he added before he disappeared inside the bar.

My gaze darted across the street, and I spotted Starlight Books almost instantly. The tightening in my chest completely vanished.

Starlight Books was home.

I'd been lucky enough to have grown up in an establishment filled with books. While money was too tight to go on grand vacations, I'd never been shortchanged on adventure. That was the beauty of being brought up with books—I had escaped into the fantasy of the books I read, which meant I had the pleasure of traveling with characters who felt like family. I'd learned that with books around, I never truly had to feel alone.

A smile spread across my face as I caught a glimpse of Pops through the storefront windows. He was organizing books, placing them back within their proper spot on the bookshelves.

After a quick look each way, I jogged across the street and whipped the door open to Starlight Books as I rushed toward him. "Pops! I'm home!"

"Beckett, my boy! I didn't know you were getting in tonight. You should have told me." He closed the distance between us, pulling me in for a big hug.

I squeezed him back and then pulled away to look at him. "I wanted to surprise you." I strolled around the store and took in the changes that Pops had made over the past few years, feeling relieved to find that not much had changed. "I'm here for two weeks."

Pops's face paled briefly. "That's great," he said as he began to walk away. "Let me finish up in the back, and I'll meet you at a table."

He didn't wait for a response and headed straight for the only customer in the store, a young woman who sat toward the back of the shop. He said something to her that caused her eyes to snap up in my direction. Our gazes locked on each other for a moment before she returned her attention back to Pops as he sat down to join her.

After forcing myself to look away, I walked to the front of the store to take a seat and positioned myself so I could continue watching their interactions from afar. I studied her, trying to take in everything that I could about her and commit it to memory.

She was captivating. She had long, wavy, dark hair—almost black—with dark eyes, a curvy figure, and skin so fair that I worried she'd never seen sunlight before. She was dressed in black leggings with a long, flowy maroon top and she didn't have a drop of makeup on her face.

Just looking at her stirred a longing I'd never felt before. She was beautiful without even trying—perfection personified. And I wanted more. I wanted to know her story and all the messy details in between. Anything and everything.

She seemed to be listening to Pops—not contributing much to the conversation, but the way they interacted gave away that they were rather close.

After a few minutes had passed, they both stood, and the woman packed up her belongings. They strode toward me as he escorted her to the door, wishing her a goodnight.

I tried to put the pieces together but came up short. "Uh, Pops." I raised my eyebrow. "Who the hell was that?"

He looked at me as if I'd lost my mind. "I'm not sure what you're insinuating, but she's a regular customer here."

"A customer"—none of this was making sense—"who hangs around late at night?"

He sighed and sat down across from me as the silence filled the space. His body looked tense, his fingers fidgeting. Something was weighing heavily on his mind and putting him through hell.

"What's going on?" I asked.

He cleared his throat and placed his hands on his lap. "I have something I need to tell you, and I'm not quite sure how to say it."

His expression was somber, and his face had lost some of its color. I leaned forward and rested my arms on the table. "It's okay, Pops. What is it? Do you need help with finances? You know I'd do anything I can to help you and this business." I found myself spewing anything I could think of while I desperately tried to put the pieces together.

His gaze dropped to the floor. "I appreciate that more than you know. I've... I've become ill." He paused. "I've recently been diagnosed with a brain tumor, and soon I'll have to make arrangements to step away from Starlight Books so I can begin treatment."

A lump formed in my throat. I felt like an asshole. Suddenly overwhelmed with emotion, I took a breath as a million questions popped into my head at once. "A brain tumor? What type of brain tumor? I know there are different types, right? Some worse than others, I think. When does treatment begin? What can I do?"

I leapt into full-on panic mode. "Tell me what I can do to help, and I'll make it happen. I can get you the best doctors back in Boston." I stood abruptly. "We can leave tonight. Let's get you packed."

I went to grab my suitcase, but I stopped in my tracks as Pops raised his voice.

"Beckett, stop. There's no need for all of that. Sit back down."

I returned to my seat as he went to the counter and began making us coffee. "Lock the door, would you?"

I did as he requested, confused about what was happening, while he grabbed our coffees and nudged his head toward the couches in the corner of the store.

After we were both seated on the couch, he picked up the conversation where we'd left off. "I'm afraid I don't have many answers right now." He sipped his coffee and let out a breath. "I'm not sure of the type of tumor yet. I need a biopsy. But don't you worry, we'll get it figured out. I don't want to go to Boston for treatment, though. I want to stay here at home in Quimby Grove."

My heart felt like it had begun to chip away. Not only did Pops have a brain tumor but he'd refused my help. "Okay, but what can I do to help?"

He shrugged his shoulders before letting his gaze find the floor. "I'm afraid I'm going to have to close Starlight Books for quite some time. I thought perhaps I could find someone to cover for me, but I don't have anyone that dependable, except for Ellawyn. I know how busy you are, Beckett. I hope you understand the position I'm in."

The thought of Starlight Books being closed for any amount of time was like a dagger to the heart. This store had been Pops's biggest accomplishment—his childhood dream. I couldn't let it end like this.

"What if I take over the operations of Starlight Books?" I watched as he hesitated, and I knew exactly what he was about to say. "I'm not too busy." I sat up straighter and squared my shoulders as if preparing for battle. "The best part about my company is that I'm the one in charge, and I can take time away from the office. The business practically runs itself, and what I can't handle remotely, my VP can handle there. What's most important to me is you, Pops. You come first. You and Starlight Books. I'm staying and helping."

As Pops's eyes filled with tears, he pulled me into his arms for a hug. His body shook uncontrollably while he let his emotions run free. The tears soaked my shirt, and my heart broke a little bit more as his sobs escaped his throat.

We'd get through this. There was no other option. I couldn't lose Pops. I refused to. If that meant taking over Starlight Books so he could seek treatment, then so be it.

☾

WHEN I WOKE up the following morning, my body was stiff from falling asleep on the couch with my laptop clutched to my chest.

After I'd gotten home, the weight of the bomb that Pops had dropped hit me like a ton of bricks. The conversation had replayed on a loop in my head for hours as I tried to imagine how things would change for us.

But I couldn't wrap my head around it. I couldn't grasp it—it wasn't tangible yet. I couldn't imagine my life without Pops, so the decision to stay in Quimby Grove had been easy. After I'd shot off an email to the VP of Walden Advertising, Kennon, letting him know I'd be in Pennsylvania indefinitely due to a family emergency, I'd fallen down a vicious spiral online and researched everything I could find about brain tumors.

My brain was full of worst-case scenarios, and I couldn't help but feel a bit defeated, but it didn't stop me from lying on the couch all night with my laptop.

And now I was sore and late getting to Starlight Books for the day. Oh, and it was pouring rain, and I didn't have a car in Quimby Grove yet.

What a great start.

I hurried throughout the house, grabbing my clothes for the day, and quickly showered and shaved before getting ready to leave for the bookstore. After tearing apart the garage, I'd managed to find an umbrella, thankful not to have to get drenched on the way in.

The walk into town seemed longer than it had last night. The sidewalks leading to the Square were deserted as the rain pelted down, and the car traffic was almost non-existent. I couldn't help but notice the irony of the morning—caught in a downpour, alone.

As I hurried through the rain, I made a mental note to get a car to keep in Quimby Grove so I would have it in poor weather or to take Pops to doctor's appointments. Pops liked to walk everywhere or, if it was a further distance, he'd take the bus, and I definitely didn't want him taking the bus with a weakened immune system.

Perhaps two cars—one for me and one for Pops.

When I finally arrived at Starlight Books, the place was bustling with business. Pops was behind the counter, giving an older woman her change along with her coffee order. He was all smiles as he waved the next customer forward. The couches and chairs in the front corner of the store were all occupied, and the tabletops were well on their way to being filled as well.

After saying hello to a few familiar faces, I headed toward Pops and noticed the same woman from last night sitting in the very same seat. I strode past her, not giving her a second glance. "Morning, Pops," I said as I hurried behind the counter. "Busy morning?"

He smiled. "Morning, Beckett." He poured two cups of black coffee and placed one in front of where I stood. "What are you doing here so early?"

He couldn't have possibly forgotten last night's conversation already, could he? "Pops, I'm here to help with the store." I took a sip of my coffee. "We agreed that I'd take over operations of the business so you can focus on your treatments."

He laughed. "Oh, you knucklehead, of course I didn't forget. I'm just messing with you." He grabbed an apron and held it out to me. "Ready to work?"

Over the next two hours, Pops and I worked side by side. He'd greet the customers and take their orders while I made the drinks and food. And then we'd both take turns serving. Whenever we had a lull in business, I'd look out into the shop and see that the dark-haired beauty was still here, hunched over a sketchbook.

The inexplicable pull toward her hadn't dulled overnight. Pushing the thoughts away, I refocused on Pops.

"Beckett, good work this morning, my boy." Pops grabbed a rag and ran it over the surface of the front counter. "The shop runs smoothly with the two of us at the helm. I could get used to this. If I weren't stepping back, that is." His shoulders slumped and he bowed his head after his admission.

The reality of the situation seemed to be hitting him. I was about to interject when his entire demeanor changed. In a matter of seconds, he plastered on his normal, happy face and turned back to me. "Well, it's slow now. Why don't we go into the kitchen and start the lunch prep?" He dropped the rag back into the bucket below the counter. "I have a bell above the door that will ring when someone enters."

He took off toward the kitchen, and I followed suit. We began prepping salads for the lunch rush in silence. After a few minutes of work, I decided to bring up the transportation issue in hopes that it would alleviate some of his stress.

"I realized today that I need to get a car since I'll be staying in Quimby Grove." I placed a head of lettuce on the cutting board and chopped it up. "I was hoping we could go car shopping together and get you one too."

Pops's movements came to a halt, and he turned to face me with his nostrils flaring. He stepped toward me and planted his legs wide. "I appreciate the offer. But I do not need you coming in and trying to fix things. You may have to take control of everything in Boston, but that's not what I need here." He sighed. "I'm sorry. I know you mean well. Your heart is in the right place, but I don't need a car of my own."

The knife stilled in my hand as I processed what he'd said. I hadn't considered that he would think that I was just trying to fix everything. Back in Boston, whenever something could be improved, I'd hop into problem solving mode, take control, and rectify the situation. If something was broken, I'd fix it. "I didn't mean to offend you, but I think this is something I could do to—"

"Do you know what I need?" he interjected. "I need you, Beckett. Not your money, or your ability to solve everyone's problems. I simply need you. I need your love. Your support. Your patience. And most importantly, your understanding." He looked at me as tears formed in his eyes. "I need my family. Can you understand that?"

"Of course." I stepped toward him and placed a hand on his shoulder. "But you need to tell me when you do truly need something and allow me to help if I can. You're my only family, Pops. You matter. And I'm here for you in any way that I can be."

He leaned toward me and pulled me in for a hug. Without another word, we both retreated into finishing the mundane task of lunch prep.

I was drenched with sweat by the time we finished the lunch rush. I snagged a bottle of water and leaned against the counter as Pops began another order. He grabbed two slices of bread, buttered them, and then walked to the refrigerator door and brought out two slices of cheese.

He finished making the grilled cheese sandwich, plated it, and then grabbed a bottle of water before he left for the front end of the shop.

I followed him out and covered the counter while he delivered the sandwich to the dark-haired woman. She glanced up at Pops with a sweet smile while she dug out her wallet and tried to pay him. He shook his head and waved her off.

When Pops returned behind the counter, he went straight for the kitchen.

The second the kitchen door swayed closed, I followed him. "Okay, Pops. What gives with that woman out there?" I raised my arm and gestured to the bookshop area, where the mysterious woman was seated. "She was here at closing last night and back at opening today. And she's still here. That's weird."

He glared in my direction as he continued to clean up the mess from the prep work we did earlier. He grabbed one of the cutting boards and let it drop into the sink with a loud thud.

"Is she... homeless?" I guessed. "There are shelters in Quimby Grove. We can take her, if needed. Shit, I'll drive her myself."

"Beckett Walden," he snapped. "How dare you judge someone so harshly."

I put my hands in the air. "I just don't want you or Starlight being taken advantage of."

"Beckett, go see the wizard and get yourself a heart, why don't you? That young lady out there has gone through something terrible. I don't know the details, and even if I did, it wouldn't be my story to share." He sighed and sat down on one of the stools in the kitchen. "Her name is Ellawyn. She showed up around town about six months ago. She's about twenty-four-years old and sweet as pie."

He took a swig from his water bottle before he continued. "She has an apartment somewhere in town, so no, she's not homeless. She doesn't take advantage of anything, and I know this because, every day, I disappear into the kitchen and come back to see that the tip jar has an extra ten dollars in it. The girl overpays for a lousy grilled cheese sandwich. She's here almost every day, all day long. I'm not sure why, but she doesn't hurt anything by being here. She's a paying customer and works on her art. She's family." He narrowed his eyes at me. "And Beckett"—he held my gaze—"I'm saying this now. If she chooses to stick around when I'm gone, you will allow it and not kick her out or hurt that girl in any way."

Pops just scolded me, and I don't even have a response. I hadn't realized she was family. "She's part of our family?" I questioned.

"She isn't. But just because she doesn't have my blood

running through her veins doesn't mean she's not my family." He stood from the stool and retreated to the front of the shop.

When I went back to the counter, I looked inside the tip jar and saw a twenty-dollar bill that hadn't been there before.

Well, I'll be damned.

CHAPTER 3
Ellawyn

Benji was the epitome of a cool, calm, collected person, even after being diagnosed with a brain tumor. Maybe even more so. I couldn't wrap my head around how well he was holding himself together. He was doing a much better job than I was, and I wasn't the one who was ill. When I thought about my days at Starlight without him, I couldn't picture it. He made me feel at home here, never once placing judgment on me for having spent all my time at his store.

Now it was my turn to repay the favor and be strong for him. This transition couldn't be easy for him, especially with his grandson back in town. It would be a lot for anyone to handle.

I couldn't deny that I was intrigued by Benji's grandson. I'd caught him watching me earlier, and I could practically feel him judging me, and then I'd seen it written all over his smug face.

His handsome, smug face.

Who wouldn't be smug if they looked like that? I wasn't in a position for anything, but I wasn't blind, either.

He was tall, probably over six foot if I had to guess. He had dark brown hair that was a little longer on the top—long enough to style—and he had a scruffy-beard situation going on. It was well maintained and suited him. His eyes, though—they were what drew me in, captivating me and holding me hostage. They were a lighter shade of blue, almost gray looking, like a rough storm out at sea, where I was destined to lose all sense of direction and be lost in the world that was him. If not for a compass to guide me back to true north, I wasn't sure I'd ever recover from a man like him.

A shatter coming from behind the counter pulled me back into the real world and away from my daydream about the mystery man. I turned toward where the noise had come from and saw him rolling up his sleeves in preparation of cleaning up the broken glass on the floor. My cheeks heated with a mixture of attraction and embarrassment. His forearms were a canvas full of artwork. An unfamiliar story spread across every inch of his skin, leaving no space untouched. He looked like a dream with his sleeves rolled up to his elbows.

I didn't think I'd ever seen anyone with so many tattoos. My hand formed a fist as I desperately ignored the desire to run my fingers across his skin—as if tracing the ink and feeling his warm skin under my fingertips would let me become familiar with the intricacies of his life, of his story. The pull to know more about him was strong.

But I was stronger.

Turning my gaze away, I refocused on my art piece. My rough draft of my mixed media piece was almost complete. The piece would have artwork that connected to my poem, along with pieces pulled from the poem itself. Alongside the canvas, the full poem would be written out.

Nausea took over my stomach as my nerves intensified. Art was subjective, but my words next to it? My thoughts, my feelings, would be crystal clear to anyone who took the time to read the poem. Bearing my soul for the world to see wasn't something I ever thought I'd do. I didn't want to be pitied or looked at differently.

Benji approached with the biggest grin I'd ever seen, holding a plate with a grilled cheese sandwich on it. "Ellie girl, I have a brilliant idea I'd like to run by you."

My stomach let out a growl, and I laughed when Benji passed me the plate. "Hey, Benji. You're in a good mood today." I gestured for him to sit with me. "What's your idea?"

I bit into the sandwich and let myself enjoy the delicious mix of the melted cheeses. Grilled cheese would always be a favorite meal of mine, and I'd been having one for lunch every day for six months.

"Well... I don't want to intrude with what I'm about to ask you."

Cue internal freak-out. *What could he possibly want to ask me that would be an intrusion?* Mentally, I start to run through all the possible scenarios. I'd been so caught up in my thoughts that I almost missed what he was trying to ask me.

"I thought you might like to display some of your completed art here at Starlight Books." He pointed toward my sketch pad. "The piece you've been working on the past few days is quite wonderful, and I'd be honored to display it."

My mouth gaped open, but no response came.

"It could also give you the chance to list it for sale," Benji quickly added. "No pressure, but I thought it might be a good start for you." He looked like he was genuinely interested—it was touching. No one had ever cared about my artwork before.

"That's so sweet," I began as I looked down to my sketch pad. "But, um, I'm not sure if my artwork would... fit? Some of my pieces can be a bit on the darker side."

He smiled. "It wouldn't matter to me if it were a rainbow or something much more sinister than that." He picked up my sketch pad and looked at the sketch. "I'm insanely proud of how dedicated you are to your art. I'd love for it to have a spot here. Starlight isn't just for books, coffee, and pastries, you know. It's for the creatives, the dreamers, and the believers. And you, dear girl, are all of those things and so much more."

"Thank you so much." I hesitated as I considered his offer. I hadn't felt so supported in such a long time. But displaying my work was a huge step for me, both professionally and personally. I'd come to Quimby Grove to start fresh, so maybe this was the next step for me. A little push to put myself out there more.

"That means so much. I'm scared, but... I think I want to do it. I had planned on finishing the piece tonight. Can I bring it in tomorrow morning?"

Now that he'd offered to display my work here, I needed to get the piece finished as soon as possible before I chickened out of a great opportunity.

"Absolutely," Benji replied. He stood and bent down to give me a hug. "I'll give you a few minutes to yourself, but then I'd like to introduce you to my grandson."

"Sure, that'd be lovely."

Anxiety took root as soon as Benji stepped away. My focus in Quimby Grove had been to fly under the radar, and I'd thought I'd done a good job. Things were quickly changing, though. Having my artwork displayed was one of those scary changes, but now being formally introduced to Benji's grandson was another.

I was almost positive he would be much more social than his grandfather. It was only a matter of time until word spread of the weird girl who hung out at Starlight Books all day.

Ugh, this is not good.

I turned my attention back to Benji as he stood behind the cash register, laughing. His grandson's smile instantly lit up the room as he wrapped an arm around Benji's shoulder.

Maybe I didn't have anything to worry about him after all. Maybe he was just as kindhearted as his grandfather. Benji said something, and in an instant, the grandson's eyes bolted up to meet my gaze.

Busted. He totally noticed me sitting here watching them. My palms felt clammy, and the heat rose in my cheeks as he smirked and gave me a wink before nodding at Benji.

Pretending to be busy, I forced myself to look down at my sketch pad again. But instead of getting back to work on my piece,

I continued watching him out of the corner of my eye as he strode around the counter and cleared his throat.

"Ladies and gentlemen, I apologize for the short notice, but Starlight Books will be closed for the remainder of the day." His voice carried over the entire shop. "We have an unforeseen family matter that we have to take care of today." He went over to the counter and reached behind it, grabbing a stack of cards. "As a thank you for your understanding, we have meal and drink vouchers that can be redeemed within the next year."

He made his way over to the door as the other customers in the store stood to evacuate. Grabbing my belongings to leave, my thoughts wandered to how his voice sounded just moments ago. There was something deeply hypnotic that had completely mesmerized me. The deep husky tone was comforting and smooth—a total surprise to how I had envisioned it. By the time I'd finished getting everything tucked away in my tote, the hand-some grandson was walking toward me.

Suddenly on alert, I watched his every movement until he stopped next to me, bending down until his mouth was near my ear. The warmth of his breath caused my reserve to melt away in a flash, and I trembled.

"You stay," he whispered before he sauntered back toward the door.

Trying to decide if I should stay or leave, I glanced around the shop for any sign of Benji, but he was nowhere to be found. After a moment of contemplation, I tugged my tote bag over my shoulder and headed toward the exit. But before I could reach the door, Handsome stepped directly in front of me, blocking my way, and locked the door.

I watched his precise movements as he flipped the OPEN sign around so that it'd now display CLOSED.

When he finally turned to face me, I crossed my arms over my chest defiantly and tried to keep my nerves at bay. Being this close to an attractive man again, especially a stranger, brought a lot of my fears to the forefront of my mind. I suddenly felt small and weak, but I held my pose like a shield of armor and refused to play into my insecurities.

He threw his head back in laughter, and just like that, he found a chink in my armor as it crumbled down.

I dropped my arms as my hands shook, suddenly feeling like crawling into a hole. My insecurities came back in flashes, and waves of shame overtook me.

He seemed to notice my demeanor change, and he stepped forward to take my hand and led me to one of the couches in the corner of the bookstore. "I'm sorry if I made you uncomfortable." He gestured toward the couch. "Have a seat, I'll be right back."

I placed my head in my hands as I realized I'd made a complete fool out of myself. He was probably telling Benji all about how weird I acted.

Would I ever be able to stop feeling so insecure and small?

The sound of footsteps nearby caused me to pull my head from my hands and sit up a little straighter.

He plopped down next to me on the couch as he extended his arm toward me with a glass of water.

"Thanks," I said without a glance in his direction.

He didn't say anything more—not that I'd expected him to. But I surprised myself by wishing he would have.

Before I could consider these feelings, Benji appeared and took a seat in the chair directly across from where we sat. He looked between the two of us until he caught his grandson's gaze. "This young lady is named Ellawyn, and she's quite the artist."

Next, he turned his attention to me. "Ellawyn, this is my grandson, Beckett. He's my only family left." His gaze flickered back to Beckett for a moment. "He has his own successful company back in Boston, and I'm very proud of him."

The corners of Beckett's mouth curved. The love and mutual respect shared between the pair was clearly special.

Witnessing the moment made me feel like an intruder and miss my own family. Not seeing them, or even talking to them, for such a long period of time was starting to take a toll on me. My heart longed to feel that sort of connection again.

To not feel so alone.

Benji cleared his throat and joined his hands together in his lap. "I wanted to discuss the future of Starlight Books and my future within it. My situation calls for transparency, and I'd like to discuss—"

"Thank you for the introductions, Benji, but this sounds like a family matter. I should probably go."

He waved his hand, dismissing the idea. "Nonsense. I want you to stay, if you don't mind." He looked me in the eyes with a silent plea, and I knew I wasn't going anywhere.

I nodded. "Okay."

"I'm scheduled for a biopsy tomorrow morning, so I'll need to be away from Starlight Books," Benji continued. "The doctors at Pennsylvania Memorial will remove a sample of tissue for testing. I'll know what type of brain tumor I'm dealing with once the lab processes the results, and then we can determine a course of treatment."

The reality of Benji's situation slammed into me like a freight train. While I'd been processing the details, Beckett had already leapt to Benji's aid.

"We can close Starlight tomorrow and I can go with you to your appointment," Beckett chimed in.

"We can't afford to close the shop tomorrow. I want business to go on as usual."

Beckett furrowed his brow. "You're not going to this appointment by yourself. We can handle closing for a day."

"No," Benji barked. "The store needs to remain open, and someone needs to run it."

Suddenly, both men's attention was on me, but I was unsure why. I blinked. "Did I miss something?"

Beckett and Benji shared a look before Beckett cut to the chase. "She can run the store," he mumbled.

Oh, hell no. There was no way I'd run the store alone. I'd almost never been allowed to do anything alone back in my old life. I stalled and picked up my water with shaking hands. The water spilled over the top as I tried to get a firm grasp of the glass and my emotions. Beckett stared at the water as I set it down without taking a drink.

"I... I'm sorry, Benji. I'm not sure I'm comfortable running the store alone." My voice shook. "I wish I could help."

"I wouldn't expect you to work here at the drop of a hat," Benji responded before he turned to look at Beckett. "You know better, Beckett."

I found myself zoning out as the two of them continued talking about Benji's appointment tomorrow. The situation overwhelmed me, and I couldn't get a firm grasp on how I felt.

Beckett walked toward the counter and grabbed something. When he returned, he subtly held out a bottle of water in my direction while he continued talking.

My gaze lingered on his outstretched hand, feeling touched by the simple yet sweet gesture. I could handle this better if my hands shook. I reached out to grab the bottle, my fingers overlapping his. Beckett didn't rush to move his hand away from mine; instead, he held it there for a long moment before he released his grasp. The warmth of his touch was replaced by a chill that raced through my body.

Did he do that on purpose?

I couldn't imagine him wanting to touch me any longer than possible, but the thought of his hands on me was enough to heat my cheeks with embarrassment. The desire to have him touch me surprised me.

I needed this conversation to end so I could head home and allow some distance between us. An idea suddenly came to me that could solve Benji's problem. "What if I accompany you to your biopsy appointment tomorrow, and Beckett can run the shop?"

They both responded at the same time.

"That'd be perfect," Benji exclaimed.

"Sounds good," Beckett said.

"Awesome." I tugged my tote onto my shoulder and rose from my seat. "I don't have a car, though."

Beckett scoffed. "Neither does Pops." He sprung to his feet and extended a hand for Benji. "How is it safe for either of you to be without cars? Especially you." He stared at me with a perplexed expression. "A woman taking the bus alone? At night?" He shook his head. "Not smart."

That annoyed me. "Listen," I snapped as I placed my hands on my hips, "I don't take the bus unless I have to. I walk mostly, and I can take care of myself."

Beckett raked a hand through his hair as he rolled his eyes. "New plan. You both meet here before the appointment, and I'll order a car service to pick you up and drop you off at the hospital."

"Fine," I muttered before I turned to Benji. "See you around ten tomorrow morning?"

As soon as Benji nodded his agreement and said good night, I stormed out of Starlight Books, letting the door slam closed behind me.

☾

THE WALK home went by in record time.

I marched into my apartment, heading directly for my bedroom, and grabbed a pair of shorts and black V-neck T-shirt. After stripping out of my leggings and sweater, I went into to my art studio and flipped the light switch. The lights flickered briefly before illuminating the messy workspace.

The walls were painted a warm alabaster white, with floral patterns outlined in black and random splashes of emerald and maroon. It was chaos and I loved it. One side of the room had stacks of unused canvases of various sizes all along the wall. The opposite side of the room housed all my completed pieces, organized by theme and then size.

The floor toward the center of the room had been covered in a black tarp to help contain the mess. A barstool and an empty easel awaited me in the center of the room.

I moseyed toward the blank canvases and eyed which size felt right for my vision. I picked up the second largest size and sat it on the easel.

I pulled over the barstool and sat down while I stared at the empty space. My mind went blank while I mentally envisioned how the piece would go. After plucking the black hair tie from my wrist, I piled my hair into a messy bun on top of my head.

I tore myself away from the easel and collected my headphones along with the materials I'd need, then put everything within arm's reach of the canvas.

Because I needed to lose myself in music, I scrolled through my mp3 player and looked for something to put on while I worked. After a moment, I found the perfect song to transport me into the mentality I needed for this piece. I queued up "Volatile" by Relic Hearts to play on a loop.

I stood in front of the canvas while I listened to the song, absorbing the lyrics and allowing myself to tap into those horrible feelings from not too long ago. I let myself latch on to certain lines of the song as if they were an anchor to my emotions. After a moment, I was ready to put my feelings onto the canvas.

"I'm constantly fighting or fading away. I can't even explain, I wish I could escape. The grip that my fears seem to have on my heart."

I snagged a handful of old crumpled-up newspapers from my supply box and flattened them out before I dug my lighter out, flicked it on, and watched the flame dance in front of the canvas.

One at a time, I'd take a piece of newspaper and run the flame over the edges before I quickly pulled it away and extinguished the flame. I ran my thumb and index finger over the edges that I'd torched, the heat from the newspaper radiating through my fingertips as it burned me back. The ashes fell to the floor with my tears.

"What if the fire is setting me free?"

☾

THREE HOURS HAD PASSED by the time I finished working on the piece. Without giving it a second glance, I ambled out of my studio and into my bathroom to look in the mirror.

Boy, I'm a mess. Paint was splattered all over my face, with random pieces of glitter thrown into the mix. When I looked closer, my eyes were red and puffy, and tear streaks stained my cheeks. I must have cried for a while.

I held out my arms and found myself covered in black alcohol ink and smudge marks from my paintbrush. Bits and pieces of other mediums lined my arms and legs as well.

Exhaustion was starting to take over from painting for hours on end.

Leaning into the shower, I turned the nozzle and let the hot water spray from the showerhead before I pulled the shower curtain closed. I tore my paint-stained clothes from my body and dumped them into my hamper before I entered the shower and cleaned myself up.

Once clean, I dressed in my sweatpants and oversized Beatles T-shirt before wandering back into my studio to check out the finished piece with a fresh perspective.

When I reached the easel, the air left my lungs, and I struggled to catch my breath. Tears formed in my eyes, but I quickly swept them away. This was by far my best piece, and my new favorite. Many mediums were incorporated into it. It was pure chaos, and in the center of the madness, a female marionette stood with strings attached that led to the top of the canvas.

The puppet looked so broken after having lost herself to her master's control. The doll had been stripped of her identity, and she was afraid of what was to come and what could have been.

The puppet was me.

And I finally wanted to break free.

CHAPTER 4

Beckett

When I entered Starlight Books, I was hit with the harsh reminder that beginning today, everything would change.

And it started with me opening the store by myself for the first time.

After I relocked the door to the shop, I went behind the counter and started a pot of coffee. While I waited for the coffee to brew, my mind drifted to thoughts of Ellawyn. But if I was honest, she hadn't been far from my mind since the day I'd first seen her.

There was something about her that pulled me in.

I'd been shocked when she offered to go to the biopsy appointment with Pops, but then, I'd been left confused as to why she wouldn't want to cover the shop instead. When I thought back to how jumpy she'd been yesterday, a thought popped into my head. Maybe she just didn't want to be alone. I just wished I could tell if the problem had been her being alone in the shop or being alone in general.

The rich aroma of coffee dragged me away from my thoughts of Ellawyn just as the pot finished brewing.

Grabbing a dark green coffee mug from below the counter, I poured myself a cup of coffee and went into the kitchen where I noticed an old-looking, banged-up small box on top of the table, with a sticky note that read Recipes.

I placed my coffee on the table and removed the sticky note before opening the box. Dozens of recipes were placed within, all carefully labeled for each time of day, including a section solely dedicated to snacks. I flipped through the breakfast section and plucked out the recipes for various muffins and pastries and got to work.

By the time I finished baking and prepping for the morning rush, two hours had passed, and I had ten minutes to spare until opening.

I moseyed out into the shop and refilled my mug before noticing a figure standing outside of the door, but I couldn't see who it was from this distance. I flicked on the lights and moved toward the door, my steps faltering when I saw Ellawyn patiently waiting outside while holding a big wrapped-up canvas in her hand. She was just as beautiful now as she had been yesterday.

I unlocked the door and held it open for her. "Good morning. Come on in."

A smile inched across her mouth. "Morning," she whispered before she brushed past me and made a beeline for her usual table. She carefully set her canvas on the floor and leaned it against her chair before she turned her attention to the wall where her painting would be displayed.

I returned to the counter and kept an eye on her as she stood still, firmly rooted to the exact spot she'd been in since she'd put the painting down. It was like she was in a trance.

I didn't think she even blinked. Deciding to check on her, I went to her table and stood in front of her. "Ellawyn."

She snapped out of whatever had sucked her in and blinked at me. "What?"

"Sit." I moved out of her way and sat across from her chair.

"Oh. Okay." She unglued her feet from where they'd been firmly planted and sat down across from me, folding her hands in her lap as she let her gaze fall. "Did you ask me something?"

"Are you okay?" I gestured to the wall where she'd been staring. "It was like you were hypnotized."

A pink hue crept into her cheeks as she tucked a piece of hair behind her ears. "Ugh." She exhaled. "Yeah. I'm just nervous to display my work for everyone in Quimby Grove to see."

Wanting to comfort her, I leaned forward and placed a hand on her knee. As soon as I touched her, she jumped from her seat as if I'd hurt her.

Pulling my hand back, I stood. "Sorry." I stepped back, wanting to give her some space. "Just trying to be a friend."

When she didn't respond, I strode back to my side of the counter—where I belonged—and started another pot of coffee so I'd be ready for the rush that was due any second. When I looked up to check the door, Ellawyn appeared.

"I'm... I'm sorry. I just startle easily, I guess." She pulled her tote bag off her shoulder and dug through it. "You didn't do anything wrong."

"Wild horses." I waved her off. "What's your usual breakfast order? I'd better learn what our biggest supporter likes." I smiled at her, hoping to make her comfortable.

She returned the smile, and it reached her eyes. This was the first time I'd been close enough to really look at her eyes in the light, and I could get lost in them. They were a deep brown full of depth and secrets, but when the light hit them just right, they melted into golden rays.

Fuck, she was beautiful. I'd do anything to see that smile for the rest of my days here in Quimby Grove.

"That's nice of you," she started. She pulled her wallet from her bag. "I like vanilla lattes and blueberry lemon scones." She extended a twenty-dollar bill in my direction.

"I'm not taking your money." I turned to grab a scone from the display case. "Heated?" I asked as I raised the scone for her to see.

"That'd be great." She watched my every move. "I'd like to pay, though."

"I don't think Pops would want me to charge you," I assured. "Why don't you go have a seat, and I'll bring this out to you when it's done."

The corner of her mouth twitched before she nodded and returned to her seat.

Just as I finished making her latte, the microwave beeped. I grabbed her scone and placed it on a plate with a few napkins.

Still flying high from her smile, I decided to see if I could earn another one.

I grabbed the latte and rounded the counter to meet her at her table. "Here you are," I said as I placed her latte on the table in front of her, along with the plate. "One warm blueberry lemon scone for the prettiest woman in Starlight Books." I gave her my most charming smile.

She turned her head to the side to hide her blush. "I'm the only woman in here, Beckett."

I leaned an arm on the table and bent down to look at her. "Doesn't make it any less true."

I winked at her before I strode back to the counter and finished filling the display case with today's pastries.

Growing up, I'd always enjoyed helping in the shop, and I hadn't realized how much I'd missed it until I came back. The vanilla and hint of cinnamon that wafted throughout the shop at all hours of the day. The distinct smell that only a book could offer. The constant chatter of the folks from around town. I loved everything about Starlight Books.

But I think my favorite memory had to be how I'd spent every day sitting in the worn-out beanbag chair in between a few of the bookshelves as the faint aroma of warm chocolate chip cookies—Pops's special recipe—comforted me, knowing they'd just come out of the oven and would be waiting for me.

The memory lingered long enough to make me want to go see if the beanbag was still here. I rounded the corner of the counter and was caught off guard by the sight of Ellawyn.

She'd pulled her hair into a bun on top of her head, keeping it in place with two pencils. A few rogue strands of hair had fallen and surrounded her face as she bent over her sketch pad, drawing furiously. She bit her bottom lip, and the sight went straight to my cock as I envisioned those pretty lips wrapped around me.

She looked up at that exact time, catching me in the act. "What are you up to?" She glanced down at her watch—not a smart watch; an actual wristwatch. "The prework crowd will hit in about thirty minutes."

She shocked the hell out of me by initiating conversation and floored me by her prediction of when the crowd would start to filter in.

She'd paid attention to Starlight Books.

And I liked that. "Observant." I sat across from her. "I was stocking up for the breakfast rush and was hit by a memory." I leaned back into the seat as I looked around the empty shop. "I grew up here—in Quimby Grove and at Starlight Books. I spent all my time here before and after school and on the weekends. I was the child of Starlight, or at least that's how people referred to me." I laughed at the memory of being called Starlight Kid. "Anyway, I was here so often that Pops bought me my very own beanbag chair. It was huge. And comfortable."

"It sounds amazing."

"It was just perfect, you know? Perfect for me to hang out in and read books, do homework. It was a special part of Starlight that was all mine. Anyway, I wanted to see if it was still out here."

Ellawyn rose from her seat. "Lead the way."

"Come on, nosy," I teased. We moved toward the far end of the store, in between the shelves of books, until I came across that corner that had been mine. "It's not here."

Ellawyn placed her hand on my forearm. The gentlest touch warmed my skin. "I'm sure Benji kept it." She let her hand linger for another moment before she slowly pulled it away and returned her arm to her side.

I felt the loss instantly.

"I doubt it. It was a long time ago." I stepped around her and left, leaving her standing in the aisle as I went back to the counter.

As soon as I got settled behind the counter, the customers poured in. For the next two hours, I served the entire Quimby Grove community—or at least that was how it felt. I was flooded with familiar faces as they lingered around the counter, catching up and asking how long I was in town for.

Others had flat out asked why Pops wasn't running the store today.

And for those two hours, I'd repeated a vague version of the truth: I'm back in town to be closer to Pops, to re-establish my roots within Quimby Grove, and allow Pops to have a break from working seven days a week.

Technically, everything was true.

It was almost time for Pops to arrive when the crowd faded out. I glanced at Ellawyn and noticed she still hadn't hung up her canvas. She'd been staring out the window of the shop, lost in her head.

I whipped up a new vanilla latte and walked over toward her table. "Hey, Ellie."

She jumped in her seat as her hand flew to her chest, and her head whipped in my direction.

I extended my hand and held out the latte for her, and her eyes lit up as she noticed the drink. She slowly reached for the coffee and grabbed it, like she was being careful not to let her fingers brush up against mine. "I noticed you didn't hang up your canvas yet." I nod toward the floor, where the canvas sat. "Need any help?"

I leaned against a bookshelf and watched as she sighed into her latte.

"Thanks for the latte. I needed it." Her gaze dropped to the canvas at her feet. "I haven't hung it up yet because... Well, because I'm scared. It's personal. There are so many what-ifs that are clouding my head."

"We only get one life, Ellawyn. You've gotta live it."

She slumped down into her seat, looking defeated.

"I know it's easier said than done, but you've got to take some risks in life. Do something that scares you. Who cares what people think? But I'm sure whatever is on that canvas is phenomenal. Don't worry."

She scoffed. "How would you know if it's phenomenal or not? You haven't seen any of my work yet."

"I don't need to," I told her. "I can tell because of how you come off as a person. You're creative, you seem insightful, and kind. It'll be phenomenal because it came from you." I pushed off the bookshelf and stopped at the corner of her chair. "Pops will be here soon. You have five minutes to hang it up or I will."

Hoping that was the push she needed, I gave her some space and went into the kitchen.

The light on the dishwasher blinked, so I unloaded the clean dishes from this morning's prep work and quickly reloaded it with the dirty dishes from breakfast. Once I'd started the dishwasher, I grabbed a bottle of water from the fridge and took a break and reflected on this morning.

The morning had gone by seamlessly. The prep work and baking went according to plan, the food tasted great, and I kept up with the food orders along with manning the register. I was surprised at how well things had gone and how much I enjoyed working by myself. It was vastly different from my job back in Boston.

Maybe I'd needed this change of scenery after all.

Plus, having Ellawyn here hadn't hurt. I'd found myself wanting to be around her more. I'd done everything I could to visit her and had sneaked glances at her from the counter.

And it'd been enough to know she was close by.

I took a few large drinks from my water bottle, emptying it, and then tossed it into the recycling bin. I grabbed two extra trays of pastries and carried them out to the display case so I could refill them.

When I looked out into the shop, I saw Ellawyn hanging her

canvas and making sure it was level. Even with her body blocking most of the piece, I could tell it was extraordinary. I hurried and put away the remaining pastries before I went over to where Ellawyn had been trying to level the canvas. "Here"—I nudged her with my shoulder—"let me."

She stepped out of the way, and I took over. When I was finished, I stepped back a few and stood next to her. "Okay, now let's see what we've got here."

Her eyes darted to the floor. "Thanks for the help. Um... Benji should be here any minute, so I-I'm going to freshen up before he comes."

She practically bolted away from me.

When she was gone, I walked back up to her art piece to examine it more closely. I wasn't an art critic, but I was really into what she created. It was dark and complex. Emotion and pain radiated off the piece and captivated my full attention. The focal point of the piece was a puppet, or a marionette type of thing. It was full of despair and looked so desperate and alone—like she was struggling to break free but couldn't.

On the left-hand side of the piece, was a poem:

Dependent on your every move
A puppeteer's doll
A real-life marionette
You tug, you pull
I bend, I move

A slap of the string
A tug of the wrist
Your hand or mine
I cannot tell which

There are voices all around me
Saying things that are not true
The words are coming out of my mouth

But it's not me, it's you

You always have me dancing around
And putting on a show
A constant feeling of disconnect
And not knowing where this will go

The walls are closing in
I'm starting to lose myself
I don't know who I am anymore
But it's not me
It's someone else

When I finished reading her words, I was speechless. Pops had mentioned she'd been through something, and this confirmed that. The pain was palpable and sent an ache straight to my heart. I had the sudden urge to find her and see if she was okay. To hold her in my arms and comfort her.

When I looked around, she was nowhere to be found.

Where the hell is she?

When she hadn't returned after a few minutes, I returned to the counter to help some customers that had come in while I'd been over by the painting.

Ellawyn reappeared when I began preparing their food. She had her head down as she made her way back to her table. She darted past her canvas and picked up her tote bag. At that exact moment, the bell on the door jingled, and in strode Pops with a grin plastered on his face from ear to ear.

The man was getting a biopsy today, and he looked like he'd just won the lottery.

After finishing with my last customer, I darted around the counter to greet him. "Hey, Pops. You sure look happy today."

His smile was infectious, and I found myself smiling back at him.

"Beckett! It's Ellawyn's big day today. She's hanging up her canvas." He stepped around me and headed straight for Ellawyn.

His good mood seemed to rubbed off on her, too, because her uncomfortable smile completely transformed into a genuine one in a matter of seconds.

I joined them as Pops praised her artwork. "Your piece is amazing," I said. "I really like it—especially the poem." I looked at it again, re-reading her words as I became more in awe of the woman who stood beside me.

"Thanks," she clipped before she turned her attention to Pops. "Benji, should we head out?"

When they started for the door, I grabbed her elbow, halting her. "Quick question. I noticed the initials ERC in the bottom right-hand corner. What does it stand for?"

She hesitated for a moment. "Ellawyn Rose Calloway."

And with that, she walked out the door after Pops.

CHAPTER 5

Ellawyn

I THOUGHT if I put distance between me and Starlight Books, I'd be able to rid my brain of all things Beckett. But like a moth drawn to light, he consumed me. Being pulled into his orbit was undeniable, and the risk of getting hurt was inevitable.

But the threat of pain wasn't enough to deter me.

I'd sworn he was flirting with me today. The thought caused a flutter to form in my stomach, rooted deep, like my entire being had been filled with butterflies taking flight.

I pushed thoughts of Beckett from my head and instead tried to focus on Benji and his biopsy appointment.

The drive to the hospital was completely silent. I watched Benji as he looked out the window and played with his hands. He'd link his fingers together. Then unlink them. And then he'd force himself to lay his hands flat in his lap.

He was a nervous wreck, which was understandable.

When we arrived at the neurosurgery unit of the hospital, a tall male nurse was at patient check-in. "Hi there," he greeted. "How can I help you today?"

Benji hesitated but recovered quickly. "Hi, I'm Benjamin Walden. I have an appointment for a biopsy."

The nurse checked something on his computer and nodded

his head. "Here we are." He pivoted and gathered a clipboard with a stack of papers on it. "Let's get you checked in, Mr. Walden. We have quite a bit of paperwork to fill out."

The nurse went over all of it with us. It was the typical paperwork you'd expect at an appointment like this—consent forms, getting information on allergies, medications, anesthesia reactions, and previous surgeries.

Benji grabbed the green clipboard and thanked the nurse before he moseyed toward a small table that sat in the lobby.

He pulled out a chair and sat down before he pulled out the one beside him for me. His hand trembled when he picked up the pen, so he laid it back down and shook out his hand.

"Nerves," he said. He tried again and wrote the date on the top, his lines shaky. He mumbled a curse under his breath before laying the pen back down.

I reached across and placed my hand on his, giving it a gentle tap. "Let me."

He nodded and slid the clipboard my way. I wrote his name down on the paperwork and went through the questions with him.

"I'm sorry, Ellie," Benji interrupted. "I wish I could lie and say I didn't know what has come over me but... I'm scared. Everything is happening so quickly."

When Benji dropped his head in his hands, I turned to face him. "It's okay to be scared. I'd be terrified too. Anyone would feel this way." I leaned over and hugged him.

"Thanks, Ellawyn."

It didn't take us as long as Benji had hoped to finish the paperwork. His facial features turned somber as he collected the clipboard and went to hand it in to the nurse.

When he walked back over, the color had drained from his face. "The nurse says the neurosurgeon will be out in about ten minutes to get me." He sat and stared out the window into the parking lot.

Deciding I needed a task, I rose to my feet. "Okay, Benji. I'm going to go grab a drink at one of the machines around the corner. Want something?" I dug my wallet out of my bag before placing my tote on the chair I'd just vacated.

"No. Thanks, though. I can't have anything to eat or drink before anesthesia."

My head whipped in his direction. "Wait, what?" He hadn't said anything about being put under for the biopsy. "I didn't know about that. What type?"

He considered the question. "The kind that will knock my old butt out. Didn't I mention that yesterday?"

I thought back to last night's conversation. Benji had made this appointment seem like it'd only be a few hours long. "No, I don't think you did," I answered. "That's okay." I waved it off. "How long will the procedure be?"

He exhaled and shook his head. "I'm not sure. We can ask once the neurosurgeon comes out."

While we waited for the neurosurgeon, Benji and I made light conversation surrounding movies, music, and our favorite board games—mine was Guess Who and his was The Game of Life. We made plans to buy our favorite games and host a game night at Starlight Books. I was thrilled. It'd been years since I'd sat down and played a game.

We laughed while confessing our favorite desserts. I had to explain what an Oreo truffle was, and we agreed our game night should include desserts as well. We had almost planned an entire event before we were interrupted.

"Benjamin Walden," a man announced as he came into the lobby.

He nodded at Benji. "Mr. Walden," he greeted before he turned to face me and stuck out his hand. "I'm Dr. Reinhart. It's nice to meet you."

I placed my hand in his, but instead of letting go after a quick shake, he gripped it a little tighter and held on. I pulled my hand from his grasp and looked to Benji.

"This is my friend, Ellie," drawled Benji. "She tagged along today so I wouldn't have to come alone."

Dr. Reinhart's gaze hadn't moved from me to Benji. I decided if I wanted this awkward moment to end, then maybe I'd better help move it along. "It's Ellawyn, actually." I gestured toward Benji. "Only certain friends get to use that nickname."

He looked between Benji and me before he settled his gaze on me again. "Ellawyn. That's a pretty name." A coy smile slid onto his face as he stared at me.

Choosing to ignore him, I stood straighter, readying to ask him the few questions I had. "This biopsy today—will it be done under general anesthesia?"

"Yes, it will."

I didn't miss a beat. "And what's the recovery time like? Basically, will we be able to return home today, or do we need to plan to stay overnight?"

Dr. Reinhart's jaw ticked, and his eyes narrowed in my direction. "Worried about missing a date tonight?"

What a tool.

"No," I clipped.

"Very well." He clapped Benji on the back. "We hope recovery time will only be a few hours, but an overnight stay might be required to monitor vitals and what not. We'll know more after the procedure."

"Great." My molars ground against each other. "Will someone come let me know once the biopsy is finished?"

"Yeah." A grin spread across his face like the Cheshire cat. "You know what? I'll personally come and let you know how it goes."

A wave of nausea washed over me. I looked at Benji, who seemed oblivious to the doctor's arrogance. "I'll be out in the waiting room the entire time," I comforted. I pulled him in for a hug and squeezed hard. "I promise everything will be fine."

Benji smiled at me. "See you after, Ellie."

Dr. Reinhart held the door open for Benji, and as he looked

over his shoulder at me, he winked. I rolled my eyes, hoping he saw.

I could admit that he wasn't bad looking. He had looked to be in his early thirties, well tanned, and with dirty-blond hair that was a bit on the longer side. Based on the way he filled out his blue scrubs, I'd say he spent a lot of time working out. But he was smarmy and inappropriate.

Hard pass.

I moseyed through the lobby, looking for a place to get comfortable as I waited for Benji. When I finally landed on a spot in the furthest corner, I pulled out my sketch pad and hoped to pass the time.

After an hour of staring at the blank page, I gave up and shoved my sketch pad back into my tote. I couldn't keep my mind focused.

When I wasn't wondering how Benji's biopsy was going, my thoughts were reserved for Beckett.

What was he up to at the shop?

What did he think about me after reading my poem?

Had I imagined the spark, the chemistry, that had ignited between us whenever we were around each other?

A hand landed on my shoulder, causing me to bolt from my chair. I turned around to see Dr. Reinhart and his megawatt smile. *Ugh, I wish he'd just knock it off.*

"Ellie."

"Ellawyn," I corrected. "How did the biopsy go?"

I hadn't expected to see him again so soon. I turned my wrist to check the time and saw that it was almost two thirty in the afternoon. I'd been so lost in my mind that a huge chunk of time had passed. I'd been lost in all that was Beckett.

Dr. Reinhart cleared his throat and waited until my gaze snapped to his before he continued. "It went well. Mr. Walden is in recovery now but hasn't woken up yet." He stepped closer. "I'd like to keep him here for a few hours for observation but may end up keeping him overnight after I re-evaluate him in the evening."

I blinked, shocked that we would be here until the evening at least. "Oh. That's an awfully long time." I tried to think of how I could get in touch with Beckett to update him.

"Standard protocol, Ellie." He grabbed my elbow and tote bag and began to lead me down a long corridor. "How about we grab some lunch while we wait?"

I came to a dead halt. "It's Ellawyn," I corrected. "And thanks, but no. I want to be with Benji when he wakes up." I held out my hand for my tote bag. "What room is he in?"

He handed me back my bag and huffed with annoyance.

He shook his head slightly, like he'd cleared away a haze of confusion. "Of course, Ellie." He extended an arm. "After you."

I sighed and walked ahead of him, not bothering to correct him on having used my nickname. Or the fact that he didn't tell me the room number.

He made sure I stayed ahead of him until we got to the door, and he stepped forward to open it for me. After that, I fell a few paces behind him.

He led us to the elevator bank and pushed the up button. We stepped into the elevator in silence, and he reached for the button for the thirteenth floor before closing the distance between us and leaning on the wall, facing me.

The elevator creeped and crawled slower than I'd thought possible.

I pulled my tote bag off my arm, hoping it'd force him to step back. "What room is Benji in? I'd like to write it down."

No such luck. He stayed glued to my side.

"Room 1313. Listen, Ell—"

A ding echoed throughout the elevator before the doors opened, and I rushed out as soon as I could squeeze through. "Thanks for showing me the way. I've got it from here." I turned the corner and desperately sought out the placard indicating which rooms were down which part of the corridor.

My heart was racing, my breathing intermittent, and my eyes blurred.

Dr. Reinhart's behavior had rocked me, and now I was incredibly nervous. He was a creep, but there was something else that bothered me about him. I hadn't been able to pinpoint it yet but knew I needed to avoid any real time spent with him in the future.

I saw the sign that pointed to the right for room numbers beginning with 1300 through 1325. I turned right and smiled at the nurse's station that I passed on my way.

When I came upon Benji's room, I opened the door and carefully closed it behind me. The room was dark, with the curtains drawn. The dim lighting made the beeping of the machines sound louder than they were. There were two chairs by the windowsill in the furthest part of the room and another by the bedside. Benji was lying in his bed, sleeping peacefully. Part of his head was bandaged up from the biopsy.

Seeing him like this made his new reality feel even more real. I hoped the biopsy came back that the tumor was benign, operable, and easy to treat. I didn't know a lot about tumors, but I was determined to find out more—even if I had to ask Dr. Reinhart. I shuddered at the thought. I'd never been an outgoing person, and it'd gotten worse the last few years, but I wouldn't let Benji's recovery suffer just because I was afraid to speak up.

After an hour passed by and Benji remained unconscious, I found myself wishing I had a cell phone to help pass the time and to update Beckett on.

Maybe he should have come instead of me.

"Ellie," whispered Benji.

He'd spoken my name so low that I almost missed it. When he attempted to speak again, he opened his eyes and tried to sit up.

I jumped up and came to his bedside. "Benji," I exclaimed. "You're awake. Let me call the nurse." I went to the other side of his bed and grabbed the call button, then pushed it so hard that I worried I'd broken it.

A nurse dressed in yellow scrubs entered the room with a smile so bright it matched her outfit. "Hello to my newest patient." She smiled and walked over to Benji's side. "We're just going to check your pupils and ask a few questions, okay?" She pulled a small light out of her pocket and flashed it in Benji's eyes. "Can you tell me your name?"

"Benjamin Walden."

"Good job. Now how about moving your fingers?"

Benji wiggled his fingers and made a fist out of both hands.

"Now legs and toes?"

Benji did as instructed, and the nurse smiled down at him. "That's great. I think we'll be in awesome shape here soon." She continued checking vitals while documenting everything in her computer system.

After a few minutes, she turned to tell Benji about possible side effects, but when she looked at him, he'd fallen asleep. She laughed as she turned to me. "Well, I guess I can tell you about those side effects." She rattled off a list a mile long, such as nausea, headaches, and the possibility of seizures. "Mr. Walden will be staying overnight for observation, and Dr. Reinhart will be around in a few hours for rounds." She typed something into the computer before she looked at me again. "Do you have any questions?"

Only one came to mind. "Are visitors allowed overnight or are there certain hours?"

She smiled. "No overnight visitors, but the hours are nine in the morning until nine in the evening." She came over to me and stuck out her hand. "Let me know if you need anything."

I placed my hand in hers and shook. "Thanks."

Then she was gone, and I was alone in a dark hospital room with a passed-out Benji.

☾

HOURS HAD PASSED since the nurse had left and Benji still hadn't woken up. I checked the time on the monitors that hung next to his bedside.

Seven.

Visiting hours would end in two hours, and I still hadn't gotten ahold of Beckett yet. Desperation took over, and I grabbed the bag that housed Benji's belongings and dug out his phone. I tapped on the screen, relieved it wasn't password protected, and saw that he had fifteen missed calls from Beckett, along with a handful of text messages. I scrolled to Beckett's name and typed out a text message, letting him know that Benji was being kept overnight and gave him the visiting hours.

He responded instantly.

Beckett: Took you long enough to check in.

Beckett: I've been worried. Are you staying overnight with him? Is he okay?

I responded, letting him know that Benji was okay so far, and that I'd be leaving tonight and would try to come back first thing in the morning.

Beckett: I'll be there in an hour. What's the room number?

Me: 1313.

When he didn't respond, I powered off the phone and put it back in Benji's bag. I hated to admit it, but it had been lonely here all day without anyone to talk to.

I got up and stood at Benji's bedside, watching as his eyelids fluttered. Feeling hopeful, I decided to try to talk to him and see if he'd wake up.

"Hey Benji. It's me, Ellawyn. If you want to wake up, I'd love to chat."

Nothing but silence filled the room. Feeling discouraged, I sat back down.

"Ellie, girl." Benji's whispered words were barely audible.

I returned to his side as he opened his eyes. They wandered around the room until they landed on the hospital water bottle. I moved to grab it and placed the straw to his mouth, and he gulped down water. "Small sips," I insisted. "You don't want to get sick."

I removed the straw from his mouth and set the drink on the tray next to him.

"Thank you," Benji said. "For staying with me all day."

I placed my hand on top of his. "Of course. Beckett will be here soon to pick me up and to visit with you before visiting hours end." With one last squeeze, I returned to my seat.

"I heard your surgery went well," I started, but when I looked over at him, the words fell flat as I watched his eyes flutter closed while his arms and legs convulsed.

"Oh my god, Benji." I jumped up and pushed his call button repeatedly. I rushed to roll Benji on his side as fast as I could, but it was nearly impossible. He'd become so rigid that I struggled to move him at all.

The air vanished from my lungs as I started to panic. Why hadn't anyone arrived yet?

Taking a deep breath, I positioned myself to try to roll him again. At that exact moment, the nurse from earlier rushed in. "He's having a seizure," I yelled between sobs. "I'm trying to roll him, but I can't. Please help me."

The nurse rushed to my side and nudged me over a little. "Count of three." She counted us down, and on three, we were able to successfully get Benji safely on his side.

Dr. Reinhart entered at that moment, took one look at me, and ordered the nurse to get me out of here.

She gently touched my arm and guided me away from Benji and toward the opposite end of the room, by the windows. She moved the chair to face the window and tugged me toward the seat before she crouched down beside me at eye level.

"I'm Lucy. What's your name, sweetheart?"

"Ellawyn," I replied. Between my ragged breathing and my crying, I'd have been surprised if she could even hear me.

"Beautiful name." She pulled a tissue from the tissue box that sat on the windowsill and handed it to me. "You did an amazing job helping Benji."

I blew my nose and kept my gaze focused on the sunset. "Is he going to be okay?" I choked on the words, afraid of the answer.

She nodded. "Of course. Seizures are pretty normal for patients with a brain tumor. This likely won't be his last, either. I know it doesn't make it any easier to deal with, but at least you know what to do now." She glanced behind us, and a tiny smile spread across her face. "Look, he's fast asleep now."

Turning in my chair, I glanced behind us and looked at Benji. Lucy was right. Dr. Reinhart had rolled Benji onto his back, and he was asleep with no twitching movements.

Letting out a breath, I looked back at Lucy. "Thank you. I'm sorry for being a basket case when you walked in."

Lucy stood up and hugged me. "You were fine. I reacted similarly when this first happened to me."

"Lucy." Dr. Reinhart's voice carried from across the room. "Why don't you go grab Ellawyn a bottle of water?"

"Sure." She squeezed my shoulder before she stepped away.

When the door closed and everyone left, I decided to stay where I was, content to look out the window. What I hadn't expected, though, was to hear footsteps approaching behind me. I stiffened, watching as Dr. Reinhart's reflection appeared in the window.

His expression was disconcerting—the look on his face that of a hunter, searching for his prey.

"Ellie, why don't you come with me to the staff cafeteria for a late dinner?" He inched closer and leaned on the windowsill, facing me.

"It's Ellawyn." I pulled my sweater tighter across my torso. "Thanks, but I'd prefer to stay with Benji."

"Mr. Walden is asleep and will be all night."

"Like... Like I said—"

A voice from behind us spoke over mine.

"She said no." Beckett strode toward us. A rush of relief coursed through me. When he met my side, he placed a hand on the small of my back and steered me away.

"Look who it is," Dr. Reinhart hissed. "Beckett Walden." He stuck his hands into his lab coat pockets. "Long time no see. Should have known Ellie was yours."

If looks could kill, Dr. Reinhart would be a dead man. Beckett led me to Benji's side and turned to face off with the doctor. He narrowed his gaze. "Her name is Ellawyn. She doesn't belong to me or anyone else for that matter." Beckett crossed his arms over his broad chest. "And if you were listening, you'd have heard that you clearly weren't her choice tonight."

"I'll have Lucy come give an update on Mr. Walden."

Dr. Reinhart stormed to the door and hesitated before he placed his hand on the doorknob. He looked over his shoulder. "And Ellie?"

I glanced in his direction and a grin spread across his face.

"Have a nice evening."

CHAPTER 6
Beckett

Watching the color drain from Ellawyn's face was enough to make me want to punch Reinhart in the fucking face.

I grabbed her hand, leading her to one of the seats by the windowsill. "Ellawyn, are you okay?"

She remained silent, but her body trembled.

Crouching in front of her, I tried to meet her gaze. She wouldn't even look at me. "You can talk to me." She dipped her head lower, avoiding my gaze. Her hands were wrapped around her shirt, clenching the fabric.

As much as I didn't want to, I gave her knee a squeeze before I pulled away to give her some space and rejoined Pops at his bedside.

His head was bandaged from the surgery, and his face was swollen. But he looked peaceful. I couldn't even imagine how his recovery would look after his surgery. I reached behind me to grab a chair and pulled it up to sit as close as I could. In a low voice, I gripped his hand and talked to him while he slept. "Hey, Pops. It's Beckett. I just wanted to see for myself that you are okay and tell you that I love you. I'll be back first thing in the morning."

I ran my hands over my face, wishing he'd wake up so I could actually talk to him. Faint footsteps sounded behind me. "You ready?" I asked without turning around.

A sniffle came from over my shoulder. "For what?"

I turned around and put the chair back. "To go home."

Her mouth hung open slightly, but she recovered quickly. I couldn't stop myself from thinking she looked beautiful, even after crying.

"You're... You're offering me a ride back to Quimby Grove?"

I cocked my head to the side. "Uh, yeah. How else would you get home?"

She lifted one shoulder. "I just thought I'd take an Uber or something."

"I've got you," I answered.

As quietly as possible, I opened the door and ushered her out, not wanting to wake Pops.

The walk back to the parking garage was quiet. Ellawyn trailed behind me a few steps, her head glued to the floor. Once we reached the car, I opened her door and waited for her to climb in.

The gesture must have startled her, because she paused for a few beats before getting inside. "Thank you," she said.

"Sure," I answered before closing her door. When I got in the car, I noticed her spinning a silver ring on her finger repeatedly. It slid fast and with such ease that I was surprised it didn't fly off her.

"Do you want to talk about it?" I started the car and turned on the radio, keeping it at a low volume.

She turned away from me to fasten her seat belt. "About what exactly?"

Throwing the car in reverse, I glanced at my mirrors, and backed out of the parking spot. "Let's start with how things went today with Pops." I drove up to the parking attendant at the exit of the garage and handed him a twenty. "How'd the biopsy go?"

She exhaled and sat up. "It went well. They performed a stereotactic needle biopsy."

I cocked an eyebrow. "A what?"

"Essentially, a needle is used to access the tumor since the tumor is deeper in the brain. Stereotactic guidance is like using a GPS in your car." She turned to face me while she spoke, and I couldn't help but notice how the moonlight lit up her features, casting beautiful silhouettes onto her skin. "A navigation system based on Benji's pre-op scans," she explained.

"It's a good thing one of us knows what's going on. It sounds a lot safer than what I had imagined."

"Everything was fine until he was recovering in his room," she admitted before she averted her gaze down to her lap.

"What happened?" I took a deep a deep breath as I braced myself for what she might say next.

Ellawyn spent the next few minutes filling me in on Benji's seizure.

Out of the corner of my eye, I caught her shoulders shaking as she swiped her fingers under her eyes. She placed her hands back in her lap, and wanting to provide some comfort, I leaned over and put my hand on hers, feeling the wetness from her tears.

"It was so terrifying," she whispered. "I felt so helpless."

Ellawyn clearly cared a lot about Pops and had beaten herself up over something she couldn't possibly have prevented. "It sounds like you did everything you could. Don't blame yourself." I squeezed her hand before returning it to the steering wheel. "What did Dr. Reinhart say when he came in after you pushed the call button?"

"Oh, um..." she fumbled. "Well, the nurse, Lucy, came in right away and helped me roll Benji onto his side, and then Dr. Reinhart made her take me toward the windows so I could calm down." She looked at me briefly before she turned her gaze to the window. "She explained how frequently seizures can happen in this situation."

Ellawyn gushed about how wonderful the nurse was, but she completely left Dr. Reinhart out of the conversation. I gave her a reprieve and kept my gaze focused on the road as I merged onto the highway.

I contemplated how to broach the subject of Dr. Reinhart and what a dick he was to her. I needed to tread carefully, or she may end up more closed off than she already was. She had finally started to open up to me, and I didn't want to ruin that. "Can I ask you a question?"

She kept her gaze locked on the window and shrugged. "Sure."

"What happened with Dr. Reinhart before I came in?"

She turned toward me, her lips pressed together tightly. "It was nothing to worry about."

I sighed and glanced at her as I drove. "I know he made you uncomfortable before we left. I just wanted to make sure he hadn't done anything worse."

Her silence was deafening.

"Listen," I continued, "I know it's none of my business, but I know Dr. Reinhart." She shifted her body in the seat so she could look at me. "We grew up in Quimby Grove together. He's not a great guy. Just friendly advice—keep your distance. He's a creep, but he's a good doctor from what I've heard."

Reinhart was more than a creep, but I wasn't about to tell Ellawyn that. Rumors ran rampant through Quimby Grove about him and his indiscretions. Word on the street was that he'd sexually assaulted numerous girls all throughout high school. I didn't know the validity of most of those accusations, but I did know at least one was legitimate. I wouldn't be surprised if there were more.

But I'd keep all of that to myself to keep Ellawyn from being even more freaked out about him.

"Yeah," she began. "Um... he just kept hitting on me, even after I'd declined multiple times." She cleared her throat. "I just didn't like it."

I exhaled. Ellawyn must have a history with assholes. "He's a real piece of work," I agreed.

The corners of her mouth tipped up, and a small smile stayed there as she turned her head back to the window.

The rest of the ride back to Quimby Grove went by fast. I put on my turn signal to merge off the highway and decided to hit Ellawyn with one last personal question before we parted ways. "Here's my phone. Why don't you put your number in it?"

She bit her bottom lip. "I don't have a cell phone."

You've got to be kidding me. I couldn't think of a single person that didn't have a cell phone. "You're twenty-something years old and don't have a phone?"

"That's correct."

"By choice?"

"Yes, Beckett." She folded her arms across her chest. "By choice."

I blinked at her. "You need a phone, Ellie."

"No, I don't," she insisted.

"What if you needed one for an emergency? Or to talk to friends or family?"

"I don't have friends," she responded flatly. "And my family knows that I'll be out of touch for a bit. I send letters when I can."

I gripped the steering wheel so hard that my knuckles turned white. Her logic was insane and totally unacceptable. She could get hurt and wouldn't have a way to call for help. Who the fuck sent letters anymore anyway?

"I just don't know what to say to that."

"You don't have to say anything. It's how I live my life."

Before I could respond, my cell phone chimed with a text notification, and the voice assistant on my phone read the text out loud through the speakers of the car.

Amber: Beckett, are we still meeting up at Remnant Hearts tonight to catch up over drinks? Xoxo.

Fuck. Couldn't that text have come through after I dropped her off? I could feel Ellawyn's gaze on me as I ignored the text and kept on driving.

"Hot date?" she asked with a forced laugh.

I eyed her. "I wouldn't call it a date, no."

"Right," she huffed. "Of course, a hookup doesn't require the efforts of dating. Makes sense that you'd prefer the hook-up over putting in the work." She rolled her eyes and looked away.

Her hostility caught me off guard. Her attitude was so out of character for the Ellawyn I'd gotten to know over the past few days—the quiet, shy, recluse of a woman who was passionate about people and art.

I never would have thought so, but apparently, she had a fiery side too. The more I learned about this woman, the more I liked.

I smirked. *Two could play this game.* "Now, now, I'll have you know that I happen to put *a lot* of work into my hookups as well."

Her head whipped to face me, and her mouth dropped open as her cheeks reddened. She snapped her mouth shut and stayed quiet.

I nudged her with my elbow. "Ellie, have I rendered you speechless?" A grin spread across my face.

The corners of her mouth twitched. "Oh, hush."

We'd finally arrived at the Square and were a block away from the shop. "Now where would the fun be in that?" I teased. Easing on the breaks, I pulled right in front of Starlight Books and parked the car. "Home sweet home." I opened the door to get out as Ellawyn did the same.

She stood on the sidewalk, waiting for me as I rounded the car to join her. Exhaustion seemed to have taken over as she let out a yawn. "You had a pretty big day today, didn't you?"

"What do you mean?" She walked toward the old red Adirondack chairs that were placed randomly throughout the Square and took a seat. "Oh, yeah. I guess I did have a big day."

She settled further into the chair, leaning her head back. She let her eyes drift closed, and I couldn't help myself from partaking in all that was Ellawyn. She looked so fucking beautiful, a majestic goddess that had captured all my attention. I couldn't look away even if I wanted to.

And knowing she'd spent the entire day with Pops, taking care of him when I couldn't, made her even more desirable. Her gravitational pull was undeniable. The more I knew about this woman, the stronger the allure. I was hooked.

She shifted her head to look at me. Worry was etched on her features; something was clearly bothering her. I tapped on my temple. "What's going on up there?" I asked.

Her giggle filled the space, and she ducked her head. "I know it's silly, but I was curious what people thought about my art piece today."

"People seemed to love it and even read the poem." I hesitated before I continued. "And they asked who the artist was."

She sat upright, her mouth dropping open. "You didn't tell them it was me, did you?" She sprang to her feet and started pacing on the sidewalk.

I knew how she felt about sharing her art, so her secret was safe with me. I waved her off as I walked up to where she was pacing in front of Starlight Books. "Nah. I just told them it was a local artist."

My mind drifted back to Ellawyn's poem and her past. I found myself thinking about who could have hurt her so badly. There were so many signs of past trauma that it was hard to miss, but I knew not to push. Someday, I hoped to earn her trust and become someone she could depend on.

And I'd spend every day until then proving to her that I could be.

She stopped pacing and stood right in front of me. "Thanks," she said. "It's just..."

I took a step toward her. "It's okay. You're entitled to your privacy without being obligated to explain." I gestured to the streets around us. "Especially in a town this small. And I've learned that there are different types of artists. Some want to create art while screaming it from the rooftops. But there are other types of artists who simply must create; it's as essential to them as breathing. They create because they have to; they don't need the attention. They need the outlet."

Her gaze hadn't left mine; she looked awestruck. "How did you know?" She cleared her throat. "How did you know it's something necessary for me to do?"

"Call it a hunch."

"Okay." She smiled at me and pointed behind her. "I should head home. I'll see you tomorrow morning." She went back to the Adirondack chair and picked up her tote bag before placing it on her shoulder.

I nodded. It suddenly dawned on me that I should have dropped her off at her place instead of coming back here to the shop. "Do you need a ride? Or I could walk you home?"

"Not necessary. Besides, you have a date waiting at Remnant Hearts." She nodded toward the bar across the street. "Your ultimate destination tonight is right there."

I didn't bother to point out that I hadn't texted that woman back, nor do I have any desire to meet up with her. I kept my voice casual and decided to ask her to come with me. "Why don't you have a drink with me instead?"

She gave me a small smile before turning to walk away. She spoke over her shoulder. "No, thank you. Have a good night, Beckett."

I watched as she crossed the street and headed down the block toward the Quimby Grove Theatre. The bright old-school lights from the theatre sign lit up her silhouette as she walked by. Her pace quickened and before I knew it, she rounded the opposite corner and disappeared into the darkness.

Regret over not demanding I take her home had started to take over, and I vowed never to make that mistake again. I turned around, casting a glance toward Remnant Hearts Bar. It had always been a favorite of mine, carefully tucked away within Quimby Grove. I appreciated the new addition that Max had placed—a deep-red neon sign of the bar's name hung in the storefront window, along with a broken heart symbol that flickered every so often. It suited the bar better than a steadily lit sign.

Remnant Hearts—a place to go to pour your heart and soul out whenever there was only a tiny piece remaining.

Reaching into my back pocket, I grabbed my cell phone out and typed out a quick reply to the woman who had texted me earlier.

Me: Sorry, Remnant Hearts isn't in the cards for me tonight.

CHAPTER 7

Ellawyn

YESTERDAY WAS EXHAUSTING.

Between Benji's biopsy, the Dr. Reinhart drama, and my surprising jealousy of the woman Beckett was spending time with, I'd come straight home and passed out. There'd been no time for eating or grabbing a shower, just hardcore REM sleep.

Thankfully, I'd remembered to set my alarm before I crashed. I didn't want to be late to Starlight Books this morning, just in case Beckett needed me to pick up Benji from the hospital.

After I brewed a pot of coffee and poured as much as possible into my to-go tumbler, I headed straight for my closet. I didn't have many clothes here in Quimby Grove, but I had enough to get by. I stared at my wardrobe, looking for a nice outfit to wear today. I'd been determined to look cute, to make an impression.

To not be invisible for once.

The sudden spike of jealousy last night fueled my fire as I continued my search for the perfect outfit. I didn't know what had come over me, but the thought of Beckett spending time with a woman was enough to make me feel ill. Which was ridiculous— I barely knew the guy.

I sighed as I grabbed the TV remote from the nightstand and flicked on the news to confirm that today's weather would be nice and warm. Turning around in my closet, I looked through my dresses, which weren't many. My clothing style had never been flashy, as I'd never had the desire to be the center of attention, nor had I been allowed to dress in anything that would draw the desire of other men. But that life was gone now, and I did have a few cute pieces of clothing that made me feel worthy.

I decided on my favorite black shirt dress. It had a plunging *V* neckline, a slight collar, loose-fitting short sleeves, and went down to about midcalf. It wasn't a very showy dress, but I still felt great when I wore it. I paired it with medium-sized silver hoop earrings and my favorite matte black key necklace.

After a quick shower, I applied minimal product to my hair and opted to let it air dry so my natural waves would come to life. When I risked a glance in the mirror, I barely recognized the girl staring back at me—a girl I could be proud of. I'd slowly started to take back control of my life again. It was surreal to have to rebuild your entire life from nothing, but I'd been getting stronger each day while putting in the work to reclaim my independence. With a final once-over at my reflection, I put on my black Converse sneakers before grabbing my tote and heading out to Starlight Books.

During my walk to the bookshop, I couldn't help overthinking everything from the night before. Beckett and I hadn't discussed what today's plans would be, or if I'd even be a part of those plans. I certainly didn't want to insert myself into their personal lives, but at the same time, I had an overwhelming urge to help them.

There'd been no denying that I was drawn to the Walden family. Benji was the sweetest old man I'd ever met, and Beckett... Well, Beckett was in his own atmosphere. He was untouchable and unattainable. But he was also easy to be around, caring, funny, and when he had to, he was an alpha male that radiated power and dominance.

But I wasn't good enough for a man like Beckett Walden. And truthfully, I didn't think I was ready to let him in on a more personal level just yet. I couldn't bring myself to deliberately allow someone access to break down the barriers I'd erected over the past six months. He could wreck me, and I wasn't sure I'd survive it.

But was the risk worth it?

I let out a breath and cleared away my thoughts as I came up to the shop just as Beckett taped a sign onto the door that read: *Starlight Books is closed for the day due to a family emergency.*

Figuring Beckett had decided to go pick up Benji, I turned around and started back down the block to head home. I only got about halfway before I heard my name being yelled. Turning around, I saw Beckett headed my way—and he looked even more handsome today than he had yesterday. He wore dark jeans that sculpted to his body and a navy blue Henley that stretched across his broad shoulders.

Casual looked good on him.

He closed the distance between us. "Hey, Ellie," he greeted. "Where are you going?"

"Uh." I pointed back toward Starlight Books. "I saw the sign and assumed you were going to pick up Benji. I was just heading home."

His eyes traveled up and down my body twice before his gaze settled on my face. "You look especially beautiful today." He ran his knuckles down my forearm, leaving goose bumps in their wake. "I have your vanilla latte and blueberry lemon scone ready. Come on."

I couldn't hide my smile even if I wanted to. "Okay."

He led us back to Starlight Books, where a warmed-up scone and a vanilla latte sat waiting for me, as promised. I picked up the latte and raised it in a silent thank-you while he laughed and poured himself a cup of coffee. "I figured we could close the shop today and go get Pops together."

Taking a bite out of my scone, I nodded my head. "Sounds good," I replied once I'd taken a drink. "How long do you think it will take until Benji receives the biopsy results?"

He rinsed out the coffeepot and took a drink from his mug before grabbing a rag. "Not sure." He wiped down the counter and placed the rag into the bucket underneath. "I hope to get that answer today, and then we can go from there. I don't have a lot of questions yet, but I'm sure I will once we know more."

"Yeah, makes sense." I took a sip of my latte and finished it before standing up to throw my trash out. "I tried to research as much as I could yesterday. I can't imagine how stressed Benji must be."

"I know, but he'll put on a strong façade and pretend everything is just fine." Beckett rounded the corner and joined me. "Let's head out the back door."

Beckett grabbed my bag before I could and led me through the kitchen and toward the back of the shop. Opening the door for me, he extended his arm, as if to guide me through. "Ladies first."

I giggled as I stepped through the door, until I came to an abrupt stop. "Oh my god," I whispered. "*That's* your car?"

In front of me was the sleekest SUV I'd ever laid eyes on. The shiny black exterior was impressive. I'd figured that Beckett was well off, but I hadn't anticipated that he was doing this well for himself. I glanced down at my outfit, suddenly feeling out of place.

"Isn't she a beaut?" He strode around to the passenger side, where I was standing. "My VP shipped it down here for me since Pops doesn't have a car." He opened my door, allowing me to slide in before he gently closed it. After he slid into his seat, he gently placed my bag behind my seat before looking at me with his charming, megawatt smile. "What do you think?"

"It's the fanciest car I've ever been in." Something struck me then. "What about the car you picked me up in last night?"

He reversed out of the back alley and turned onto High St, heading toward the highway. "Last night, I borrowed my buddy's car."

The leather interior was smooth, and the dash impressive.

"It's amazing," I admitted. I'd meant what I'd told him—this was the nicest car I'd been in, and I hoped I wouldn't ruin it somehow.

The rest of the drive to Pennsylvania Memorial was spent with us listening to a podcast we both enjoy, Crime Junkie. Beckett had been ecstatic to find out I loved true crime as much as he did. We ended up pausing the episode and sharing our theories with each other. It was surprising how much I enjoyed Beckett's company. Slipping into easy conversation made the ride go by quickly, but because we spent so much time talking, we didn't get to finish the episode before we arrived at the hospital.

Beckett navigated the parking garage and managed to snag a spot next to the elevator, just in case Benji was tired. Just as we approached room 1313, he hesitated and gently placed a hand on my arm, stopping me. "Are you going to be okay when Dr. Reinhart comes into the room?"

I exhaled, feeling touched by the consideration but also embarrassed by it. In that exact moment, I could physically feel how tense I'd been. Pushing my shoulders down from my ears, I forced myself to relax. "Yeah, I think so." At least, I hoped I'd be okay, and hopefully Dr. Reinhart had taken a hint last night.

He squeezed my arm and gave me a nod before he opened the door to Benji's room. Benji was lying there watching the news. A smile spread across my face, and Beckett's was soon to follow.

When Benji finally noticed us, a grin spread across his face. "Beckett, my boy! Come give your Pops a hug."

Beckett wasted no time rushing to Benji and leaning over his bedside to grasp him in a hug. He pulled up a chair and sat down. "How are you this morning?"

Benji patted his hand. "Much better. Although, I don't remember much from yesterday besides the biopsy with Ellawyn." He turned his attention to me, his smile reaching his eyes. "I need a hug from you, too, Ellie girl."

I peeled myself away from the corner of the room and joined Benji at the other side of his bed. I leaned down and gave him a hug. "I'm so glad you're feeling better," I whispered before I pulled away.

We spent the next several minutes filling Benji in on everything that happened yesterday with his seizure and how Beckett had decided to close the shop today.

Benji surprised us all by not commenting on the loss of business for one day. When he didn't say anything, Beckett visibly relaxed. I could tell how stressed he must be with all of this, but his love for Benji was always present and at the forefront.

Our conversation was interrupted as the door to Benji's room was shoved open, and Dr. Reinhart walked through the threshold. He did a quick sweep of the room, looking from Benji to Beckett, until finally turning his attention to me. A wry smile creased the corners of his mouth as he took me in before he turned his attention back to Benji.

As Dr. Reinhart talked with Beckett and Benji, I found myself pulling away from the conversation. I didn't want to hear Dr. Reinhart's voice, let alone look at him. Memories of my past ran through my mind. Suddenly it was as if I were outside of my own body, on the outside looking in. Everything felt so far away and out of reach. Closing my eyes, I counted down from ten as I focused on my breathing. By the time I got to one, I felt a little more like myself again, but the uneasiness that I'd felt still lingered.

Beckett's stern voice pulled me back to reality. "When will we get the results of the biopsy," he questioned.

"We'll have the results in a week at most. They'll go to Benji's PCP, where they'll meet with you to discuss the best course of treatment."

Beckett moved to extend his arm to shake Dr. Reinhart's hand. "Thank you."

Dr. Reinhart glanced down at Beckett's outstretched arm before he placed his hand in Beckett's for a quick shake. "Of course." He turned to Benji. "I'll go prepare your discharge papers. Your nurse will bring them in." He shook Benji's hand before he turned away from the hospital bed. Instead of leaving right away, he lingered by the door and glanced in my direction. He reached into his coat pocket and pulled out a card and scribbled something on the back. When he stepped toward me, he extended his hand with the card. "Ellie."

Instead of taking it I stayed frozen where I was. My heart pounded out of my chest as my vision narrowed. I couldn't see in front of me any longer, as everything distorted and blurred out of focus. Closing my eyes, I counted down from ten again. My vision started to clear right as a hand landed on the small of my back. Beckett's touch was like a tether that reeled me back to reality and kept me grounded. It was a silent show of comfort.

A sign that I wasn't alone in this.

Beckett stepped around me and went to grab the card out of his hand while Dr. Reinhart tried to pull it back.

Beckett was faster, though. He stepped back to my side and held up the card in front of both of us. The front had his name, title, and contact number. He flipped the card over to read the handwritten note: *Ditch Beckett and come out with me. I'm off in an hour.*

Beckett laughed out loud and threw the card back toward Dr. Reinhart, which landed right next to his feet. "She isn't interested. Now go get our discharge papers so we can get the hell out of here."

Dr. Reinhart bent to pick up the card and slid it back into his coat pocket. "She will be eventually. They always are." He left out of the room without so much as a glance back.

A throat cleared behind us.

Shit. I'd forgotten Benji was here to witness all of that. I could practically feel my face turning red with embarrassment. When I turned around, I found Benji staring at us.

"That guy's a real asshole," Beckett grumbled. "He harassed Ellie last night and just tried to take her home with him today." He walked back to the chair next to Benji's bed and sat down.

Benji looked at me as if I were fragile and about to crack. He was probably right, but I still hated that he could see it. "Sorry he treated you poorly, Ellie."

I managed to give him a half smile. "It's okay." I made eye contact with Beckett and mouthed the words "Thank you" to him.

After a few minutes, Benji's nurse from last night, Lucy, came into the room with her huge smile and a stack of paperwork that would give Benji his get-out-of-jail-free card.

As they went over paperwork, I decided to give them some space and went over by the window to sit down. I was lost in my own little world until Lucy came up behind me. Her gaze found mine in the reflection of the window, and her smile was replaced by a look of sadness.

"Are you okay?" she asked. She lowered her voice before continuing. "I overheard Reinhart being a bit... much earlier."

"I'm okay." I turned to look directly at her. "He just made me uneasy, that's all."

"I've got to go check on my patients, but I just wanted to check in. It's not the first time he's made someone uncomfortable around here. Just be careful and stay alert, okay?"

I stayed silent but nodded my head.

Lucy smiled and gave my shoulder a squeeze before she turned and sauntered out of the hospital room.

Her words seemed ominous and replayed in my head as I tried to figure out what she had been trying to say. All I knew was that she was warning me of things to come.

CHAPTER 8

Beckett

THE NEXT FEW days had come and gone quickly. Pops returned to Starlight Books, acting as if nothing had happened. Ellawyn continued showing up at opening and leaving when I'd close the place down. She'd been staying busy, creating new art pieces and reading books throughout the store, and I'd been running Starlight Books and taking care of my business back in Boston during whatever down time I had with Starlight Books.

Which meant long days and late nights.

With the lunch rush fizzling out, I glanced down at my watch and realized Ellawyn had never come for her lunch today. I looked out into the shop and found her hunched over her sketch pad, drawing furiously with a pencil between her teeth while looking completely stressed out. I rubbed a hand over my face as I worried about her.

She'd retreated into her shell over these past few days, not speaking unless spoken to and keeping to herself. Things had been strained around here for all of us, and it seemed as if we were all coping differently. With Ellawyn, though, I couldn't pinpoint what exactly caused her to revert to her old ways. Was it waiting for Benji's diagnosis? The fact that her artwork was on display in a public place? It also could have been that asshole Reinhart. Any of those reasons would warrant a reaction, but I just wished she knew she didn't have to deal with these things alone. I could help her if she'd let me in. I wanted to help her.

Mostly, I just missed her. I missed her company. I missed the easy conversation.

After checking the shop one last time for new faces, I walked back into the kitchen area and grabbed what I'd need to make Ellawyn lunch. I'd just placed the sandwich on the skillet when Pops joined me. "Hey, Pops."

He gave me a knowing look. "I don't recall anyone ordering a grilled cheese sandwich."

"It's for Ellie. I've noticed she gets so laser focused on her work that she forgets to eat sometimes."

He laughed. "Yeah, I figured it was for her."

After I flipped the sandwich over again, I grabbed a helping of mixed fresh fruit and a bottle of water from the refrigerator. I placed the grilled cheese on the plate, cut it in half, and then added the small bowl of fruit on the side. When I turned around with the food and water in my hands, I spotted Pops looking at me with his eyebrows quirked.

"Don't look at me like that. You should go eat too, old man." Pops broke out into a fit of laughter as I left the kitchen.

When I got closer to where Ellawyn sat, I could see her staring at something. I turned to look and saw her gaze fixated on two women who were looking at her artwork on the wall—which meant Ellawyn was probably freaking out over her work getting any sort of attention.

Deciding to distract her, I walked right in front of her line of sight, blocking the two women, and sat down directly across from her with a big smile plastered across my face. She jumped at the sudden intrusion.

"Why are you staring at the two women that are eyeing your masterpiece?"

"It looked like they were reading something underneath." She craned her neck to see around me. "But I can't see what it is from here."

Turning in my seat, I noticed that the women are looking at a little card that I'd added below the canvas. A card that indicated the piece was for sale. "That's my fault. I added a card for interested buyers."

She frowned. "How could you make that choice for me?"

"I didn't. Pops said you agreed to try to sell the artwork. Is that no longer the case? I can remove the card." I pointed toward her plate. "Eat before it gets cold."

Her body language softened. "I forgot about that conversation. But you're right, I did agree to that. It's just so weird to think about someone buying something so personal to me." She picked her sandwich up and took a bite before reaching for her water. "Hopefully it doesn't end up in the wrong hands."

"Do you want me to remove the card?"

She exhaled. "No, let's leave it. I need the money anyway."

I stood up, ready to let her eat in peace, when I suddenly had an idea. "Stick around after closing tonight? I want to talk to you about something."

"Yeah, sure. I actually want to talk to you, too."

I tapped my knuckles on the table. "Excellent. I'll catch you later. Enjoy your lunch."

The rest of the afternoon flew by, along with most of the evening. Pops and I had been preparing to close the shop for the night when I brought up that Ellawyn and I planned to talk after closing.

He smirked. "Oh, what about?"

I used my pointer finger to circle his face in the air. "Stop with that look. It's nothing like that."

"I wish it were," he confessed. "You and Ellawyn would be a sweet couple. I like knowing you'll both have the other after I pass."

I sighed and gave him a sad look. "Don't go there, okay? One step at a time."

"And Ellawyn?"

"Ellawyn and I are friends." As much as I'd like to take her out and be more than that, Pops didn't need to know that. I grabbed the coffeepot and dumped the leftover coffee down the drain. "I wanted to offer her a part-time job."

His eyes widened briefly, then his features softened about offering Ellawyn a job. "Probably a good idea." He grabbed the rag I had in my hand and began scrubbing away at the dried-up coffee stains on the counter. He scrubbed and scrubbed, even after the mess had been cleaned up.

Something was wrong. Stepping closer to him, I placed my hand on top of his. "Pops. When did you find out the results of the biopsy?"

His hand stilled as he looked up at me, a crease in his brow. "Go close up the shop." He turned and shuffled away from me, heading into the kitchen.

The look on his face was one I'd never forget—fear combined with pain while he desperately tried to hold it together. I grabbed the keys to the front door and went out into the shop. When I rounded the counter, I spotted Ellawyn sitting in her usual chair with headphones on, bobbing her head as she smiled to herself.

When I made it to the entrance, I locked the door and flipped over the sign on the window, then I dimmed the lights in the shop so it'd be relatively dark inside.

As I went back toward the kitchen, I couldn't help noticing that I was much like the bookshop now—relatively dark inside, the light dimmed for the time being. Ever since Pops's diagnosis, things had been heavy, which was to be expected. But I hadn't realized how suffocating it'd be or how dark this space could get. How lonely it could all be.

In the kitchen, Pops was pretending to clean the grill. But he was actually staring off into space, his arm moving in circles over the spotless appliance. I walked over to him and placed a hand on his shoulder.

He looked at me with tear-filled eyes as he began to crumble. I grabbed him around the waist and wrapped his arm around my shoulder so I could support his weight in case he fell. His shoulders shook uncontrollably as the tears spilled down his face. After a few moments, I led him into the shop and steered him toward the couches.

Ellawyn noticed us and rushed to support his other side. When we made it to the couches, we gently lowered him onto the cushion, and I sat down beside him while Ellawyn rummaged through her bag for tissues. She pulled one out and handed it to Pops.

He grabbed it from her, then clutched it to his chest as he emptied out the well of tears. Once he finally calmed down, he looked from me to Ellawyn and back again. Ellawyn's eyes watered as she sat perched at the edge of her seat.

"Pops." I looked at him with pleading eyes. "Tell us," I prompted.

He cleared his throat. "I received a call from my doctor, and they had the results of my biopsy. Yesterday afternoon, I had an appointment."

A silent stream of tears rolled down his face and onto his shirt. "Beckett, can you get us some coffee? I'll feel better with coffee."

"Uh..." I stammered. "Yeah, sure." I stood from my spot next to him and glanced at Ellawyn. "Would you like something?"

"Hot chocolate, please. I'll help." She rose from her seat and gave Pops a hug before she followed me to the counter. "He's a wreck, Beckett," she whispered while I made our drinks.

"It must be bad." I poured her hot chocolate into a mug and slid it toward her. "I just wish he'd let me help him."

She nodded her agreement while she looked all around the counter and frowned.

I pushed the glass of tiny marshmallows over to her. "Looking for these?" I poured creamer into Pops's coffee, gently stirring before I rinsed off the spoon.

She smiled sadly as she picked up the tiny tongs and plopped seven marshmallows into her hot chocolate. "Thank you, Beckett."

The sound of my name coming off her lips sparked something inside me—a straight shot to the heart that longed to be heard again.

I shoved the thoughts of Ellawyn from my mind and picked up the coffees, refocusing on Pops. He had pulled himself together enough that the tears had subsided. I handed him his coffee, and as he took a drink, he frowned into his cup but didn't say anything.

Ellawyn and I returned to our seats and sipped our beverages while giving Pops some space.

It didn't take him long to break the silence.

"I've... I've been diagnosed with grade four Glioblastoma."

I racked my brain to remember what exactly grade four meant. If it was anything like stage four, then I knew we're in for a fight.

Before I could ask, Pops continued. "Glioblastoma is an aggressive type of cancer, mostly in older males." Tears formed in his eyes again, and this time, I let mine fall right along with him. He took a deep breath and then let it back out. With a pained expression, he said, "It's known as the meanest and nastiest of all cancers; like a tornado, destroying everything in its path."

I pinched my lips tight as I dropped my head into my hands. My heart sank at the news and my palms turned sweaty. I felt like I was about to pass the fuck out. When I looked at Ellawyn, she was as white as a ghost, with a tear-streaked face.

"Some of the symptoms of Glioblastoma are reoccurring headaches, nausea, vomiting, seizures, blurred vision, speech diffi-culty, and changes in mood," Pops explained. "The symptoms don't paint a pretty picture, but as you can tell, the outcome isn't bright either."

I couldn't process the information he was throwing at us fast enough, but once it sunk in, it hit me like a freight train.

"Like a tornado, destroying everything in its path."

This diagnosis would completely alter Pops's life, destroying him in the process. Everything was about to change, and there'd be no going back. My arms felt weak as numbness set in, my heart breaking a little more as each minute passed.

A flash of movement caught my eye when Ellawyn darted to the other side of the couch and sat on the edge next to Pops. She pulled him into her arms, cradling him as she stroked his hair while he cried. Whispers escaped her lips in a quiet mantra.

Scooting closer to Pops, I rubbed his back in small circles, hoping to relieve some of the tension. When his sobbing dwindled into slower, silent cries, I pulled back to look at him. "I'm so sorry, Pops," I whispered. Concerns and questions whirled around in my mind, but instead of voicing them, I shoved them deep inside, knowing that wasn't what Pops needed in that moment.

"I'm scared, Beckett," he confessed.

I didn't hesitate this time. I pulled him into my arms as I held on to him as tight as I could, my own tears releasing. Another pair of arms wrapped around us, and I closed my eyes and squeezed Pops tighter as Ellawyn did the same to me.

Quiet tears turned to loud, angry sobs. By the time we'd managed to pull ourselves together, we were left with red puffy faces and damp clothing.

"There's more," Pops said with a frown. "I have surgery on Friday to remove the tumor."

"Today is Tuesday," Ellawyn mumbled before she looked at Pops. "You have surgery in three days?"

"Yeah," he said with a sigh. "It's to remove as much of the tumor as possible. I'll be awake during the surgery so that they can map out where the tumor is and try to avoid crucial areas. Special marker-like things will be placed on my head to target the location of the tumor. That will help the surgeon to determine which portions of the tumor are safe to remove." He stood from his spot on the couch. "It will take five to eight hours to complete."

Three days didn't give us a lot of time to prepare ourselves to handle a major surgery.

"There's so much to figure out," Pops fretted. "Like how much insurance will cover and how much will be out of pocket. But I can't worry about that right now."

"Don't worry about that," I offered. I'd make damn sure that Pop didn't have to pay a penny toward the cost of surgery and treatment afterward. I'd cover it in a heartbeat. "I'm coming with you on Friday."

"Me too," Ellawyn chimed in. "If you'll have me."

"Of course," Pops replied with a small smile. "I'd like that." He moseyed toward the door of the shop and hesitated. He looked around, as if in a trance, like he'd been trying to commit the shop to memory. "I think that's enough of this for tonight. I'm going to head home." He opened the door and looked back. "Love you both."

Then he walked out, closing the door behind him.

Turning around, I met Ellawyn's gaze. She had tear-stained cheeks and a downcast expression. She looked completely wrecked.

But damn if she still wasn't the most beautiful woman I'd ever seen.

Not feeling like talking tonight, I decided to put off our conversation. "How about we take a raincheck on our conversation and you come in and help me with prep tomorrow? We can talk then."

She nodded, understanding lacing her features. "Sounds good. See you in the morning, Beckett." She grabbed her tote bag and walked by me on her way to the door.

"Good night, Ellie."

I let out a curse as I stood alone inside a dark, quiet Starlight Books. Deciding not to stay any longer, I went to the door and locked up. But when my feet hit the sidewalk, I was rooted in place, unable to decide what to do or where to go. A vibration in my pocket grabbed my attention, and when I slipped my phone out, I saw a text from Max.

Max: Remnant Hearts tonight?

Perfect timing. I could use a drink, or four, to get my mind off everything. I typed out a text and went to the corner of the block to cross the street to Remnant Hearts.

Me: You're buying. On my way.

CHAPTER 9
Ellawyn

I HAD such a great idea that I was literally running to Starlight Books, excited to tell Beckett. I hit the sidewalk in a steady rhythm. The sound of my shoes smacking the pavement and my heavy breathing were the only noises I registered.

When I turned the corner on Quimby Grove Square too fast, I ran smack dab into a surface so hard that I fell backward. A set of hands reached out to grab my arms before my ass hit the pavement, their hold remaining strong while I steadied myself.

"Sorry for running into you. I wasn't watching where I was going—" I stopped talking when I realized he hadn't let go of my arms yet. I tried to pull away slowly, but instead of letting go, he gave me a quick, painful squeeze before he loosened his grip on my arm and released me.

As I ran my hands over my clothes to smooth them out, I noticed I couldn't get a good look at the man's face. He had a hoodie on with the hood pulled over his head. And with it still being dark out, I could only make out the lines of his face. I bent to pick up my bag, but the man beat me to it. He passed the bag from one hand to the other before handing it over to me.

The guy was starting to weird me out, so I decided to just get out of there. "Thank you," I repeated and moved to step around him. He turned his back to me and moved with me so that as I walked away, he was watching.

A shudder ran through my body as I picked up speed and jogged the last block to Starlight Books. I knocked on the door excitedly and watched through the glass as Beckett looked up. He looked rough, like he hadn't slept in days.

He plodded over to the door, unlocked it, and let me in. "Morning," he mumbled incoherently.

I arched an eyebrow. "Everything alright?"

He shrugged. "I could ask you the same question. You knocked on the door like something was wrong, but when I opened it, you're standing there smiling. That's a little weird for you."

"Fair point. But what's weird about smiling?"

He pulled the door closed and locked it behind us. As he strode toward the counter, he talked over his shoulder. "For most people, nothing. But you're generally a stoic person, so it's a bit unlike you."

My smile faltered. He was right. It had been such a long time since I'd been genuinely happy and excited like this. He didn't know this part of my personality. That part of myself had been locked away for a long, long time.

"Now that's more like it," he joked with a smile.

"Yeah," I mumbled. "Anyway, I had an idea and I'm really stoked to tell you about it."

Beckett tilted his head for me to follow him into the kitchen. As he began the breakfast prep for the day, I walked across from where he was working and sat on the counter so I would be facing him. He went through the prep work for muffins, and I could tell that he was just going through the motions, not really paying attention. He looked beaten down, not acting like his normal self at all.

I kicked the leg of the table he'd been working on, and he looked up at me, startled.

"Are you okay?" I held eye contact instead of looking away like I would normally do.

"Sorry, Ellie. I had a rough night and went out with my buddy Max and may have had too many drinks."

Suddenly, I felt silly. Of course he'd had a rough night after the bomb Benji had dropped on us. "Sorry. I wasn't thinking..."

Beckett waved a hand in the air, dismissing my apology. "It's fine. I know you meant well. What were you so excited to tell me?"

"Oh, um... it's nothing. I didn't mean to bother you. I'll let you get back to prepping." I felt myself slipping back into my shell and shutting down. I didn't want to be this way. I wanted to break free and be myself. After being conditioned to feel as though my thoughts and feelings weren't valid, that what I'd thought didn't matter, it didn't take long for me to revert into those bad habits of my past.

Sliding off the counter, I turned to leave without waiting for him to respond.

He caught my elbow. "Not so fast. Get back here, hop your ass back up on that counter, and talk to me."

His eyes were full of compassion and a silent plea. When he seemed satisfied that I wouldn't leave, he let go and smiled at me before he went to pop the muffins in the oven. After setting a timer, he returned to where I'd been standing and hoisted himself up on the counter. He stared at me and patted the spot next to him.

With a sigh, I hopped up next to him and placed my hands in my lap, fiddling with them.

He placed one of his hands over mine, stilling my movements. The contact spread warmth through my hands and up my arms. "Do you want to talk about why you just shut down on me?" His voice was soft and gentle, but it hadn't been enough to let my walls down just yet.

Instead of answering, I shook my head no and gazed down to our conjoined hands as he flipped my hand over and laced our fingers together. My breath hitched and my eyes closed as I took in the moment—all it meant and all that I wanted it to mean.

He leaned over, brushing a piece of hair behind my ear, and let his hand linger on my face. When I opened my eyes, I was enchanted by him and wanted more. The space between us radiated with secret feelings that were hidden just beneath the surface, desperate to be freed.

"Tell me about your idea. I want to hear about it." His voice pulled me back to reality. "You were so excited about it when you first came in."

"Oh," I mumbled, feeling saddened by the intimate moment ending. "After last night, I had a strong urge to do something to help. I thought maybe we could lessen the financial burden that Benji will face. I'm sure the cost of surgery and treatment is astronomical." I paused to see if Beckett would shoot the idea down, but when he stayed silent, I continued. "I was thinking we could do a fundraiser here at Starlight Books. Not only will it help Benji financially but he will also see all the support he has in Quimby Grove."

Beckett turned his head to look at me with that megawatt smile turned on full blast. "That's such a great idea. What type of fundraiser did you have in mind?"

Having his support lit something within me. A purpose. I hopped off the counter and began pacing back and forth as I talked. "Well, when I took Benji for his biopsy appointment, we talked about our favorite board games and desserts and joked about having a game night here." I gestured to the bookshop. "We can take our idea and turn it into something bigger."

Beckett hopped off the counter and pulled me into his arms, then spun us around in circles. I laughed and resisted the urge to bury my face in the crook of his neck. Instead, I wrapped my arms tighter around him and enjoyed the feel of our bodies pressed together. Every rigid line of his body melded to mine, like our bodies were meant to become one.

When he finally put me down, he placed his hands on top of

my shoulders before running down the length of my arms and stopping to lace our fingers together. "You never cease to amaze me," he whispered. Then he planted a kiss on my forehead. "Thank you for everything you've done for Pops and me."

When I looked into his eyes, I could see so much emotion running deep within him. We stayed like that for a long moment, getting lost in each other. A current ran between us, binding us together in this moment. I could feel the shift, and I knew nothing would quite be the same again.

A loud buzzer startled us, breaking the trance. We both jumped back, dropping each other's hands as Beckett went to the oven to get the muffins out. Disappointment filled me as the loss of the moment with Beckett overwhelmed me. It had ended too quickly.

Beckett placed the muffins down on the table and put the batch of scones into the oven next. "So." He turned back to me after he closed the oven doors. "What do we have to do to make this fundraiser come to life?"

As we worked together, we also tossed ideas back and forth for the fundraiser. By the time the prep work was finished, we'd nailed down quite a few details.

Tickets would be sold for thirty dollars for those who wished to attend the game night, and we'd also have a bake sale during the event. While the money we brought in wouldn't be enough to make a huge dent in the cost of Benji's treatment, it would most certainly put a smile on his face, which was the most important part.

As I took down notes, I realized Beckett hadn't given me his favorite board game and dessert yet.

"Battleship and... chocolate chip cookies," he responded confidently as he stocked the display case with today's selection of pastries.

I let out a laugh. "Battleship, huh?"

"Yes, Battleship," he quipped. "I get to figure out where my opponent is and then sink their fucking ship. It's satisfying."

"Agree to disagree," I joked.

We continued to work in unison until it was time for Beckett to unlock the shop doors and assist customers.

While he was busy running the shop, I took up my usual residence in the corner and began working on an art piece I'd started last night—a sculpture of the human brain, but with an artsy spin.

When lunchtime rolled around, I'd finished the sketch of the sculpture and had written out fundraising ideas just in time for Beckett to plop down beside me and handed me a plate with a grilled cheese and a bottled water.

My stomach growled instantly as I reached for the plate and took a bite out of the sandwich. Holding back a moan, I savored the gooey goodness. "Thank you." I opened my eyes to find him focused on my mouth. Embarrassed, I wiped my mouth with my napkin and put my sandwich down before grabbing my notebook. "I think we should do the fundraiser *before* Benji's surgery."

His eyes snapped up to meet mine. "Wait... that would mean we'd have to do it tomorrow." He sat up straighter, leaning his arms on the table. "Okay," he agreed.

Relaxing into my chair, I grabbed the bottle of water and took a drink. This was a good thing—albeit rushed—but I wanted to make sure Benji got to enjoy this event before his world was flipped upside down even more. I also didn't want to ambush him either. "Do you think you could go talk to Benji about the fundraiser?" I questioned. After grabbing my sandwich for a bite, I continued. "Just to be sure he's okay with the idea and okay with people knowing what he's going through."

Beckett glanced around the shop, then he went over to the door and flipped the sign from OPEN to CLOSED and locked the door before visiting each of the customers one at a time. Each one looked over at me before Beckett would walk away.

"All right, Ellawyn," Beckett said as he sat back down across from me. "Here's the plan. I've closed the shop for the rest of the day and told everyone to let you know once they're done so you can let them out and lock up again as they leave."

Nerves shot through me as I realized that he wanted to leave me here. *Alone.* He couldn't possibly think it was okay for me to be here alone. I'd never had this much responsibility before. I'd screw up. "You... You want to leave me here alone?" I stammered. "Where are you going? What if someone wants to buy something? When will you be back?"

He leaned across the table to grab one of my hands, then laced our fingers together. The warmth of his skin on mine instantly calmed my nerves. "You'll be fine, I promise. The cash register is so easy that it practically does the work for you. I want to go talk to Pops and make sure he's on board, and then I'll start getting things ready for us." A smile grew on his mouth. "What if you design some flyers for the fundraiser while I'm gone?"

Having a task to complete instantly calmed my nerves. Excitement raced through me, I grabbed my sketchbook and flipped to a fresh page. "I can do that." I dug into my bag for a pencil. "When you get back, I can show you how to recreate it on the computer."

He cocked his head to the side, looking bewildered. "I have a computer in the office." He nudged his head toward the kitchen. "You can just use that while I'm gone."

He was entrusting me to use his computer. Nobody had trusted me like that in a long, long time. I dipped my chin down as I tucked a strand of hair behind my ear. "Oh... I don't know. What if I break it?"

Beckett reached under the table and grabbed the leg of my chair before pulling me to his side. When my chair was practically next to his, he reached over and pulled me onto his lap, wrapping his arms around my waist. "You won't break anything." He nuzzled his head into my neck. "And if something does break, we'll fix it together."

Momentarily, my body stilled at his affection before I let myself give into my feelings and out of my mind. My arms instinctively wrapped around his neck as the butterflies in my stomach took flight, and I soared up into a bliss I'd never known could exist.

As my feelings took over, I ran my fingers through his hair and brushed my lips against his forehead. Leaning my forehead against his, I let out a content sigh. "Thank you," I whispered. "For reassuring me that I won't completely fuck everything up."

He pulled back, placing his finger under my chin. "You could never fuck everything up. Not here and certainly not with me. I think you're absolutely perfect."

"I'm not perfect."

"You're perfect for me."

Tears welled in my eyes at his sentiment. I swiped them away before he could see and stayed silent, unsure of what to say. There was so much I wanted to say, to do, but I didn't know where to start.

Beckett gave me a reprieve as he gently rubbed my legs before helping me stand up. "We better get a move on. Did I tell you how beautiful you look today?"

Heat rushed to my cheeks as I pivoted to pick up my bag and put my things away. "Thank you," I muttered.

"I've got the keys to the shop for you," he mentioned as he pulled his wallet out of his back pocket. "I'll call the store landline once I talk to Pops." He held out the keys and some cash that he'd folded in half. "And here's some money. I was thinking maybe you could go to the store to pick up some raffle tickets once you're done with the flyer."

"Okay," I said as I reached for the keys and the money. Our fingers brushed together, the energy between us palpable. I swallowed and pulled my hand back, gripping the keys way too tightly.

"I'll be back as soon as I can."

A wave of nausea washed over me as I watched Beckett walk out of Starlight Books. Working through my anxiety, I decided to busy myself with a task. I pulled up a stool from the kitchen and sat behind the counter so I could work on the flyer and keep an eye on the shop.

After about an hour, the store had cleared out, and I was finished with a rough draft of the flyer. I went to the shop entrance and double-checked that the door was locked, and then I went into the back office to work on Beckett's laptop.

After about an hour on the computer, the flyer was done, and the file had been sent to the local printer for copies. I'd just gotten back from the store with a bag full of tickets when the phone rang. "Hello," I answered.

"Ellawyn, as I live and breathe," Beckett replied. He let out a little laugh before he continued. "Pops is on board with the fundraiser. I'm heading back now. Want to run some errands with me and move on to phase two?"

"Absolutely."

After hanging up the phone, I gathered my things and waited for Beckett to arrive. I couldn't believe all the things I'd felt for him today. I finally felt like I was free from my old life and excited to spend time with someone other than myself. I'd been letting my guard down carefully while Beckett had been slowly tearing down the walls that surrounded me.

I hoped I was worth the effort.

CHAPTER 10

Beckett

We spent the rest of the day getting everything squared away for tomorrow night's fundraiser for Pops. After picking up the flyers, we posted them all over Quimby Grove, even going door-to-door to local businesses and personally inviting them to the event.

Everyone we talked to had been in complete support of Pops and wanted to do anything they could to help. Most people even made an additional donation on top of buying a ticket to attend the event itself.

And Ellawyn... Well, she was phenomenal. The timid woman I'd gotten to know had grown into her own during our adventure around town. We talked to the first few businesses together, and then we eventually split up to cover more ground. She was shining out there today. A beauty all her own radiated off her. She was confident, personable, and completely committed to making this event a success. She was always beautiful, but today, she was pure magic. I was in awe of her.

It was close to seven in the evening by the time we made it back to Starlight Books.

Ellawyn made a beeline for the coffee maker, starting a fresh pot. "Okay, so we sold a total of two hundred tickets, right?" She grabbed two coffee mugs from the cabinet. Her eyes grew wide as she found her answer. "We just raised six thousand dollars toward Benji's treatment."

I smiled back as I went straight for the couch and sat down. Her excitement was contagious, and I found myself growing anxious to make the numbers rise—just to continue to see Ellawyn so happy.

She grabbed our cups and met me at the couch. She placed our coffees on the table in front of the couch and then allowed herself to flop down onto the cushions. A yawn caused her eyes to close as she stretched her arms up over her head. She burrowed deeper into the cushions and laid her head on my shoulder. "What's next?" she mumbled.

I let out a sigh and lifted an arm to wrap it around her shoulders. "A lot. I'm not even sure where to start."

Through her long lashes, she peeked up at me, her gaze darting around my face. "Permission to take control?" She bit her bottom lip as she blinked up at me, waiting for a response.

"Permission isn't necessary. What's your plan?"

A grin spread across her face as she sat up and pivoted on the couch to face me. "Okay, so since you're the one with the wheels, you're tasked with going out and finding board games for tomorrow. We absolutely need Guess Who, The Game of Life, and Battleship."

"I can handle that. How many different games do you think we should get?" I stood up and pulled my sunglasses out of my pocket.

She tapped her upper lip with her index finger. Let's go with ten board games. Oh, and I have a deck of cards and bingo that I can bring in as well."

I nodded. "Sounds good." I walked to the door and held it open for her to go out first. "You coming, Ellawyn?"

"Oh. No, I have my own task. Well... I mean..." she stammered. "I do if that's okay with you." She ducked her head and looked toward the floor.

She was cute when she was nervous. "What's your task?"

"Well..." She hesitated. "I was going to start the baking process. All our favorites plus some other options. I was hoping to use the kitchen here"—she motioned toward the back—"since I don't have a lot of space in my apartment."

Immediately, I want to say no. That the thought of leaving her here alone at night isn't something I'm fond of. "You want to stay here all alone while I'm out robbing Quimby Grove of all of their board games?" I joked.

Batting her eyelashes, she looked up at me. "If you're comfortable with me being here, then yes." She looked around the store. "Or I can wait outside until you return."

I pulled her into me, wrapping my arms around her waist. "I just want you safe, that's all." After a moment, she lifted her arms and wrapped them around my neck. "But of course, you can stay here while I'm gone."

Bending down, I gave her a tight hug and spun her around. "I have something for you." I stepped away and went behind the counter to grab a small gift bag. When I returned to where she was standing, I held it out for her. "Here you go."

She walked to the couch and took a seat and then moved the tissue paper around to pull out a box. When she opened the box, a brand-new cell phone slid out onto her lap. She picked it up and flipped it over in her hand. When she looked up at me, tears swam in her eyes and slowly slid down her face. "Beckett... you didn't have to do this."

I sat down beside her and took her hands in mine. "I know, but I wanted to. I worry about you."

She took a breath. "This is the nicest thing anyone has ever done for me. I don't deserve this."

I caught a few of her tears with my thumb and brushed them away. "Ellawyn, you deserve everything."

Our gazes caught, and I felt like we were staring into each other's eyes for a lifetime. It was as if we were each other's lifeline. I wanted nothing more than to kiss her lips, but instead, I learned forward and placed a kiss to her forehead. "Always remember that, okay?"

"Thank you, Beckett."

Giving her hands one last squeeze, I stood up. "You're welcome. You should have plenty of supplies in the kitchen for baking. Just shoot me a text if you need anything more. My number is already in the new phone." I winked at her. "Lock the door after I leave."

After going to seven different stores in and surrounding Quimby Grove, I finally found the last game we needed three hours after I'd left. As I was driving back to Starlight Books, my phone chimed, and the voice assistant in my car read the text aloud.

Ellawyn Calloway: You're really missing out. These chocolate chip cookies smell amazing.

My mouth curved as I listened to her message. When I arrived at Starlight Books, I parked outside of the shop and grabbed the box that I had filled with board games.

As soon as I stepped inside, the sweet aroma of freshly baked cookies hit my nose and my stomach growl. After placing the board games down on one of the tables, I relocked the door and closed the blinds before joining Ellawyn in the kitchen.

"Need any help?" I asked.

Ellawyn peered over her shoulder. "Always," she said as she wiped her hands on her apron. "But now it's my break time." She plucked a chocolate chip cookie from the cooling rack before hopping up on the counter. She took a bite, the warm chocolate dripping from the cookie and down onto her chin. "Can't take me anywhere, huh?" She smiled as she cleaned up her face with a napkin.

I laughed and got to work boxing up the chocolate chip cookies. Grabbing a cookie, I popped it into my mouth. When I went to grab another one, Ellawyn's hand came down on mine, smacking it.

"No more cookies," she teased. She finished boxing up the

remaining cookies and exhaled before speaking. "Beck, do you remember when I wanted to talk to you about something yesterday?" She picked up a spatula and twirled it in her hand.

"First, I like it when you call me Beck. And second, yes, I remember."

She rested her palms on the counter and looked down at the table. "How does it work with selling my art piece? Like, do I set a price? Or does someone just put an offer on it?"

"Either way. We can list it at a price you'd like to set, or we can take offers." I hopped up on the counter and sat. "Do you have a preference?"

"Gosh, this is so embarrassing," she mumbled. "I'm running low on money, and while I'm not thrilled about a stranger buying my art, I don't have much of a choice."

"How ironic," I answered. "I actually wanted to offer you a job here at the shop as a part-time employee. We need the help here, so it seems like a win-win. You would still have time to work on your art, and you could earn some extra cash."

She smiled up at me, and it was almost blinding. "Are you serious?" She jumped up on the counter next to me. "Thank you, thank you, thank you." She lunged into my arms and hugged me tightly.

We spent the rest of the night in the kitchen, working on the remaining baked goods for the bake sale. Ellawyn had made a big dent before I'd arrived. She had six dozen of each type of cookie made and had just started baking a chocolate cake from scratch.

We cranked up the music and danced around the kitchen with flour in our hair and on our faces, laughing as we went. I hadn't felt this carefree and happy in quite some time. This woman had become a part of my life and my heart. A little bit at first and then all at once.

The hours passed quickly. By the time we finished and cleaned up, the clock read four thirteen in the morning. We both went out into the shop, ready to leave for the night. Ellawyn twirled around and then plopped down on the couch. She stretched her arms out over her head and arched her back. My mind instantly went to all the things I'd love to do to her that would cause her to arch her back like that. Shoving the fantasy aside, I gathered up our stuff while she relaxed.

"You totally came through tonight, Ellawyn." Her cheeks turned a light shade of pink at the praise. I held my hand out above her and helped her stand. "Here's your bag." I handed it to her.

We crossed to the door, and I flicked off the lights while Ellawyn hung up a sign that said we'd be closed until the fundraiser. When she exited, I locked up and joined her on the sidewalk. "Care if I walk you home?" I asked.

She quirked her eyebrow at me. "Sure," she responded before turning to head down the block.

We walked the next few blocks in silence. It was comfortable just to be beside her. I dropped my hand to dangle next to hers, our fingertips brushing, and I slowly linked our fingers together so that we were holding hands. A small smile played at the corners of her mouth.

She stopped suddenly. "This is me."

We were just a few blocks away from Starlight Books, standing outside of a huge brick building. The front was covered in vines that nicely framed the double emerald green doors. Above the doors was a green canopy that read The Quimby Grove Ribbon Mill. There was a sidewalk leading up to the entrance with bushes and flowers surrounding it. It looked beautiful. Classy, even. It was as charming as Ellawyn. "This place looks nice, Ellie. Are there a lot of apartments inside?"

She looked up at her building and smiled. "Not many, no. Which is mostly why I picked it." She started walking up the sidewalk toward the door. "There are less than eight apartments in this building. I have the entire top floor. It allows me to have the space to do my art and live comfortably. The other floors each have two apartments." She looked around once more. "It's not much, but it's mine."

I took a step toward her and leaned in to give her a hug. I held on to her a little tighter and then stepped back from the embrace. "It's beautiful." I took a step back, ready to start down the sidewalk. "Want to walk to Starlight Books together tomorrow?"

She nodded. "Sure. Text me before you leave your place."

I winked at her as I started walking backward down the sidewalk. "Good night, Ellawyn."

"Good night, Beck."

I watched as she unlocked the door to her building and stepped inside. She opened a door—to a stairwell, I thought—and glanced over her shoulder at me. Her face broke out into a huge smile as she found me watching her.

I smiled back as she gave me a little wave.

CHAPTER 11
Ellawyn

Last night, sleep came quickly for the first time in a long time. I'd decided to wake up after a few hours so I could create a gift for Benji and make sure it would be dry in time for me to take it into Starlight Books later today.

Beckett texted me when he was on his way to my place, and I met him outside of my apartment building. We walked to Starlight Books together, laughing and cracking jokes about our overnight stay in the shop last night. While we talked, it dawned on me that last night had been one of the best nights I'd had in a while. I finally felt like I belonged again, like I was a part of something special.

Butterflies formed in my belly, preparing for takeoff. Knowing Beckett felt the same way was the cherry on top. I hadn't known I could feel that way again. I'd never thought I'd be worthy of this level of affection, but I knew now.

Beckett snapped me back to reality. "What do you have wrapped up there?" He jerked his head toward the gift-wrapped square I'd been holding.

"Oh." I held the present closer to my body. "I decided to wake up early today and make Benji a little surprise. Just something small to give him tonight at the fundraiser."

"That's awesome. What did you make?" He nudged me with his shoulder as we waited for the crossing sign to change.

"Not telling," I repeated. "Besides, it's just a small gift. Nothing to get excited about, I swear."

"Everything about you is worth getting excited about." He winked at me as he pulled me closer to him while we crossed the street to Starlight Books.

When we arrived, we immediately went our separate ways and started getting everything ready for the event. Beckett got to work setting up the extra tables and chairs within the shop while I finished packaging up our bake sale items into individual portions for people to purchase.

After five or so trips back and forth, the display case and the counter were both filled to the brim with baked goods. The cake slices, brownies, and Oreo truffles were stored in the display case, and six different kinds of cookies took up residence on the L-shaped counter Beckett had completely cleared off for me.

My stomach let out a long growl as I eyed the sugary confections that were on display right before my very eyes.

Beckett quirked an eyebrow. "Whoa there, killer. Don't tell me you're going to murder me if you don't eat soon," he teased.

I rolled my eyes and chuckled. "Maybe." I held my arms out toward the baked goods. "You can't blame me after looking at all of these options for tonight."

He stepped up behind me, wrapped his arms around my waist, and propped his head on my shoulder. "It looks amazing, babe." He kissed my cheek before he unwrapped his arms and grabbed my hand in the process. "Come on, we're going out for an early dinner." He pulled me out the door and locked it behind us.

I let him lead me down the block and across the street. "Where are we going?" I asked. When I looked around, I spotted an old antique store, an art gallery, and a bar.

"I thought it would be obvious." He stretched out his hand in the direction of the three shops I'd seen.

"I go from home to Starlight Books every day. That's about it." I shrugged as if that were normal. "I don't get out much."

His steps faltered. "You're serious?" When I didn't respond, he continued. "We're going to Remnant Hearts Bar. My friend Max owns it."

Just the thought of going somewhere new had sweat forming on my palms. Beckett tugged me along until we reached the bar and went inside, where he pulled out a barstool for me and waited for me to be seated before he took his own seat.

I took a moment and glanced around the place. The walls on the bar side appeared to be a sort of dark wood paneling, while the bar top itself was black with a wooden trim. The shelves behind the bar were well stocked with alcohol and multiple beers on tap. On the opposite side of the room, booths lined the wall. This place screamed English-style pub. There was even a red telephone booth.

Beckett slid a menu toward me, and I was shocked by the vast selection of food they offered. From English classics like fish and chips or Shepherd's pie to burgers, soups, and salads. My mouth was watering at the descriptions on the menu, and I was so distracted that I didn't hear someone approach us.

"Well, well, well. Of all the pubs in the world, Beckett Walden walks into mine."

Beckett burst out laughing as he leaned back on his stool. "Hey, man. Ellawyn, this is Max. Max, meet Ellawyn."

Max turned his attention to me and offered his hand.

"Nice to meet you," I said. "Beckett told me you're the owner. That's awesome." I glanced around. "I love the atmosphere."

Max grinned. "Nice to meet you too. And thank you. I've put a lot of work into this place." He tapped the bar with his knuckles and looked to Beckett. "What can I get you two to drink?"

"How about two waters for now, and we'll let you know if we want anything else after Ellawyn checks out the menu."

Max grabbed two small glasses and placed two Remnant Hearts Pub coasters in front of us. After filling the glasses, he placed them on the coasters and rubbed the back of his neck. "Listen, man, I'm not sure if I'll be able to make it to the fundraiser tonight. Closing manager called off."

Beckett waved him off. "Don't worry about it. You've got your own business to handle. Stop by when ya can, if you can. Pops would love to see you."

Max turned his attention to me. "Miss Ellawyn," he crooned. "You up for a hot date with a pub owner?" He leaned down on the bar to get closer. "We can ditch this tool and have a good time."

I choked on my water, nearly spitting some out as Max and Beckett laughed.

Max slid a few napkins over to me. "I was just teasing."

I rolled my eyes as I took the napkins and cleaned up the mess I'd made. "Jerks."

Beckett put an arm around me before addressing Max. "Off-limits, dude."

"You know I can't help fuckin' with you," Max teased.

The three of us chatted about Benji's fundraiser, and the men swapped childhood memories until our food was delivered. The meals looked and smelled wonderful. I'd ended up ordering the chicken pot pie while Beckett had ordered a dish called "Prince of Cambridge," which was Max's version of Cuban pork.

We fell into silence as we devoured our meals. With clean plates, and both of us feeling stuffed, Beckett paid the tab and we sought out Max so we could say goodbye. Max promised to do his best to make an appearance tonight.

After our dinner, Beckett and I went back to Starlight Books and made sure that everything was set up and ready to go. Checking the time on my phone, I realized it was almost five in the evening, and I still needed to head home to change. I went into the kitchen, seeking out Beckett to let him know. I found him putting away the last few dishes we had left.

"Hey, Beck. I'm going to head home for a quick shower and to change for tonight."

"Sounds good. I have to do the same." He put the muffin pan away and turned to join me by the door. He jiggled his car keys as we walked to the door. "Want a lift?"

"I'll walk. But I won't object to a lift home tonight." I looked up at him with a coy smile.

His movements halted at the doorway as he leaned against the frame and crossed his arms over his chest, making his black V-neck T-shirt stretch tight across his chest. He cocked his head to the side, a small smirk playing at the corners of his mouth.

Damn, that was sexy. My face flushed with heat as I thought about how good-looking and wonderful he was. He beckoned me over with his index finger before he recrossed his arms.

I took the few steps between us and stood directly in front of him, but not too close.

He laughed and pulled me into his space, bringing his arms up and around my waist. I melted into the embrace and smiled up at him. "I'd love to give you a ride home tonight. Go get dressed and text me if you need anything."

I stepped out of his embrace, feeling the loss instantly. I spent the entire walk home wondering how it would feel to be wrapped up in Beckett in every way imaginable.

☾

TONIGHT, I was dressing to impress.

I stood in front of my full-length mirror, evaluating my outfit. I'd chosen a sleeveless halter skater dress with a high neckline. It was a dark shade of blue with hints of floral overtop. My makeup was simple—a light coverage foundation, mascara, and blend of earthy brown for my eyeshadow. I topped it off with light eyeliner and some glossy nude lipstick. My hair had been curled in loose curls that were flowing freely down my back.

When I glanced in the mirror, I felt beautiful for the first time in a long time. Before coming to Quimby Grove, this side of me had been suppressed and locked away deep within. Whenever I'd get dressed up like this, or do my hair and makeup in general, I'd get berated by my ex-boyfriend. Eventually, I ended up just conceding to avoid a fight.

That life had been exhausting.

But here I was, wearing a gorgeous dress with my hair and makeup done, and I didn't have to stress over a man's negative reaction.

I was finally starting to live my life again, and on my own terms. I knew what not to tolerate in future relationships, and I recognized that I didn't deserve to be stripped of my identity and be manipulated to what someone else wanted.

My thoughts were interrupted as the alarm on my phone echoed throughout my apartment, a gentle reminder that I needed to get moving if I wanted to get to Starlight Books on time for the fundraiser.

I slipped on some nude wedges and opted for my black cross-body purse instead of my usual tote bag. After shoving my wallet, phone, and lipstick inside, I was on my way.

The walk to Starlight Books seemed shorter this evening, but I imagined that was due to my excitement. I'd almost made it to the shop without anything setting me back, but as I turned the corner toward the Quimby Grove Theatre and read the marquee, I was completely surprised. Instead of listing out this weekend's movie title, it read: *Game Night Fundraiser at Starlight, by Ellie and Beck.*

I stopped in the middle of the sidewalk, staring up at the beautiful old-school marquee, feeling overwhelmed with happiness, when a voice caught me by surprise. "Do you like it?"

Turning around, I caught sight of Beckett looking at me with the most devastatingly handsome smile. He eyed me up and down, more than once, and I did, unabashedly, the same to him. He was wearing a white long-sleeve button-up with the sleeves rolled to his elbows, which put his tattoos on full display, and a pair of black form-fitting dress pants with a narrow black tie.

I don't think I'd ever been as smitten as I was right then.

Moving around the crowd on the sidewalk, I made my way over to him and linked my arm with his. "You did this?" I questioned while I looked up at the marquee again. "It's beautiful."

"It really is a sight to see; beautiful in all its elegance and grace, lighting up the sky on even the darkest of nights."

When I turned to look at him, I found his gaze on me instead of the marquee. I smiled at him before turning away to hide my blush.

He leaned in and pressed a kiss to my cheek. "Shall we?"

We walked the last block to Starlight together, arm in arm, while we snuck glances at each other the entire way.

My breath hitched when I saw the outside of the store. Beckett had hung strands of twinkle lights and included a black hostess-style podium that would be manned by someone who would collect tickets.

It looked stunning and elegant.

"Beckett," I started. I spun around in a circle, taking in the decorations once more. "You did so much more than we'd planned..."

"I wanted to add a few more special touches. There are also tons of the little fairy light things inside as well. It looks like a fairy tale threw up inside, but I think you'll enjoy it."

When we went inside the shop, I laughed because he was right about the lights. Beckett and I decided which roles would be best for us throughout the event. I'd be collecting tickets at the door, while Beckett would be inside getting everyone situated for the event and greeting folks on a more personal level.

By the time seven rolled around, there was a line outside circling the block. Beckett unlocked the door, and we both went outside together so he could make a small announcement to welcome everyone.

After Beckett went inside, I was ambushed with people eager to get in. Everyone in line took the time to introduce themselves and welcome me to Quimby Grove. Most offered hugs or handshakes as well. The process was ongoing for about twenty minutes, until I finally got a break in the rush of people.

I glanced inside the shop and watched as everyone laughed and caught up with Beckett. My heart warmed at the sight of this man in all his glory, hosting a fundraiser to help Benji. I'd been so enthralled with watching Beckett that I hadn't noticed that someone had approached my podium. I turned to greet them. "Hello, welcome to Starlight Books's game night fundraiser." Then I saw who was standing in front of me. "Dr. Reinhart. What are you doing here?" I stood a little straighter, squaring my shoulders.

He gave me a wicked grin. "I'm here for the fundraiser for Mr. Walden, of course."

"That's kind of you, but our event is sold out." I placed my hands on my podium to steady myself.

Dr. Reinhart took a step closer and peeked inside the shop. "I think I see a few spots available inside, don't you?"

"Um, well, people are still arriving. Those seats will be taken soon."

He leaned down on the podium. I could feel the heat of his breath on my face and pulled back. "I think I heard that Max may not be able to attend. I'll pay double for his seat."

I began to answer, but another voice came in over mine. Beckett came to stand at my side, his arm wrapping around my waist.

"You've heard wrong, Jace. Max will be here."

Dr. Reinhart clocked Beckett's move and narrowed his eyes on me. He was just about to respond when Benji arrived.

"Dr. Reinhart, is that you?"

I caught Dr. Reinhart plaster on a smile when he turned around and saw Benji walking up to us.

"Mr. Walden." He let out a forced laugh before continuing. "I heard about the fundraiser and knew I had to show up for my favorite patient."

My eyes rolled. Hard.

Beckett chimed in. "Yeah, certainly is a kind gesture, but we're all sold out for the event." He pointed inside. "It's a full house in there."

Benji narrowed his eyes at Beckett before turning to Dr. Reinhart and holding out his hand. "Nonsense, come on in."

Dr. Reinhart watched as Benji entered the shop before he returned his attention to us. "Glad we could clear that up. See you inside."

As he disappeared, Beckett pulled me in closer and whispered, "I'm not sure why he has such a hard-on to attend tonight, but I don't think anything good can come of it."

CHAPTER 12

Beckett

DESPITE REINHART DECIDING TO CRASH, the event was off to a great start. Pops played games with everyone, laughing nonstop, while I was busy catching up with Quimby Grove business owners and residents. Ellawyn was manning the bake sale, and there hadn't been a single time when there wasn't a line.

I was grateful she'd been so busy. The only reason I'd kept such a close eye on her was because Reinhart had placed himself at the closest game table to Ellawyn. He even sat himself so that she would be in his line of vision. What was amusing, though, was that he sat at the game table for Clue, and Reinhart couldn't seem to catch a clue that Ellawyn hadn't spared him a glance all night.

The rest of the evening flew by without any issues from Reinhart or otherwise. Toward the end of the evening, I grabbed the microphone and got everyone's attention by calling both Pops and Ellawyn up to the front of the store with me.

Pops joined me first, while Ellawyn had ducked into the kitchen to grab her gift for him. I headed up the conversation, thanking everyone for coming out and expressing how much it meant to Pops and me. I recognized Ellawyn for her brilliant fundraiser idea and for helping to throw the event at the last minute.

When I handed the microphone to Pops, tears pooled in his eyes, and he stayed quiet for a moment. The rest of the room followed suit as the silence spread. Finally, Pops cleared his throat and brought the microphone to his mouth. "First and foremost, I'd like to acknowledge my grandson, Beckett, and the lovely Ellawyn." He looked at us, a smile growing on his face. "For those that don't know, Ellawyn is relatively new to Quimby Grove, and she holds a special place in my heart." He locked eyes with her as he continued speaking. "She's kept me company every day for the last six or so months and has grown to feel like family to me." He turned his attention back to his guests. "She will soon be working at the shop. Please welcome her with open arms."

The crowd broke out in applause while Pops turned to hug a now crying Ellawyn.

She whispered something in his ear and then looked him in the eyes as he responded. They hugged again before Pops turned back to the crowd.

"Everyone knows who my boy, Beckett, is. He's grown up from the little boy who always had chocolate around his lips from our chocolate cookie adventures each day after school."

The crowd chuckled at the memory.

"Beckett has grown into a fine man." He looked at me with such love in his eyes as tears flowed down his face. "Successful, driven, kind, loyal to his family, and so much more, Beckett is by far my biggest success in life. He's everything I'd hoped he'd be, and I'm so glad he's here with me during this difficult time. I love ya, boy." Pops placed the microphone down and turned to pull me into a hug. This hug said so much that couldn't be put into words. It meant everything.

Ellawyn stepped up to us and placed a hand on Pops's shoulder. "Benji, I have something for you."

Pops pulled away, turning to give Ellawyn his attention as she handed him the wrapped-up canvas. He laughed. "Cat-themed wrapping paper, huh?"

She shrugged. "It was all I had."

As Pops unwrapped the gift, one of his hands came to his mouth, and he gasped and looked at Ellawyn. "Ellawyn... this is so touching. Did you paint it?"

She shifted her weight on her feet, nerves taking over. "I did. I hope you like it." She pointed to a section of the painting. "The colors on it indicate love."

A few tears slipped free, sliding down Pops's face. I walked over to them, looking at what Ellawyn had created. It was a painting of a brain. The brain itself was painted gray, and there were parts within that were painted red, orange, yellow, and green. Above the main image of the brain were two words painted, and then below the brain was another word. The words read: YOU ARE LOVED.

Ellawyn leaned in and pointed out other small details of the painting to Pops. She wiped the tears from her face as she laughed with him.

Glancing around Starlight Books, I worked to commit this moment to memory. The folks of Quimby Grove were all looking at Pops with adoration and respect while he and Ellawyn talked and looked over the gift she'd made. I continued scanning the crowd until my eyes landed on Reinhart and his glaring gaze, which was pointed directly at me. I smirked in his direction and then turned my attention back on the people that mattered.

After the emotional speeches, people finally filtered out while stopping to wish Pops good luck on his surgery. Meanwhile, Ellawyn and I started to clean up after the fundraiser. I worked on the decorations outside while she dealt with the aftermath of the bake sale.

I'd just finished taking down the string lights when I glanced through the window, not seeing anyone else inside. I went to open the door of the shop and was surprised to see an uncomfortable looking Ellawyn standing beside Reinhart.

His hand reached out to touch the small of her back, and she dodged his attempt by pretending to clean up the other side of the counter. He pulled his hand back and shoved it inside his pants pocket.

Pulling the door open, I stepped inside and shut it louder than necessary. When Ellawyn looked up, a gasp escaped her mouth, and her shoulders lowered from her ears. "Hey, Beckett."

I shook my head at the sight and closed the distance between us. "Hey, Ellie." I gave her a reassuring smile and turned to him. "Reinhart."

His gaze stayed on Ellawyn, unwavering. "Good night, Ellie. I have to head home and get some rest since I have a big surgery tomorrow." He winked at her. "See you soon." He turned and moved for the door.

I followed him and locked the door as soon as he left. "Was he being weird again?" I asked before I turned off the lights.

She exhaled, placing her hands on the counter. "Just a little." She narrowed her eyes. "Hey, we haven't finished cleanup. Why did you turn off the lights?"

I joined her behind the counter, pulling two bags from beneath it. "I figured we won't open tomorrow anyway, and after we make sure Pops is okay, we can come back here to clean more, count donations, and celebrate a successful event."

I picked up two slices of individually wrapped chocolate cake and deposited a slice into each bag. I grabbed for two packs of her infamous Oreo truffles next and added them as well before I grabbed some chocolate chip cookies.

I handed her one of the bags along with her purse.

"That sounds like a plan." She peeked inside the one I'd just filled with leftovers. "What's this for?"

"For our inevitable late-night cravings." I grabbed her hand and led her out the rear exit of the shop. After we were both in the car, I took her hand in mine again and held on to her until we parked outside of her apartment building.

Instead of getting out of the vehicle right away, I pulled her hand to my lips, gently brushing them across her skin. "I've had a wonderful time tonight. You're incredible, you know that?"

She blushed, ducking her head. "I had a great time tonight."

I gave her hand one last squeeze before I hopped out of the car and went to her side to open her door. As we walked toward her apartment building, we held onto each other, neither of us wanting to break contact. Stopping just outside the entrance, I brushed a stray strand of hair out of her face and tucked it behind her ear before I rubbed her neck a little.

She leaned into my touch, shifting her face as she planted kisses all over my palm.

Wanting to respect her space but still needing to touch her, I ran my thumb over her cheek one last time before removing my hand from her face. "Good night, Ellawyn."

"Good night, Beckett," she whispered.

I watched as she entered her apartment building, keeping an eye on her until I saw her enter the elevator.

☾

THE HUSTLE and bustle of the hospital waiting room had slowly been driving me crazy. The constant chatter, the sounds of metal banging against metal out in the hallway, trays being placed, and beeps constantly going off had been incessant.

As I ran my hands over my face, I exhaled and leaned forward, propping my elbows on my knees while my hands held my head.

I was exhausted.

Sleep hadn't come easily last night. For anyone, apparently. It turned out that Pops, Ellawyn, and I were all plagued with a sleepless night. Poor Ellawyn hadn't slept at all. She was in the chair next to me, curled up with her feet on the seat, arms wrapped around her knees, and fast asleep.

She looked unbothered and absolutely beautiful.

While she slept, I replayed the conversation we'd had with Pops on the drive to the hospital this morning. He had been so vulnerable when he spoke. He'd confided that he had been having trouble accepting and grieving the loss of the plans he had for the rest of his life. Uncertainty had hit him hard—wondering what dying would be like for him, for his family, and even what would happen to Starlight Books.

I'd been at a loss for words. So instead of filling the space with more uncertainty, I'd gripped his hand while I drove, an offer of silent reassurance. Ellawyn had listened intently while silently crying in the backseat. She'd been incredibly sweet the entire time. When she'd finally spoke up, it was in a way that both acknowledged Pops's fears and reassured him that he wasn't alone in this.

She had reminded him that the best thing that we could all do, and not just him, was to live life to the fullest as much as possible. The sentiment seemed to have struck a chord within her as she let the words sink in. As I had stolen glances through the rearview mirror, she'd closed her eyes and nodded to herself.

I'd wished I knew what was going on in her mind.

☽

A LIGHT TOUCH gently nudged me. "Hm?" I mumbled as my eyes drifted open and then closed again.

"Benji is out of surgery."

I jolted awake and sat up in my seat. I looked to my right and found Ellawyn still asleep. "Sorry about that. How is Pops doing?"

When I looked up, it was the same nurse from when Pops had his biopsy. *Lilly, I think her name is?*

She smiled at me. "My name is Lucy. I'm Benji's nurse."

Okay, so not Lilly.

"Nice to meet you, Lucy." I stood up and led her away from where Ellawyn slept.

"The surgery went well. Dr. Reinhart will provide an official update, but I wanted to let you know that Benji is back in his room, and you can go back whenever you're ready."

"Glad to hear it." I checked the time on my watch. "Surgery took five hours?" I asked.

"It did." She pulled a paper out of her scrub pocket. "Here is the room number for Benji." She extended her hand to give me the paper.

I glanced at the paper with the number 1325 sprawled across it. "Thank you, Lucy. We'll be up soon."

When Lucy left, I went back to Ellawyn and gently rubbed her arm. "Hey, Ellie. Pops is out of surgery."

Ellawyn's eyes fluttered open a few times before she stretched and sat up. "How long have I been asleep?" she mumbled.

"About five hours. Come on, let's go get some coffee before we head to see Pops." I extended an arm and helped her up before I bent down to grab her bag.

When we entered Pops's room, he was fast asleep. Ellawyn quietly shut the door while I moved the two chairs next to each other at Pops's bedside.

Just as we settled in, Reinhart appeared. He gave a curt nod. "Afternoon."

I nodded back without offering a greeting.

He slid his hands inside his lab coat pockets. "Let's just get down to business. As you know, Mr. Walden had a craniotomy today. He was put under for the initial incision and then was awake for the rest of surgery. The surgery itself took a bit longer than expected due to Mr. Walden having a seizure while on the table."

"A seizure?" Ellawyn questioned. "Is he all right?"

"Yeah." Reinhart's stance relaxed as he addressed Ellawyn. "Seizures are to be expected. We were able to remove all the visible tumor. He fell asleep shortly after surgery, which is normal, but we won't know how the surgery affected him until after he wakes up."

"Thank you."

Reinhart exited the room without further commentary, leaving us alone with a passed-out Pops.

We spent the next few hours waiting for him to wake up, and

we both agreed that waiting was the worst. The feeling of helplessness was settling in.

A gentle knock on the door came before it was slowly pushed open. "Hey, you two. Just wanted to let you know that visiting hours have ended for the day." Lucy gave us a sad smile before closing the door again.

Ellawyn stood from her chair and bent down to give Pops a kiss on the cheek. "Get better, Benji. See you soon." She crossed to the other side of the room and waited by the door.

"Hey, Pops," I said as I grabbed his hand. "I've been here all day. I'm sorry that I have to leave before you've woken up. I wish I could stay. I'll be back first thing in the morning. Good night, Pops."

Ellawyn and I headed back to Quimby Grove and went straight to Starlight Books. Our ride had been filled with silence. No radio or podcasts this time, just both of us alone in our thoughts, desperate for an escape.

When we entered the shop, I grabbed her by the hand and led us to the couch. I sat down, pulling her down with me.

She giggled. "What are you doing? I thought we were going to count the money we raised last night."

"I just wanted to sit next to you somewhere more intimate than two hospital chairs." I lifted my arm and she scooted in; I wrapped my arm around her. I breathed her in, appreciating her scent. She smelled amazing, even after being in a hospital all day. "Let's go on a date."

She shifted in my arms so she could look up at me. "You want to take me on a date?" She looked at me with vulnerability in her eyes, her gaze darting across my face as if trying to get a read on my intentions.

"Not only do I want to date you but more than that, I want to know everything about you, Ellawyn. I want to know more of your silly quirks and what makes you light up inside. I want to know your secrets so that we can share them, and I can carry them with you, and you can help me carry mine. I want it all, Ellawyn."

Her breathing quickened. "More of my quirks? Meaning you already know some?"

"I know that you stick to yourself because you're afraid of letting anyone get too close. I know you tuck your hair behind your ear whenever you get nervous or anxious about something. You care deeply about those close to you and don't ask for anything in return. I know you love to create as a form of escape—whether it be creating art or baking, it's therapeutic for you and I respect that." I brushed her hair out of her face. "I want it all."

She sat up, looking at me. "You're serious?"

I reached my hand out and cupped her face, gently rubbing my thumb across her cheek as her eyes rose to meet mine.

In an instant, everything changed.

Ellawyn launched herself into my arms. Not wanting to wait another second to feel her against me, I pulled her on top of me so she was straddling me on the couch and sitting on my lap. I grabbed her face, bringing her mouth to mine in a quick motion.

Lips fused together in a frenzy; her gasp turned into a moan as my tongue explored her mouth. Hearing the noises that came out of this girl was enough to keep me wanting more. Grabbing the back of her head, I maneuvered her so I could deepen the kiss while her hands roamed my chest as our exploration continued.

I kissed the corner of her mouth as I ground my length into her core. Her head fell back, another moan escaping her lips as she rolled her hips. Taking my time, I slowly kissed my way down her neck as my hands went to her waist.

She lifted onto her knees as I gripped her firm ass. Her fingers weaved through my hair as I kneaded her ass in my hands, desperately wanting to remove the layers between us. "Touch me, Beckett," she breathed. "Please."

Pushing my cock up against her center, I let her feel what she was doing to me before I leaned forward, stopping just outside of her ear. "Baby, you don't need to beg," I whispered. "But it's so fucking sexy when you do." I reached between us to lift her dress up to her waist and slid my hand inside her panties. "Fuck." I slid a finger through her slick folds. "You're fucking drenched for me, aren't you?"

She let out a moan as she moved herself against my finger. "More," she pleaded.

I lowered my hand and slid a finger inside her pussy, letting out a groan at how tight she was. Moving my finger, I gently bit her earlobe. "So fucking sweet." I added a second finger and picked up the pace as she moved her body with my hand, matching the movements. "That's right, baby, ride my hand." Her pussy clenched around my fingers; she was close to coming already. "Come for me, sweetness." The pad of my thumb grazed her swollen clit once before she detonated beneath me.

Ellawyn collapsed on my chest as she rode out her orgasm. Her breathing was ragged, and she clutched my shirt as if her life depended on it. "You're so fucking beautiful," I reminded her.

I gently pulled my fingers from inside her and slid my hand out of her panties before I righted her dress and let it drop back down. Wrapping my arms around her, I placed a kiss on her forehead.

The sound of her moans echoing throughout the shop had become my favorite fucking soundtrack, and I couldn't fucking wait for it to repeat.

CHAPTER 13

Ellawyn

THE NEXT FEW days went by in a whirlwind.

Beckett and I decided to keep Starlight Books closed while we stayed with Benji as he recovered from his brain surgery. When Benji finally woke up, we learned that he had some paralysis in his left arm, but thankfully his speech, vision, and leg mobility was fine. Because of the paralysis, Benji had been receiving physical and occupational therapy to help regain his strength. Beyond that, he'd had a couple seizures and severe headaches since the surgery, but he was doing much better than expected.

Today, Benji was being released from the hospital, which was a huge relief to everyone. After so many days at the hospital with scary side effects, we were all about ready to leave. While Beckett went to go pick up Benji this afternoon, I was in charge of opening Starlight Books. We'd decided on a delayed opening for my first solo day so I could avoid both the breakfast and lunch rush.

As I waited for the clock to strike two, my mind wandered back to Beckett and our time on the couch just a few days ago. The heat crept into my cheeks as I looked toward the couch and pictured us together, in the dark, while he played me like a fiddle with his fingers until I reached oblivion. There hadn't been an end in sight, and I hadn't been ready for it to be over.

I'd been desperate for more, but we'd both kept some boundaries in place over the last few days. Our coziness with each other hadn't faltered, and while we hadn't had any more intimate moments since, we'd spent every waking moment together.

But I knew deep within myself that I was ready to surrender to Beckett. To give myself over to him completely. To let him devour me.

My cell phone dinged, tugging me from my thoughts. I pulled it from my back pocket, seeing a text from Beckett on the screen. I smiled down at my phone as I read the message.

Beckett: Good luck with opening, babe. I know you'll do amazing.

Me: Thank you. How is Benji?

Beckett: About the same as yesterday. Severe headaches all day. We're meeting with his neuro-oncologist at 4 and plan to go over the suggested course of treatment.

Beckett: I miss you.

Beckett: Can I take you on a date tonight? 8:30 at your place?

Watching his texts come through one right after another made my stomach leap. I responded to him and let him know that I missed him as well and agreed to a date this evening.

A smile spread across my face as I tucked my phone back into my pocket and went to unlock the doors to the shop.

It didn't take long for folks to trickle in. Most ordered drinks and spent time browsing the books while others just came by to ask how Benji was and how his surgery went. Everyone seemed pleased to know that it went well and that Benji would be heading home today.

When seven o'clock finally rolled around, I was eager to close the shop and head home. Just as I was about to round the corner of the counter to go lock up, the bell above the door rang.

Without looking up, I greeted the customer. "Hi, we're just about to close for the day," I called out toward the entrance while I walked toward the door. My steps faltered when I saw who was standing just inside the door. "Dr. Reinhart. Hi."

He wandered further into the store, glancing around the empty space. "I was in the area and decided to stop in and say hello." He turned to face me again. "No Beckett this evening?"

My throat went dry. "No, he's helping Benji with a few things." I fiddled with the edge of my apron, unsure of what to say. "I was just about to lock up, actually." I moved toward the door and held it open for him to leave.

He sauntered over and stood in the entryway. "Would you like to go out with me tonight?"

Flustered, I stammered on my response. "Oh, um... Dr. Reinhart, I—"

"Call me Jace." He reached out to grab my hands and pull me closer.

I yanked myself from his grasp. "Right. Jace. Like I said, I'm getting ready to leave." I took a deep breath in, preparing to put an end to this once and for all. I stepped outside, and as expected, he followed me.

I took a few steps back toward the door and locked it from the outside before depositing the keys into my bag. "Listen, I appreciate you stopping by, but I have to go so I'm not late for my date."

When I turned back again, he was there, standing right in front of me, blocking me from leaving. My arms broke out in goose bumps, and suddenly, I couldn't swallow. Wrapping my arms around myself, I mumbled, "Excuse me" as I tried to side-step him.

He hesitated and then moved out of my way as a smile appeared on his face. "A date, huh?" he mumbled. "Is it serious?"

I moved around him, planting myself in the middle of the sidewalk. "It's new."

He nodded, mostly to himself, before he looked at me. "New doesn't mean serious. You'll end up on a date with me sooner or later." He turned to leave. "Have a good night," he called over his shoulder.

As soon as he rounded the corner to head down a different block, a shudder ran through my body as I let out a breath. After waiting a minute or two for him to get a decent distance away from me, I headed toward the square.

My mind rehashed the situation repeatedly, trying to figure out why this man seemed to be so interested in me. Even after telling him I was dating someone, he was still relentless. I thought back on past conversations with him to see if I'd led him on in any way, and I just couldn't see where that would have happened.

Infatuation was a bitch.

I was sure he'd move on soon, though. There were plenty of other women out there that would probably enjoy dating him. When I made it to the Square, I pressed the crosswalk button and waited for the signal to change. When it did, I crossed the street and walked down the block toward the movie theatre. As I got closer, I looked up at the marquee to see what was playing this weekend, but when my gaze returned to eye level, I froze dead in my tracks.

Dr. Reinhart was leaning against the outside wall of the theatre, looking right at me. "I'm just enjoying the Square before I head home," he said with a shrug of his shoulders.

I nodded my head and unrooted my feet from the sidewalk to stride past him, increasing my speed with each step. I turned the corner and broke out into a jog for my apartment.

When I finally got to my building, I doubled over and placed my hands on my knees as I tried to catch my breath. After a few moments, my heart rate slowed, along with my breathing. I pushed my hair out of my face before I looked down the street where I had just come from. Kids were playing hopscotch on the sidewalk, and a young mother watered her flower beds.

With no sign of Dr. Reinhart, I headed inside my apartment so I could get ready for my date with Beckett.

Beckett.

Did I need to tell Beckett about what had happened with Dr. Reinhart? Would it be keeping something from him if I chose not to tell him? Would Beckett be angry with me if I didn't tell him? Maybe what happened wasn't a big deal. People stop by an individual's place of work to ask them out occasionally, right? And running into him a few blocks away could have been a coincidence. It wasn't like he bothered me.

Was I making a big deal out of nothing?

By the time I finished with my shower, I'd decided to tell Beckett about what happened. Not because he would be mad at me if I didn't, but because something about Dr. Reinhart still didn't sit right with me.

Grabbing my purse, I went back into my bedroom and glanced at my reflection. My outfit was simple, but also a bit dressy. I turned in front of the mirror, checking on the back before turning around. I wore a teal ruffled minidress with spaghetti straps. After pairing it with some white strappy sandals, I was good to go.

A knock on the door echoed throughout my apartment.

I pushed down my nerves from the Dr. Reinhart incident, and when I opened the door, Beckett was standing on my doorstep with a bouquet of the most beautiful blue and purple orchids.

My smile stretched across my face as I stepped into his space, giving him a long, tight hug.

He laughed as he carefully wrapped his arms around me. "Did you miss me?"

"You have no idea." I gave him one last squeeze before stepping back. "Let me grab my purse and we can head out."

Beckett handed me the flowers and followed me inside while I placed them into a vase and grabbed my purse. "You look beautiful, you know that?"

When I turned back to Beckett, he was looking at me with such adoration. I didn't think I'd ever had someone look at me that way, as if I was something precious and valuable. "You're too sweet." I smiled. "And thank you for the flowers. They're beautiful."

Beckett led the way to his SUV, which he'd parked right outside my building. Pulling away from the curb, he intertwined our fingers. "I have two options for our date night," he said. "The first option is more laid back, with a nice dinner out. The second option is more intimate, and if chosen, I'd like to keep the activity a surprise until we get there."

I must have given him a look, because he was quick to continue. "Intimate does not mean sex, by the way." He turned onto High Street and passed the Square. "I swear the plan isn't to just take you to a hotel and fuck you six ways to Sunday." He considered something before adding that he wouldn't be against that option, though.

I almost admitted that I wouldn't have minded the hotel idea, but I kept the thought to myself. "I pick intimate," I replied instead.

He winked at me as he drove past the on ramp for the highway and instead went in the direction of the countryside, heading toward the mountain.

The drive was beautiful. The road was scarce as we took the twists and turns along the mountainside, making our way up. Trees and the surrounding forests lined both sides of the road, engulfing us as we went.

The mystery of the mountains had always captivated me—a keeper of secrets, a fortress of solitude. I felt at ease as we ascended. Rolling my window down, I leaned my head back onto the headrest, tilting it toward the window. The wind grazed my face as I closed my eyes, getting lost in the peacefulness of the moment.

When we finally made it to the top of the mountain, Beckett

pulled into an open field filled with beautiful wildflowers. "We're here," he said as he put the car into park.

"Did you bring me here to kill me?" I teased.

He laughed as he got out of the car and came around to open my door for me. "I would never. Here, hold this, please." He passed me a wicker basket before he reached into the backseat for a large cotton blanket.

He led the way through the open field until he found a grassy spot that was level. He tossed half of the blanket into the air before he guided it down onto the grass. It was huge, probably bigger than I'd ever seen before, and it was beautiful with white-and-navy striped, and fringe embellishments on the sides.

After slipping off my shoes, I stepped onto the blanket while Beckett did the same. He reached for the picnic basket and took it from me, then placed it down on a corner of the blanket before he moved to stand behind me.

Wrapping his arms around my waist, he placed his chin on top of my shoulder while he held me tight. "I hope this is okay."

"Mm, more than okay." I tilted my head and kissed his cheek before I leaned into his strong arms. "What made you pick this location?"

He leaned me back a little bit more before he pointed for me to look up at the sky. I gasped when I saw how beautiful it looked. All the stars had begun to light up as the sun set for the evening. I'd never seen anything like it.

"Without the darkness, you wouldn't be able to see the stars and how they shine so bright," he mused. "Sometimes the most beautiful things have been hidden away or taken from us, but if you search deep within, you'll find what you've been looking for all along."

Turning in Beckett's arms, I watched as he looked up into the night sky, taking in the beauty surrounding us. When he glanced down at me, it was as if he was looking deep into my soul and truly seeing me.

Seeing the pain of my past that still haunted me.

Seeing the fragile, broken woman that was desperately trying to heal past wounds.

Seeing the scars that lay within me while my future was standing before me and knowing that, together, we would overcome the darkness that still lingered.

"I'm searching," I whispered, mostly to myself.

Beckett sat down onto the blanket and grabbed my hand, pulling me down with him. He positioned me between his legs and gently guided me to lean back into his broad chest. "What's your biggest dream?" he asked.

My answer came without hesitation. "To be happy. To be safe."

"It's that simple for you?" His voice was gentle and nonjudgmental.

"It is. I know there's a lot in life that I can't control, like my career, or loss within life, or even the people I encounter. But I can make the best of it and work around any obstacles. My only hope is that I remain happy and safe."

"That's a beautiful dream, Ellawyn."

I craned my neck to look at him. "What about you? What's your dream?"

He sighed. "I've never been one to dream, and to be completely honest, I don't even recall having dreams as a kid, either. I just always thought things would work out exactly how they were supposed to. Now, as a man, I think of things a bit differently. My dreams are constantly changing depending on where I'm at throughout the course of my life." He hesitated as he considered something. "My biggest dream now would be for Pops to be all right. Beyond that, my company is doing well, and that's a dream in and of itself." He was quiet for a moment before he spoke again. "I think maybe I need to reevaluate my dreams and how I view them."

"Don't you dare," I said as I shifted so I could see him. "There's nothing wrong with your dreams and how you view them. You're right, though. Dreams do constantly change."

He brushed a finger over my lips before he leaned forward and kissed me softly. I practically melted at the touch, sinking further into his strong arms. He gently pushed me forward and out of his arms. "Let's eat," he said as he reached for the picnic basket.

We gorged ourselves on the perfect spread of food that Beckett had prepared. We had salad, blueberry lemon scones, strawberries, grapes, bread, a cheese plate, and some wine. As we ate, we talked about our favorite silly things—our favorite movies, holidays, and colors. We laughed as we fed each other little bites of food like we'd seen in movies. But somehow, between making fun of it and being silly, we ended up feeding each other without even thinking about it.

It was strangely intimate.

When we were finished with dinner, we lay down on the blanket and watched the night sky as we continued talking. I was tucked under Beckett's arm, my head on his chest as I listened to the beat of his heart. It was a rhythm I could listen to forever, a song I wanted to know all too well.

His hand was in constant motion on my back while I used my fingers to trace circles on his chest, and I didn't think I'd ever felt more content than I did in that very moment.

"Tell me about your family, Ellie. What are they like?"

My fingers stilled at his question. The need to shut down was automatic and second nature by now. But I knew if I wanted to build something with Beckett, I'd need to be more open about my past. Continuing to move my fingers across his chest, I dove into my old life. "Well, I have a small family. It's just me and my parents. They live back in Moon Harbor, Maine, so I don't see them as often as I'd like. But I do write to them frequently." The circles turned into figure eights, the repetition soothing. "What about you?"

He winced. "There's not much to tell, unfortunately. My parents died when I was ten years old." His hand stilled on my back. "It... It was a car accident," he said. "Drunk driver hit them.

I moved to Quimby Grove and have been with Pops ever since. He's all I have left."

I threw my arm around his waist, squeezing tightly. "Oh, Beckett." I couldn't imagine losing my parents at such a young age and growing up without them. My heart broke for the ten-year-old little boy that had been Beckett. "I'm so sorry for your loss. I can't imagine how hard that must have been."

He rubbed my back and kissed the top of my head. "I was lucky to have Pops, though. What about you? How did you end up in Quimby Grove?"

In an instant, it was as if everything froze. My body went rigid. I sat upright, moving out of Beckett's embrace. My breaths quickened—I couldn't slow them and catch my breath. I felt like I was running out of oxygen. Squeezing my eyes shut, I clenched my fists as I rocked back and forth.

A hand landed on my back, moving slowly in small circles. I hadn't heard him come up behind me. His breath tickled the outside of my ear as he slowly breathed in through his nose and out through his mouth. He was guiding me on how to get my breathing under control.

"It's okay, Ellawyn," he whispered gently. "You're okay."

He repeated his words, like a mantra, over and over again until I nodded my head and agreed with him. "I'm okay. It's okay."

I opened my eyes and gazed at the stars as tears flowed down my face. I knew I was safe here, with Beckett. I desperately wanted to give him everything I could—the good, the bad, and the ugly.

And my god, there was a lot of ugly.

I pulled my knees up to my chest and wrapped my arms around myself. "I... I don't talk about this often. I don't like to think of it. But with you, I don't want anything between us. And I feel like you deserve to know the story."

Beckett's hand on my back stilled and then gently pulled away, as if he knew I needed some space to get this out.

I let out a breath, readying myself to open all my wounds and display them before the man I'd been falling in love with.

"A few years ago, I started a relationship that seemed too good to be true. He was hardworking with a stable job, devoted to his family, an active member of the community, and a real social butterfly, if you will. The relationship started out normal. We went on a few dates. We met each other's parents. Our worlds began meshing almost seamlessly together."

The tears that trickled down my face turned into a full cascade, unstoppable at this moment. Suddenly, I was exhausted and numb as I forced myself back in the past.

"Things started changing." I sniffled. "Small things at first, you know? Like not being able to see my family when I had planned to. Stupid things. Then, gradually, things ended up getting worse. I wouldn't be allowed to see my friends at all. Or if I did have plans and refused to cancel, he would just join me instead of letting me go alone."

I picked up one of the wildflowers surrounding us and twirled it in my hands before slowly picking off the petals as I continued. "Then things escalated more. He took control of my job choices, which ended up with me having to find a new job every few weeks. If I developed a friendship with a male coworker, I'd be punished for it. Or even if I just spoke with another man, there'd be hell to pay. It wouldn't matter if it were a stranger at the super-market, or an older gentleman asking for directions. It didn't matter to him."

Beckett's hand gently returned to my back as he started the circles again. I leaned into his embrace, thankful for the connection.

I cleared my throat. "After that, things seemed to become stag-nant for a while. If I complied to every rule and demand, then life was good. It's embarrassing now, but I used to falsely believe those periods of time meant we were experiencing an upswing; that our problems were getting better, that he was changing. I was too naïve to realize that things only appeared that way because I was behaving. But I paid the price for those 'happy' times. I had noth-ing. No relationships with my family and friends. I burned all those bridges because of the behavior I was conditioned to display. The friends that noticed the red flags and tried to warn me were cast aside as friends who didn't want me to be happy. That's what I was made to believe."

Beckett leaned in, pressing a kiss to my forehead. He swiped away a few tears as he held my face in his hands. "Ellawyn, that's abuse. I hope you realize that. You didn't deserve any of that. I'm so sorry, baby."

"I do realize that now. At the time, I thought it was love. But it was all an illusion. After a certain point, I realized I was alive, but I wasn't really the one living my life. He was. He was in control of every aspect of my life. If I stepped out of line, I was punished. And I know I don't have to tell you what type of punishment I endured.

"Once I made the decision to leave, I slowly began putting things into place to make that happen. I met secretly with my parents, who helped me devise a plan. I began saving and storing money away where he couldn't find it. I would be more compliant so that I could earn some of his trust back and some freedom. When I had ten thousand dollars saved up, I stuck it in the bottom of my shoe and told him I was going to the grocery store while he was at work. He knew I typically walked to the store, so that's exactly what I did. I went to the store, bought the usual amount of groceries with his credit card, and then began my walk home. This time, though, a car picked me up, and I left the groceries sitting on the side of the road. I had it all planned out. The car that picked me up, a car he's not familiar with and not linked to my parents or old friends, would be untraceable. The car also contained a suitcase full of clothes, along with some shoes. I was dropped off at a gas station a few towns over, and the driver used their phone to call a car service to take me to Pennsylvania. Then I asked to be dropped off a little bit outside of Quimby Grove, and I decided to walk the rest of the way. I haven't seen my parents since I arrived in town almost a year ago."

Beckett pulled me into his arms as I cried harder. My body

convulsed as I sobbed into his chest. He pulled me back down onto the blanket, lying behind me while he plastered kisses across my hair and shoulders as he held me.

After what felt like an eternity, my sobs began to fade into a silent cry, until eventually, I cried myself to sleep.

CHAPTER 14

Beckett

Ellawyn had been passed out in my arms for over an hour, and I refused to move from her side, even after she had fallen asleep.

A lot of things about Ellawyn made much more sense now that she'd shared her story with me. Why she didn't have a cell phone, or why she only went to the bookshop and home. She'd been scared. How brave she must have been to have given up her entire life, including her family, to break free from a bad situation and start fresh. No wonder she'd taken to Pops like she had—she missed her family.

Her story broke my heart. But it also pissed me the fuck off to know that her dickhead of an ex had treated her so horribly. I wanted to find that fucker and beat his ass. My girl was fearless and strong as hell. And I'd be damned if I treated her as anything less than the queen that she was.

As the wind started picking up, the air grew colder, and Ellawyn shivered in her sleep. I carefully inched myself away from her, peeling my arm out from underneath her. I grabbed the picnic basket, took it to the car, and opened the passenger side door. Once I got back to where she was sleeping, I wrapped the blanket all around her and picked her up off the grass. I carried her to the car and slid her into the passenger seat without waking her, then reached across to buckle her up before I eased the door shut.

The drive back to Quimby Grove was quiet as Ellawyn's story continued to permeate my entire being. A sense of pride had taken root and grew within me. I was so damn proud of her.

I parked in front of her apartment building and turned off the car. When I looked over at Ellawyn, her hair was strewn across her face, and her delicate lips had parted slightly. She looked even more beautiful than usual. I unbuckled her before I went around to her side of the car. I rubbed her arm. "Ellawyn, we're back at your place."

She stirred as her eyelids fluttered open. "We're home?" She stretched her arms out in front of her.

"Yeah, baby. We're at your place." I helped her sit up and unwrapped her from the blanket cocoon I'd concocted for her. "Let me walk you in."

She took my hand, and together, we walked inside her apartment building and directly into the elevator that had been waiting. Once we were outside her door, I took a step back to give her some space so she could dig out her keys.

"Stay with me," she whispered.

When I looked into her eyes, all I could see were the nerves she must have felt about asking me to stay and thinking that I might have said no. "Okay," I said. "I'll stay."

She looked down and away. "I can understand if you're no longer interested in me now that you know my story. If you no longer want me, I get it."

"I will always want you, Ellawyn." I took a few steps toward her, closing the space between us.

Electricity sparked, a lust-filled current flowing freely, and suddenly, we were unable to resist. In a flash, we lunged for each other, and her back was pushed up against the door. My mouth claimed hers, her hands in my hair while I wound mine around her waist. I pushed my cock up against her stomach, and she let out a gasp.

"Door," I whispered into her ear as I kissed down the column of her neck.

She moaned and gripped my hair as I sucked on her fair skin. "Hmm?" she murmured.

"Open the door, baby." I flipped her around to face the door. "Unless you want fucked in the hallway."

Her fingers fumbled to get the correct key into the lock. Once it was opened, she pushed me inside, and the door slammed shut behind us.

I picked her up and her legs wrapped around my waist as our mouths met. I glanced around her space, looking for the closest surface to have my way with her, until my eyes landed on the kitchen island. Shoving everything to the floor, I deposited her down onto the surface as the electricity between us intensified.

Her hands flew to my button-up, and she quickly worked to undo each button while I untied the straps of her dress. She shoved the shirt off my shoulders and pulled the sleeves from my arms as I ran my nose down her neck, inhaling the sweet aroma of cherry that lingered on her skin. I grazed over her collarbone and every expanse of skin I could find until I finally got to the area that covered her.

Wasting no time, I yanked the dress down, exposing her bare breasts. My mouth went to one of her breasts while my hands caressed the other. Ellawyn arched her back and let out a moan as I sucked on one of her nipples while flicking the other. Her breathing quickened with every touch. Every squeeze. Every lick. Every flick.

"Beckett. More," she whimpered.

I looked up at her while I sucked on her breast, and I swear she was about to explode just from that. I let her breast fall from my mouth and kissed my way back up to her lips before capturing them with my own. "Slide back on the counter, baby," I mumbled against her mouth.

Her lips left mine as she slid back until her feet dangled off the edge. I reached under her dress, found her lace panties, and slid them down her legs. After tossing them onto the floor, I grabbed her dress and pulled it down before throwing it aside and leaving her completely bare for me. I licked my lips as I took her in. "Spread your legs for me, angel."

She spread her legs wide for me, revealing her dripping wet pussy.

She was a fucking masterpiece.

I dragged her a little closer to the edge and slid my fingers up through her slick folds. "You're so fucking wet for me, Ellawyn." Her head dropped back as I ran my fingers through her slit again while I kissed my way down her chest, to her stomach and thighs, and then finally, to her swollen clit. I flicked her clit with my tongue and Ellawyn's body quivered. "So close already, baby?"

Lapping at her clit, I slid two fingers inside her and slowly pumped them in and out, setting a steady rhythm. When I added a third finger and picked up the pace, her hands flew into my hair. She gripped my head while she thrusted her pussy against my mouth. Placing a hand on her stomach, I held her still while her grip on my hair tightened. Her pussy clenched around my fingers as she reached climax. I lapped up everything she gave me. When I came up from between her legs, she was breathing heavily and lying down on the counter, covering her face with her arms.

Grabbing her hands, I pulled her up so she could sit upright. She wrapped her arms around my neck as she licked my lips. Kissing her back, I opened my mouth, letting our tongues collide so she could taste her essence on mine. "You're so fucking perfect," I whispered into her ear.

I undid my belt and let it drop to the floor. When I stepped out of my pants and briefs, her eyes were glued to my cock, and I pumped it a few times. Her eyes went wide as she looked me up and down, biting her lower lip in the process.

"You're... um... wow."

I leaned forward, planting a kiss to her lips. "I know, baby. I'll be gentle."

Her head shook. "What if I don't want gentle?"

My gaze met hers and she nodded, confirming what she'd just said. I reached down to grab my wallet and snagged a condom. I had just ripped it open when her hand landed on mine, stopping me from removing the condom from the wrapper.

"I don't want anything between us." She grabbed the condom and tossed it onto the floor.

Grabbing her legs, I pulled her to the edge of the counter and draped one of her legs over my shoulder. The tip of my cock nudged her entrance as she looked up at me and gave me a slight nod.

She screamed out as I slammed into her all at once. Her tight pussy enveloped my cock like a vise. I pulled out slowly, grabbed her hips, and slid into her hard and fast. She held on as I quickened my pace with each thrust.

Ellawyn leaned in and found my mouth, meeting me for a rough and messy kiss. Before long, she started to meet the pace, silently driving the need to go harder, deeper. Thrust for thrust. Kiss for kiss. We took from each other as we gave everything we had. I picked her up off the counter and carried her over to the couch. After laying her down, we picked up where we left off as I pounded into her again while she screamed out in pleasure.

She writhed beneath me as she gave me everything she had. Her body. Her soul. In this moment, she was all mine. And I wouldn't have it any other way.

Her pussy clenched around me as her orgasm built. I reached down, finding her clit, and swirled the pad of my finger against it, watching her combust as I continued to chase my own release.

I unloaded into her, burying myself deep within her body, and I hoped like hell I made a mark on her heart, too.

☾⋆

WE SPENT the early morning hours in between the sheets of Ellawyn's bed as we continued our journey of discovering each other's bodies and catching up on things we'd needed to fill each other in on.

When I filled Ellawyn in on Benji, we had to bring a box of tissues into the bed to try to rein in the crying.

Yesterday, I learned that Pops would have radiation therapy for six weeks, along with an oral chemo pill that would be taken five days a week during those six weeks. The neuro-oncologist explained that after the treatment was complete, Pops would have a new MRI done and be reevaluated. Depending on how that went, he might be eligible for a clinical trial or could possibly have to have another round of chemo. After Pops's appointment, he and I had gone back to his apartment, and he'd dropped the bomb on me that not only was he officially stepping down from Starlight Books but he also didn't want me to come care for him during his treatment.

That blow had been a hard one to take, and I'd protested that decision until he explained. He had given me a hug and said that he didn't want to push that burden onto me or Ellawyn, and instead, wanted to hire someone for that kind of help.

To add to the shock of that news, those interviews for an aide were happening this afternoon.

Ellawyn and I had both gone into Starlight Books that morning and had worked together all day. We completed the prep work for the day, and then Ellawyn had started taking orders and filling them while I worked on inventory until I had to leave to join Pops for the aide interviews.

When I got to Illusion, a local wine bar, Pops was already chatting up an employee. I sat down and joined him just as the staff member left the table. "Making friends already?" I joked.

He chuckled. "That was the owner. Great guy. He's grabbing us some water."

I nodded as I looked over the interview list Pops had organized. There were eight names on this list. I couldn't imagine how he'd gathered so many applicants in such a short time. Made me wonder if maybe he'd been planning this for a while now.

After a few hours of interviewing several applicants, none of which seemed to be the perfect fit, I was beginning to lose hope, until Pops leaned over and whispered, "The real contender has arrived."

Turning in my seat, I watched as a woman walked our way. She must have been in her early to mid-twenties. She had bright blonde hair and blue eyes and was dressed in a pair of black scrub pants and a tie-dye scrub top.

"Hello." She extended her hand toward Pops first and then me. "I'm Rhiannon Kastanowski." She sat down and gestured toward her top. "Sorry about the clothes. I'm just now leaving work for the day."

Pops smiled at her, pushing aside the interview questions we'd been going over. "No apologies necessary."

Pops seemed completely taken by Rhiannon already, and she had barely been here for two minutes. Deciding to interject, I started the interview process. "Rhiannon, please tell us about yourself."

"Well, I'm twenty-three years old and obsessed with golden retrievers. I currently work as a home health aide, but the hours aren't nearly enough."

After a few more questions, mostly from me, Pops hired her on the spot and offered to have her start tomorrow. When she walked out the door, I turned to him. "What the hell was that?" I asked.

He shrugged and put his hands in the air in mock surrender. "Okay, okay. So I knew I was going to hire her from the beginning."

My mouth dropped open as a laugh escaped. Of course he would have found someone but still interviewed folks for hours. "Why didn't you just tell me that instead of spending all evening interviewing people?"

His eyes softened. "I just wanted to spend some time with ya."

My annoyance vanished. "I'm glad we did it, too, Pops." Suddenly it dawned on me that I should be spending more time with him before he was sick from the side effects of chemo and radiation.

Pops picked up his water glass, holding it in a salute to the owner standing behind the bar as he did the same back to Pops.

Over the next hour, we worked our way through Illusion's menu, trying the various drinks and ordered some dinner. Throughout the meal, we talked about things that weren't tumor or business related. It felt nice to enjoy Pops's company without the pressure of anything else getting in the way.

When I told him that Ellawyn and I had started dating, a huge grin spread across his face. He got up from his spot at the table and rushed out of Illusion, presumably to go see Ellawyn. I pulled out my wallet and tossed enough money on the table to cover the bill and a generous tip. I nodded to the owner as I made my way after Pops.

When I finally caught up to him, he was pulling open the door to the shop. "Making a run for it, old man?"

He elbowed me in the stomach, causing me to let out a groan, and stepped inside the shop. When I entered after him, Ellawyn had just come out of the kitchen wearing a smile as big as her face. "Benji," she greeted, "I've been thinking of you. How're you feeling?"

Pops pulled her into a hug. "I'm fine, dear, but I've heard that you are dating my grandson."

She pulled back, looking at him, and a smile slowly took root. "Guilty." She laughed.

Pops pulled her back in, hugging her again. "I always knew you two would hit it off."

We spent the rest of the evening chatting with Pops while we played board games together. Pops won every time. This memory of the three of us would be forever imprinted in my memory. A moment of normalcy before everything changed again.

After he left, Ellawyn and I closed the store together. It wasn't until we were about to lock up that she mentioned she hadn't brought in the mail from today. When I brought it in from our mailbox, I flipped through it to make sure nothing urgent stuck out. Nothing was out of the ordinary until I came across an envelope with Ellawyn's name on it.

I called for her as I walked through the shop. "There's something for you, actually."

She popped out of the office, taking off her navy apron and hanging it up. "That's weird." She grabbed the envelope, flipped it around, and examined it before shoving it into her tote. "It's probably some weird junk. Let's get out of here."

We started our walk home hand in hand, and I filled her in on the aide interviews. When we got the old theatre, I pulled her close and she snaked her arms around my neck. "This is where we go our separate ways."

She rested her head on my chest. "I'm not happy about it."

"Neither am I," I replied as I gave her a squeeze and dropped a kiss to her head. "How about you stay with me tomorrow night? You can pack a bag and bring it to work so we can walk home together."

"That sounds lovely." She beamed. "I'd like that."

We parted after one last kiss goodbye. I watched as she turned the corner to head home, waiting until I could no longer see her, then I pressed the crosswalk button and continued the walk to my place.

Today had been a damn near perfect day—waking up with Ellawyn in my arms, spending time with Pops over dinner, and then the three of us playing board games. It was simple, but it was nice. My time here in Quimby Grove, while complicated, had been life-changing in more than one way.

When I got home, I started cleaning up the place and making it presentable for Ellawyn. I foresaw her spending a lot of nights here. After clearing out a drawer in the bathroom and making room on a shelf in the shower, I made one of my dresser drawers available for her, just in case. I had no intention of springing all of this on her, but if it happened that she spent a lot of time here, then I'd be ready.

My phone vibrated in my pocket. When I pulled it out to make sure it wasn't Pops, I was surprised to see Ellawyn's name on the screen with a text message.

Ellawyn: Um, so you know that letter that came to Starlight for me?

Me: Yes. Why?

My phone vibrated again with an image notification. When I opened it, a piece of lined notebook paper filled the screen with the words "you slut" written in a bold red. My blood boiled at the thought of someone talking to her in this way and harassing her. I threw my phone on the bed as I paced the room. Who the fuck would do that?

I grabbed my phone to text her back and asked if she wanted me to come over. All that came through after that was a simple response that said "No." It would have to be her asshole ex-boyfriend from Maine. I couldn't just let this go, and I had to do something since she wouldn't let me come over.

Me: Do you think it's from your ex back in Maine?

The three dots appeared right away, only to stop after a moment. The cycle repeated a few times until she finally responded.

Ellawyn: No. If he knew where I was, he would have come in person. He wouldn't have hidden behind a letter.

Ellawyn: I'm going to bed. Good night, Beckett.

Me: Good night, Ellawyn. Call if you need anything.

She stopped responding after that, not that I could blame her. My sweet girl had such a sensitive soul, and I knew she must have been devastated after seeing that piece of paper.

Deciding to distract myself, I headed into my home office and logged into my email for my company back in Boston. I managed to respond to a few emails before I got sucked back into thinking about the paper. I needed some sort of plan.

I texted Max and filled him in on what had happened. He was

equally as pissed off as I was and agreed to keep an eye on Ellawyn and stop by whenever I wasn't able to be around. We both agreed that nothing about this scenario made sense. She only ever went to Starlight Books and home. Beyond a few hospital visits with Pops and organizing a fundraiser, she hadn't done anything out of the ordinary.

It had to be the ex-boyfriend who had somehow managed to see Ellawyn and I together around town. There was no other explanation.

That would be tomorrow's problem. There wasn't anything I could do tonight, so instead of focusing my energy on being angry, I decided to go back to handling work emails. I'd been pleasantly surprised to see how well everything was going with me working remotely and seeing that had just solidified my most recent decision: work remotely permanently and stay in Quimby Grove.

The only downside now was that I'd need to plan a trip into Boston to get some files, equipment, and to sign off on various projects.

And I had to do it soon.

CHAPTER 15

Ellawyn

AN UNEASY FEELING settled in after I'd opened the envelope. As I paced back and forth in my apartment, my heart rate skyrocketed, and it felt like an elephant was sitting on my chest. I couldn't breathe.

Forcing myself to calm down, I walked into my studio and sat on the floor with my back leaning against the wall. Pressing my cheek to the cold wall, I closed my eyes and pictured Beckett. My focus was on him as I breathed in and back out again. When I felt like my breathing was more manageable, I opened my eyes and glanced out the window. From where I was sitting, I could see the moon, full and bright, and I found myself wishing for the same. I snapped a picture of the moon from this angle. Just as I tucked my phone away, a loud pounding blasted throughout my apartment as somebody banged on the door.

Who would be stopping by at this time of night?

The only person who even knew where I lived was Beckett. I pulled my phone out again to see if Beckett had texted about coming over, but he hadn't.

Bang. Bang. Bang.

The knocks rang through the apartment once more, only this time, louder. It felt as if the walls were shaking from the force on the other side of the door. I stood up slowly as the pounding continued, and I carefully slipped off my sneakers and stepped into my slippers.

Sliding my feet along the wooden floor of my apartment, I made my way out of my studio and into the kitchen without making any noise. The feeling of unease intensified as I got closer to the door. I felt nauseous. I inched my way through the kitchen until I was right beside the door.

Holding my breath, I counted to ten. When the knocking subsided, I inched myself in front of the door, eye level with the peephole. Just as I lined my eye up to look through the hole, the knocking started again in the exact spot where the peephole was.

I dropped down to the ground as I tried to muffle my sobs. My mind flashed to Beckett as I considered calling him, but this wasn't his mess to deal with. Pulling my legs to my chest, I sat balled up in front of the door for a whole hour, silently crying until the knocking stopped. When I finally got the courage to check things out, I stood and slowly lined my gaze with the peephole again.

Nothing.

I saw nothing. The hallway was empty. Whipping the door open, I looked to my left and was greeted by an empty corridor.

Rubbing my hands over my face, I turned and went into the kitchen. I grabbed a glass from the cabinet and filled it to the brim with water from the faucet. After guzzling down most of it, I dove into the medicine basket on my counter, seeking out my sleeping pill container. I popped two into my mouth, finished off my water, and set the dirty glass into the sink. Before I left the kitchen, I hesitated by the knife block. I chose a huge butcher knife on impulse and brought it with me to the living room. I placed it within arm's reach underneath the carpet. Then I grabbed my pillow and favorite blanket from my bedroom before returning to the couch. After placing my pillow toward the end of the couch that would allow me a visual of the door, I lay down and watched.

The last time I checked the time before falling asleep, it was three thirteen in the morning.

☽

WHEN I WOKE UP, my phone was vibrating in my left hand while a knife was clutched in my right. Feeling disorientated, I dropped the knife to the floor and listened to the sound of it smacking the ground. After a quick look around my living room, I accepted the call. "Hello," I mumbled. My voice was groggy, and I didn't even have the energy to mask it.

"Ellawyn," Becketts voice cut through the line. "Are you okay?"

I sat up immediately and eyed the knife on the floor. "Uh, yeah." I cleared my throat. "Why do you ask?"

"Because..." He hesitated. "Because it's almost eight thirty in the morning, and you're usually here when I do the prep work."

Removing my phone from my ear, I glanced at the time. "Oh, fuck," I cursed before I jumped up from the sofa, tossing the blanket off me, and rushed into my room. "I'm sorry. I overslept," I said as I grabbed my duffle bag from underneath my bed.

Placing my phone on speaker, I looked for items to pack. First, I found a pair of pajamas and tossed them into the bag without folding them. Scouring through my closet, I found my favorite pair of jeans and my favorite graphic tee that featured a stack of books that read "You'll always find adventure within a book." I tossed those inside the duffle before I grabbed the finishing touches of my intimates and toiletries.

"Ellawyn," Beckett snapped through the phone.

I'd forgotten we were even on the phone. "Sorry, forgot." I zipped up my bag and slung it over my shoulder. "I was just packing a bag."

"It's okay." His tone turned lighter. "Do you need me to come pick you up?"

I bent down to pick up the butcher knife and placed it in the sink. "What? No, that's okay. I just didn't sleep well last night." While I brewed a pot of coffee, I leaned on the island, watching as the dark liquid dripped into my cup. "I'll be in soon."

"Okay," he said. "Take your time. I was just worried about you."

After we hung up, I sipped my coffee while standing in the kitchen. Just hearing Beckett's voice had been enough to calm my anxiety and make me feel a bit more grounded. Feeling better, I grabbed my coffee and took it into the bathroom to get ready for the day.

Armed with more caffeine, I grabbed my tote and duffle bag and headed out the door. When turning around to lock my door, I noticed a note taped to it. Glancing down the hallway, I checked for signs of anybody lurking around. When I didn't see or hear anything, I turned my key, secured the lock into place, and ripped down the note.

Once outside, I headed down the block in the direction of Starlight Books. It wasn't until I turned the corner and saw the Quimby Grove Theatre that I allowed myself to stop and open the note.

The color drained from my face as my coffee cup slipped from my hand, dropped to the ground, and broke into tiny pieces, making a mess everywhere. I reread the note once more before shoving it into my tote bag.

The message rang in my head the whole way to the shop.

It should have been my name you were screaming instead of his. Next time, it'll be me.

Making it to the shop in record time, I whipped the door open so quickly that I was surprised it didn't come off its hinges. My gaze darted around in search of Beckett as I quickened my pace while weaving through the tables and bookshelves. When I stormed into the kitchen, I was out of breath. "Beckett," I cried out.

The door to the office whipped open as he walked into the kitchen. "Ellawyn, what's wrong?"

My duffle and tote bag fell to the floor as I ran into his arms and held on as tight as I could. Tears soaked his shirt as he rubbed my back and tried to soothe me. "Baby, what's wrong?" He pressed a kiss to my hair. "Whatever it is, we can get through it together."

After a few moments, I tore myself away from his hold and walked back over to my tote bag before pulling out the note. I handed it over. "This was taped to the outside of my door this morning." I hiccupped a sob. "And last night, someone was pounding on my door." I wiped the tears from my cheeks. "The person who was pounding on my door must have been the one to leave the note."

Needing some space, I left Beckett alone to read the note while I went into the employee washroom to wash my face. When I glanced in the mirror, it felt like I'd taken a time machine back to my previous life. The sullen, broken girl from my former life was in the mirror, staring back at me. I braced my hands on the sink and forced my gaze away.

I wasn't that girl anymore. I was no longer chained to a home that felt like a prison. I had a life here that came with freedom and a man that respected me. I didn't have to look over my shoulder here.

Until now.

After splashing some water on my face to try to wash away the lingering pain from my past, I left the washroom and went to find Beckett.

I went out front, into the shop, and spotted Beckett sitting with Max on the couches. Their hushed tones told me they were talking about me and that damn note.

I was just about to join them when a customer approached to place an order. As I handled the customer, I made eye contact with Beckett. He held up an index finger before turning his attention back to Max.

After I was finished waiting on customers, I finally had a moment to myself. When I was busy, my mind was occupied, and

I could focus on the task at hand. But now, standing here alone while those two talked about what was happening, I'd begun to feel like I was in the dark again. Like people were making decisions for me.

Annoyed, I marched over to where the two men sat and crossed my arms over my chest while I stood above them, staring them down.

"What?" Beckett questioned as he looked between Max and me.

"Whatever is happening around here"—I waved my arms around as I spoke—"is happening to me. Not you"—I pointed at them both—"but me. Do not talk about these things without me as if I'm not here or able to defend myself."

Max rose from his seat, stepping toward me. "You're right." He leaned in for a hug and I reciprocated. "I'm sorry," he said as he sat back on the couch. "Join us."

Beckett looked dumbfounded as he watched me take a seat. "I didn't think you'd want to be involved in this." He lowered his voice before he continued. "Because of your past, I mean."

"That's the exact reason why I need to be involved."

Beckett's face flooded in understanding as he took in what I'd been trying to say. In a split second, he stood from his spot on the couch and pulled me up for a hug while he apologized.

Advocating for myself had been like a rush. I suddenly felt like I could handle anything that came my way. It felt good to handle last night's scare alone, and it felt good to stand up for myself while I'd reminded Beckett that I needed to be involved and have control of what happened to me or how to react.

And he'd given me that.

All three of us discussed what had happened within these past twenty-four hours. Max seemed adamant that whoever was doing this was escalating things. First, someone had mail delivered here, proving they knew where I worked. And next, they'd shown up at my home, now proving they knew where I lived.

"What do we do?" I questioned. "I feel like we're at a loss. I'm not sure who's doing this. Or why."

"I know you told me last night that it wouldn't be your ex-boyfriend, but are you sure?" Beckett poked.

I shook my head, although doubt was creeping into my mind. My ex couldn't be bothered to play games like this. If he'd wanted me to know he was around, he'd have made sure I saw him. He was direct. He didn't hide behind letters and locked doors. But would he? He was the king of mind games and control. "Maybe," I confessed. "But I'm not sure. It's hard to tell."

"We could file a complaint with the police," Max offered with a shrug. "They could at least have these two examples on file and have a record of it."

"No," I blurted out. "No police. Not yet anyway."

Max tapped his knuckles against the coffee table. "Alright. But consider it. In the meantime, I'll keep a close eye on this place while I'm at work." He stood, getting ready to leave. "And just be vigilant, okay?"

"Will do." I waved at him. "Thanks for everything."

The rest of the day went smoothly while Beckett and I worked at Starlight Books together. He was never far from my side, always keeping a watchful eye on me and the entrance of the shop.

His caution made me question if I was doing the right thing about not reporting the notes to the police. Under normal circumstances, I would have done that already, but because of my past, I'd been hesitant. I wanted as few traces of myself within Quimby Grove as possible. If this weirdo wasn't my ex-boyfriend, Joshua, then I certainly didn't want the police nosing around and trying to question him.

I could let this play out a little more.

As things quieted down in the evening at the shop, Beckett let me clock out early so I could work on sketching out my next art piece. I could use the distraction, and I was sure he could tell. Settling into my favorite chair, I put on my headphones and turned my playlist on shuffle. Closing my eyes, I waited until a song came on that lit the creative fire within me.

Of course, it had been one of the saddest songs buried within my playlist that lit that match—"Jar of Hearts" by Christina Perri.

Placing the song on repeat, I pulled out my sketch pad and began drawing out a rough sketch of the first design that came to mind. My pencil started outlining the smooth lines of a mason jar, filled about three quarters of the way with hearts.

A literal representation of a jar of hearts.

By the time I decided on how to bring this idea to life, Beckett had finished closing the shop and joined me at my table with my bags and his car keys. "Come on, baby." He bent down, placing a gentle kiss on my lips. "Let's go to my house."

WHEN WE ARRIVED at Beckett's place, I was completely shocked at what I was seeing. He had a charming split-level family home with a two-car garage. It had a gorgeous bay window, which I'd always dreamed of having.

"Wow" was all I could muster.

He looked at me with a perplexed look on his face before he exited the car and came around to my side. "Wow, what?" he questioned as he reached for the bags that had been settled on my lap.

"I just expected more of a bachelor pad vibe," I answered as I got out of the car and shut the door. "This is a family home. It's beautiful, though."

He led me inside, and I halted in the entry way as I took it all in. The living room area had hardwood floors and a brick accent wall with a fireplace, along with a cozy area rug directly in front of it. There was a glass coffee table and the most comfortable-looking leather couch I'd ever seen, paired perfectly with a recliner and loveseat. Above the fireplace hung a large flat-screen television, and on the opposite wall, abstract artwork adorned the space.

I'd only seen one room and I was already smitten. "I think I'm in heaven now," I joked. "But seriously, I love this room."

Beckett placed my bags onto the floor before moving into my space, pulling me flush against him as he led us to the couch. Sinking into the soft leather of the couch, I let out a sigh and melted into the cushions. "Okay, so we can never stay at my place." I slipped off my shoes and pulled my legs up onto the couch. "My furniture is crap compared to this."

Beckett laughed. "Your place is great. But yeah, my couch is better."

Sticking out my tongue, I playfully kicked him with my foot. "What do you feel like doing?"

He gave me a smirk. "Besides you?"

Blushing, I turned away. "That's not what I meant." I'd suddenly become embarrassed of the thought of wanting sex and acting on it. In my previous life, I was always told when we'd have sex. I wasn't ever the one to initiate it. What if Beckett thought I didn't want him? "I mean, I do... want to... with you again sometime." I'd choked on my words and ended up even more mortified.

He leaned in, giving me a kiss on the lips. "I know, baby." He stood and pulled me up with him, then led us toward the kitchen. "Let's get you fed. You haven't eaten all day."

Beckett continued to charm me all throughout dinner, where he served me grilled cheese and tomato soup. The man knew my heart.

Our conversation over dinner mostly stayed on his home and how beautiful his kitchen was. Although the kitchen was rather quaint, it was lovely. There was a skylight in the middle, which I imagined would be stunning during the daytime. The floors were a neutral shade of gray—a nice contrast against the white cabinets, the backsplash, and his stainless-steel appliances.

The kitchen became my second most favorite room in the house so far.

After dinner, Beckett offered me his shower so I could get

ready for bed. I'd been so touched to find he'd made counter and shelf space for me in his bathroom. And I was even more relieved whenever he said we were still taking it slow, but the space was there if I wanted to use it.

I did want to use it.

Things with Beckett had been moving at warp speed, and instead of getting whiplash, I'd been feeling giddy over our momentum.

When I came out of his en suite bathroom, I found Beckett propped up against the headboard with a laptop resting on his lap. "Your Boston business?" I questioned as I placed my dirty clothes into my duffle bag.

He looked up from his computer and smiled. He turned the covers down and patted the empty spot next to him. "Come on in, beautiful."

When I climbed into his bed, I scooted as close to him as I could and laid my head on his shoulder. "Thanks for this."

He placed a kiss on my head. "You're welcome here anytime. And yes, I am answering a few emails for work. They need me back in Boston soon to sign some paperwork and consult on a few accounts. I've been putting it off, but I think I better go while Pops is still feeling pretty healthy."

I nodded. "You're right, the timing with Benji is perfect. You should just get it over with." I turned my head and kissed his shoulder before I sat up and scooted over a few inches to give him some space.

His fingers flew over the keyboard as he answered an email before shutting down the device. "Want to come with me?"

Admittedly, I wanted to go. I could use an escape from Quimby Grove after these last two days. But I knew I couldn't. "Someone needs to run the shop," I reminded him.

"Oh." He sighed. "You're right. But are you even comfortable doing that?" He wrapped an arm around my shoulder, pulling me closer. "I mean, are you okay with being left alone after receiving those two notes? I know you can run the store just fine. I just don't want to leave you alone."

"You won't be leaving me alone," I reassured him. "Max will be around."

That didn't settle his fears in the slightest. But after we argued for about twenty minutes, and I convinced him I'd be fine, he finally agreed to go on the trip with a promise to return to me soon.

What I didn't admit to him, though, was that I was scared, too. But I knew Beckett had to go, and I wasn't about to stand in his way.

CHAPTER 16

Beckett

THE NEXT FEW days were spent making sure everything was going smoothly at Starlight Books and with Pops before I left for Boston.

Rhiannon had been a godsend. She had been taking Pops to physical and occupational therapy appointments for his arm, and he seemed to be improving. She and Pops clicked effortlessly. I'd been grateful they were able to bond before the effects of radiation and chemotherapy set in.

Things at Starlight Books had been going flawlessly as well. Ellawyn had been busy learning the ins and outs of the business since she'd already mastered the food prep, making the drinks, and closing the store. Now, after a crash course in inventory, invoices, and all things business, she was ready to take over.

The sense of pride that she had found while learning everything about the Starlight Books made me so damn happy. She had focused all her attention on Starlight Books after the incidents with the notes, and I think between working and her art, she was able to not obsess over what had happened.

Thankfully, after those two incidents, things had been quiet. There hadn't been any new notes left and Ellawyn hadn't been alone at her place since. We either slept at my place or both of us were at hers. But I refused to take any chances, especially while I'd be out of town. Max was prepared to be in and out of the shop constantly, along with walking her to and from work.

It might have been a little overdramatic, but we'd rather be safe than sorry.

As I left the office and went out into the shop, the bell above the door jingled. A smile spread across my face as I watched Ellawyn greet Pops in a hug while they both laughed at something.

Pops spotted me walking toward them. "Come on, my boy," he shouted with excitement. "Ellie and I are starved."

As if on cue, Ellawyn's stomach growled, and her eyes went wide at the noise. "Oh, my goodness." She giggled. "I guess I'm hungrier than I thought."

I locked up the store and joined them on the sidewalk as we walked the few blocks to our destination. We had decided that we'd all have dinner together tonight since I was leaving for Boston tomorrow morning.

"Where are we going anyway?" Ellawyn asked as she nudged me with her elbow. "No one ever told me."

Pops and I shared a look over her head and responded in unison. "Illusion."

She shrugged as I pulled her into my side. "You'll love it," I assured her as I pointed to the building we were walking toward.

She eyed it up and down. "I approve," she declared. "It looks unique." She laughed as she ran ahead of us and held the door open for Pops and me.

Dinner was a great time. The drinks were out of this world. Ellawyn opted for a spiked orange cream slushy, Pops ordered a Cider Mule, and I decided to try their newest mead that was on draft. The food was spot-on as well. Ellawyn went with a flatbread that she raved about, Pops had the brisket melt, and I kept it simple with tacos.

Once finished, we relaxed into our seats at the restaurant, talking and enjoying each other's company. Pops told us he was anxious for his treatment to start but was determined to remain positive. And when I told him about Ellawyn taking over Starlight Books while I'd be in Boston, he'd been thrilled and over the moon excited for her.

I found myself zoning in and out of the conversation as I realized how easily Ellawyn fit perfectly into our lives, as if she belonged there the entire time.

The missing piece of the puzzle.

"Earth to Beckett." Ellawyn's voice snapped me back to reality as she waved a hand in front of my face.

I brought her hand to my lips and tenderly kissed the top. "What did I miss?"

She melted into my side at the contact of my lips on her skin. "I was asking what time your flight leaves for Boston," she repeated.

"I believe my flight boards around eight thirty."

"Excellent." Her excitement seemed to grow as she spoke. "I can drop you off at the airport in the morning so we can say goodbye."

My smile fell. Kennon was going to have a car pick me up at my place in the morning and take me to the airport. It was what we'd always done. I hadn't even considered that Ellawyn would want to drop me off.

Seeing my expression, Ellawyn started to backpedal. "It's okay," she blurted. "I mean, I don't have to. I just thought—"

I cut her off. "I'd love to have you drive me to the airport," I reassured her. "Having you see me off would make my day."

Pops gave me a knowing smile as I pulled my cell phone out underneath the table and texted Kennon that I didn't need the car service this time.

"Perfect." Ellawyn beamed as she sipped her spiked slushy.

☾

WE SPENT the rest of the evening at my place, lying on the couch and watching true crime documentaries while eating popcorn. My focus had mainly been on her, though. She was perched on the edge of her seat with a notebook on her lap.

"Stay here while I'm out of town," I offered. Her head whipped around to me as she stumbled to pause the movie. I laughed. "I like your priorities—pausing the movie before answering."

She mock glared at me. "Well, yeah." She pivoted on the couch, settling her legs underneath her. "I think what you just said requires my full attention." She hesitated as her gaze lingered over my facial features. "You want me to stay at your house while you're away?" She looked around the living room. "Like in this beautiful living room?"

"Well, you can move around. You wouldn't have to stay in just the living room." I chuckled. "I'd feel safer knowing you were here while I'm gone. Whoever wrote those notes knows where you live. We haven't seen any signs that indicate he knows where I live." I shrugged. "But it's just an option. You don't have to stay here if you don't want to."

Her gaze dropped to the floor as she let out a breath. "He could follow me here, then this wouldn't be a safe place anymore," she said quietly. When she lifted her gaze to meet mine, the pain within was evident and raw as the tears began to gather. She swallowed and took a breath before continuing. "I'd rather stay at my place and not risk yours."

I pulled her into my arms and held her close as she buried her head into my chest and cried. I'd give anything to reassure her that everything would be fine regarding this stalker situation, but I'd never been one for false promises, so I whispered into her hair that we'd get through this and promised she wasn't alone anymore.

She fell asleep nuzzled perfectly within my arms. Letting her be, I reached around her and dug my phone out of my pocket and checked to see if Kennon had responded.

Kennon: Since when do you not need a car service?

It was a valid question. I'd always used a car service when traveling. When I responded, I dropped the bomb that my girlfriend was going to be dropping me off instead and then also requested that he coordinate getting both me and Ellawyn top-of-the-line security systems for both of our places as soon as possible.

After filling Kennon in about what was going on, he was equally as pissed off as I was. He promised to start working on it first thing tomorrow.

Feeling a bit better about being able to provide Ellawyn with some extra security, I glanced down at my girl while she slept. Her braid, which she had so carefully put into place earlier, had strands falling out. Pieces of her hair were draped over her face. Carefully, I pushed her hair out of her eyes before I shifted her in my arms so that one arm went under her knees and another under her back. When I stood, she shifted into my chest, getting cozy. I managed to get up the stairs without waking her and gently placed her in my bed and then covered her up.

Tiptoeing away from her, I went into the bathroom and got myself ready for the evening. As I reached for my toothbrush, I noticed her purple one housed in the toothbrush holder. I caught myself smiling.

It felt strangely intimate.

When I finally joined Ellawyn in bed, she rolled into me and laid her head on my chest. She stayed asleep, cradled into me, and I fell asleep knowing I had my girl safe in my arms tonight.

☾

I WOKE up to gentle kisses on my forehead, my cheeks, my lips, and eventually trailing down my bare chest.

Ellawyn kissed her way back up my chest and to my lips again as she laid her body on top of mine. I pressed my erection into her, and she let out a gasp and opened her mouth. I slid my tongue inside and kissed her.

She reciprocated and slid her tongue inside my mouth as we

both got lost in the kiss. Her lips turned up as she smiled against my mouth. "Good morning," she whispered against my lips. "Time to get up. I'll start the coffee."

Glancing at the alarm clock, I groaned as I took in the time. "I wish we had time to finish what *you* just started," I reprimanded.

"Me too," she called out as she left the room and went down the stairs.

By the time I finished getting ready, the aroma of freshly brewed coffee had drifted toward the top of the stairs. Following the scent, I found Ellawyn in the kitchen with both hands wrapped around her mug. "Finally," she joked. "I made you breakfast."

When I looked around the kitchen, there was nothing. I crossed my arms over my chest and tilted my head. "And you ate it?"

She let out a giggle as she placed her mug down and walked toward the toaster. She pulled something out and placed it on a napkin before turning to me. "Here ya go."

I looked down at her hands and saw a napkin wrapped around two Pop-Tarts. I laughed and gave my head a shake. "How domestic of you."

After sharing the Pop-Tarts and finishing our coffee, Ellawyn grabbed my bag and dragged it outside to the car. When she struggled to lift it, I helped her, and we placed it into the trunk together. She closed the trunk and let her hand linger on top. She looked devastated. "That bag is pretty heavy for a quick trip to Boston..."

Placing a finger under her chin, I lifted it so I could look her in the eyes. "Say the word and I'll stay."

She shook her head and pulled away from me before walking to the passenger side of the car. Not waiting for me, she opened the door herself and slid inside.

Most of the ride to the airport was silent. Ellawyn had turned her body to face the passenger window and completely closed down on me.

"Talk, babe," I prompted.

"Does it even matter?" she answered.

"I'm not sure what you're asking, but I'll always care about what you think and your feelings. Those are important to me, and I want you to voice your emotions rather than keep them bottled inside."

Reaching over, I grabbed her hand and laced our fingers together.

"I'm not used to people caring about what I think or how I'm feeling," she confessed.

"I know," I said as I squeezed her hand. "But rest assured that I will always care about you, your thoughts, and your feelings. You're safe in this relationship."

She squeezed my hand three times and smiled over at me before she turned on our favorite true crime podcast.

☾

THE PLANE RIDE BACK to Boston was uneventful.

I tried to catch up on emails, but I couldn't. I tried to fall asleep, but it wouldn't happen. My mind constantly drifted back to Ellawyn and how heartbroken she had looked when she dropped me off at the airport. She had looked absolutely crushed to be going back to Quimby Grove alone.

When I landed in Boston, I immediately turned my phone back on in case Ellawyn had texted. But I was left disappointed when I saw I had no message notifications. It wasn't until I was settled in the back of the car that had picked me up that I decided to reach out to her instead of waiting. Trying not to worry, I sent her a text to make sure she had made it back to Quimby Grove okay. I left the screen open, waiting for those three little dots that might appear. But when they didn't pop up after a few minutes, I closed out of the app and let my phone go back to black.

It didn't take long to arrive at Walden Advertising. When I stepped out of the car, I looked up at my building, and a warm feeling took over. At first, it was a feeling of comfort. This building had been my home for so long. But then, a feeling of sadness took over as I realized it was no longer associated as home.

I began my journey into the building, taking in everything for the first time in a while, and it was all exactly the way I left it. As soon as I walked into the main entrance, I saw our smiling receptionist. She was perched in front of a wall with a nice wood grain that gave off a barn-style plank type of feel. It was made of rough-cut lumber with the blade marks still visible. Centered above her was the name of the company in sleek silver lettering.

She greeted me with a huge grin. "Mr. Walden, welcome back! It's so good to see you again."

Her enthusiasm wasn't even bothering me like it used to. "Morning, Mrs. Lively. Nice to see you again."

Mrs. Lively had been with my company since the beginning. She had a bit of a grandma vibe about her. She was a nice older woman and had curly gray hair. She always offered everyone candy and loved bright colors and bold patterns. Everyone adored her.

She scurried around the corner of her large desk and came around to pull me into her arms for a hug. "Are you back to stay, dear?"

I smiled down at her. "I'm sorry, Mrs. Lively, but I'm not. I'm needed back in Quimby Grove to help care for my grandpa and..." My words faded away as I thought about Ellawyn. I did consider her my girlfriend; I'd just never used that sort of label here in Boston, and Mrs. Lively had never seen me with a steady girlfriend.

Her eyes narrowed. "I sense there's something else keeping you in Quimby Grove." She nodded her head toward the couches that sat in the corner of the reception area. "Come along, dear."

I joined her on the couch as she reached into her pocket to pull out a piece of candy. "Butterscotch?"

"Thank you." I reached for the candy and placed it into my pocket.

"Alright, dear," she started. "You alluded to having to take care of your grandpa. Is he alright?"

Mrs. Lively had a special way of caring about others, so when she asked about Pops, I couldn't hold back. I filled her in on everything we'd been through so far. From the biopsy to the surgery, and now to him starting chemotherapy and radiation this week. She was sympathetic and understanding. She placed her hand on my knee, patting it gently. "Oh, honey. That's terrible. It's understandable that you need to be there for him. Who is running his shop while you are out of town?"

The corners of my mouth tipped up at the thought of Ellawyn. "Ellawyn is taking care of the shop until I get back." My hand went to my pocket, wanting to see if she'd responded to my message, but I fought the urge and forced my hand to my side.

She pursed her lips as she narrowed her eyes. "She's special to you, isn't she, dear?" She didn't wait for me to answer. Instead, she leaned back, getting comfortable, and pulled a butterscotch from her pocket. Popping it into her mouth, she winked at me. "Tell me about this Ellawyn."

I rubbed a hand over my face as I considered how to even begin. I shared a bit of Ellawyn's past and how helpful she had been since Pops's diagnosis. "Somehow during all of that, we became friends. Then, we became more."

"Sounds like you're in deep with that girl," she observed. "The entire time we've been visiting, our conversation has been normal. You were your usual serious, businesslike self. But the moment you mentioned that girl's name, your eyes lit up and came to life. Even your tone of voice changed."

"I do care deeply for Ellawyn," I agreed. There was no denying that. "Our relationship is relatively new, but I'd do anything for her."

"That's love," she declared. "You love this girl, I can tell."

"It's too soon for that." I waved her off.

She chuckled. "Love has a way of sneaking up on people, dear. Your heart feels it. You've just got to get your head to accept it."

Ignoring her assessment of my relationship, I steered the conversation back to Walden Advertising and then we chatted about her grandchildren, her garden, and how much she dislikes reality TV.

When I stood up to head toward my office, Mrs. Lively stopped me. "Mr. Walden," she called. "I have a question I forgot about until now."

"Sure, what is it?"

She slowly walked back around her desk. "You mentioned that Ellawyn organized a fundraiser to pay for your grandfather's medical bills. Why? You could easily pay for those yourself."

Letting out a sigh, I decided to answer her question honestly. "Ellawyn was so excited about her fundraiser idea and doing something nice for Pops, and I couldn't tell her and break her heart."

A mischievous smile spread across Mrs. Lively's face. When she didn't comment, I playfully rolled my eyes and smiled at her before turning to leave the lobby area.

It wasn't until my back was turned that she finally spoke up. "You love that girl."

CHAPTER 17
Ellawyn

I CAUGHT myself staring out the window of Starlight Books off and on all day. Most of my day had been spent looking out that window, if I were being honest. First, I found myself searching for anybody that could be coming to leave me a hateful note. Then, I had been looking for Beckett, hoping he'd walk through the door with his arms wide open and say he was back to stay.

But instead, I was left with a heaviness in my chest and a revolving door of customers. I barely registered the people that had come into the shop today. I'd been on autopilot just going through the motions of the mundane. And now, the shop was closed, the closing work had been completed, along with balancing the drawer, and I'd even completed the food prep for tomorrow.

But here I sat, glued to the couch, staring off into space while thoughts of Beckett filled my head. I'd kept my phone off and in my bag all day so that I wouldn't text him too much. I knew how busy he would be. Caving, I pulled my phone from my bag and powered it on. I couldn't help but smile when I saw I had three missed text messages from him.

Beckett: Ellawyn, just checking in. Did you make it home okay?

Beckett: My receptionist wants to meet you.

Beckett: Okay, not to sound like a creep, but I'm starting to get worried.

Feeling bad about ignoring him all day, I typed out a response letting him know I'd been working all day and refusing to look at my phone. His response was instant.

Beckett: Glad to hear you're okay. Why were you refusing to look at your phone, though?

Me: Avoidance.

Beckett: Explain, please.

Me: Truth? I missed you more than I expected. There has been a hollowness inside me all day, but I didn't want to risk becoming the girl who texts her boyfriend constantly while he's away.

My phone started ringing immediately after my text had been delivered. "Beckett," I answered.

His laughter filled the line, and I swore I could almost feel his presence through the phone. "I miss you, too, Ellie," he said. "You're right, though," he admitted. "This—us—it's definitely more than I expected."

Heat rushed to my cheeks. We spent the next hour on the phone together, me talking while curled up on the couch in the shop, and him relaxing in his living room at his place in Boston. Just as we were about to hang up, I decided to ask him the question I'd been avoiding. The question I didn't want the answer to but needed. "How long do you think you'll be in Boston?"

He sighed into the phone. I could practically envision him rubbing the back of his neck with his hand while he tried to answer the difficult question. "Probably longer than I had anticipated. As I got reacclimated today, I realized there's a bit more that I need to do before I can come back and transition to working remotely all the time."

Pulling the phone away from my mouth, I exhaled and sat up on the couch. "Oh, okay," I mumbled. "Well, it's getting late. I should probably head home."

We ended the call with the promise to reconnect tomorrow, and I immediately texted Max that I was ready to walk home to my apartment whenever he was.

I couldn't handle being at Beckett's house tonight.

It would have just been too much.

☪

ROLLING OVER, I slapped the top of my alarm clock to turn off the loud noise coming out of the speaker. Only, it didn't work because it was my phone ringing, not my alarm. Opening one eye, I glanced at the clock and looked at the time. Four thirty. I reached for the phone blindly and accepted the call. "Hello," I answered.

"Can you take Benji to his follow-up appointment with the neurosurgeon today?"

Wait, what? "Rhiannon?"

"Yes, it's Rhiannon. Can you take him? The appointment is at eight this morning."

"Sure."

Rhiannon rushed off the phone with a quick thank-you before the call disconnected. I rolled back over in bed and tried to fall back asleep. When that didn't work, I begrudgingly got out of bed and admitted defeat.

☪

WE HADN'T BEEN in the waiting room of Pennsylvania Memorial Hospital long when Lucy entered and called Benji's name.

After he left, I pulled a book out of my bag and started to read. I had only been a few pages in when I was interrupted.

"Ellie." His voice grated on me like nails on a chalkboard.

Refraining from rolling my eyes, I kept them down as I

turned a page in my book. "Dr. Reinhart," I greeted. "Shouldn't you be back with Benji?"

He sat down next to me, leaning over to see what I was reading. I shifted in my seat, trying to put some distance between us without being outwardly rude.

"Lucy is taking his vitals. I heard you were out here, and I couldn't resist the chance to see you and say hello. It's been a while."

As I nodded, I could feel Dr. Reinhart's gaze on my face, staring at me while I continued looking down at my book. I flipped the page again and tried to get myself to focus on the words this time.

"No Beckett today?" he asked.

I jumped in my seat at the sound of his voice. "No, he's out of town on business."

He slid an arm around the top of my chair. "Dinner tonight?"

Did he just ask me out to dinner after I barely spoke to him? Getting pissed off, I slammed my book shut and shoved it back inside my bag. "I'm not interested," I blurted out. "I have a boyfriend, and this is inappropriate." I rose from my seat, slung my bag over my shoulder, and started to walk away. "I've got to make a call. Excuse me."

After some much-needed caffeine and a fake phone call, I went back to the waiting area and was relieved when Dr. Reinhart was nowhere to be found. Pulling my book back out, I waited for Benji to finish up his appointment so I could drop him off and head to Starlight Books for the rest of the day.

☪

TODAY WAS EXHAUSTING. From being woken up early, accompanying Benji to his appointment, and running Starlight Books the rest of the day, I was beat. And the radio silence from Beckett wasn't helping either.

Hoping he'd reach out had been driving me crazy.

When the clock struck six in the evening, I decided to call it an early night. The shop hadn't been busy in an hour or so, and there were no customers, so I took the opportunity and flipped the OPEN sign and locked the door.

I'd just come in tomorrow morning and do prep after a good night's rest.

I pulled my phone from my back pocket, hoping Beckett would have reached out by now. But there was nothing. Guilt started to seep into my body as I replayed our conversation from last night.

Could he be mad at me for getting upset over him staying in Boston a few extra days? I shook the thought from my head. No, Beckett wasn't like that. He was probably just busy at work.

Resting my head in my hands, I debated what I should do for dinner. As if on cue, my stomach growled. "I'll go to Illusion for dinner and a drink," I said out loud to myself. "I deserve a treat after today."

When I walked into Illusion, I was surprised at how packed it was considering it was a weekday. I found the only vacant table in sight. It was a small two-seater table right next to the main window, with a pair of purple velvet chairs at each end. Claiming the space, I sat down and pulled out my book so I could enjoy some reading. It wasn't long until the waitress came to drop off a glass of water, a menu, and the promise to be right back. After examining the menu, I settled on a caprese salad and the Illusion hypnotic red wine.

All throughout dinner, I kept my book open as I ate, getting lost in the magic of the fairytale story. The wine had been the real winner of the evening, though. The coloring featured hints of purple, and it had a blackberry aroma along with hints of strawberry. It was so delicious; I'd almost ordered another glass. Between a great book, excellent food, and the most amazing wine I'd ever tasted, it was safe to say this solo dining experience had gone well. I'd always loved my own company and never had any issues going out alone before, but I'd lost that independence all those years ago up until recently.

It felt great to get that piece of myself back.

As I returned my book to my bag and dug out my wallet to pay, the waitress came over and placed a folded piece of paper on the table in front of me. When she didn't offer an explanation, I furrowed my brows and questioned her. "What's this?"

Her smile was blinding as excitement took over. "Your bill has been paid for," she said in a rush. "And the handsome gentleman wishes to remain anonymous." She picked up the dirty plate and wineglass. "He also asked for me to give you that note." She pointed down toward the table. "It's very romantic, yeah? Anyway, have a good night."

Smiling down at the note, I bit my lip in anticipation that Beckett had come home early. I grabbed my things, along with the note, and went outside. Moving off to the side of the building so I'd be out of the way, I opened the paper.

My smile vanished as everything around me seemed to fade away. My eyes snapped up, and I looked around the square for anyone that looked familiar and could have left this note.

But there was no one I recognized. And certainly no one that seemed to be focused on me. Panic set in as I turned to run down the block.

I hadn't made it far when I heard someone yelling my name. When I turned around to see who it was, I was relieved to see Max running toward me. "What's wrong? I saw you when I was across the street, and you looked upset. I hurried as fast as I could."

Without responding, I handed him the note and started to walk home again without waiting for him. It wasn't long until he fell into step with me. "I'm coming home with you," he fumed.

I nodded.

We walked the rest of the way in silence.

☪

SAFELY INSIDE MY APARTMENT, I locked the door before turning to Max. "I'm going to lie down for a few minutes. Make yourself at home." The nausea came in waves as I turned from him, went straight into my bedroom, and pushed the door most of the way closed.

Pulling the duvet down, I slid inside my bed while still dressed in the day's clothes and burrowed underneath the covers. Turning on my side so I could see the light shining in from the living room, I listened as Max took a seat on the couch. A few seconds passed by when I heard Max say Beckett's name.

My heart started to beat a little faster. I hadn't spoken to Beckett all day and now he had to hear about what happened from Max. Pulling the covers up to my chin, I listened in on the one-sided conversation.

"Yeah, man. I'm at her apartment right now," Max said. There were a few beats of silence before he spoke again. "She was at Illusion when someone paid for her bill anonymously and then had the waitress give her a note before she left." The sound of a crumpled-up piece of paper being unfolded filled the air as I held my breath for the reading of the note. "It said, 'You and I belong together, and soon we will be. I'll make sure of it. See you before someone gets back from Boston.'"

My stomach turned, a ball of knots forming deep inside. This stranger told me we'd be together soon. Whoever it was knew that Beckett was out of town. I threw the covers off me and rushed out of bed and into my bathroom. I barely made it in time to avoid getting sick on the floor. I crawled over toward the door and pushed the button on the knob to secure the lock into place. I started the bath and added in some of my favorite lavender bath salts, attempting to soak my troubles away.

☾

"ELLAWYN," a hushed voice called. I almost thought I was dreaming until I heard it again. "Ellawyn," the voice echoed.

The bottom of the bed dipped slightly. My eyes opened as I tried to remember what happened last night. "Max?" I mumbled as I sat up and leaned against the headboard.

"You look like shit," he said with a laugh. Max didn't hold back.

I laughed with him. "Feel like it, too," I responded. I'm sure I did look like hell. After my bath last night, all I managed to do was get dressed in old sweats and brush my teeth. My hair had been neglected. I don't even know if I washed my face. "You stayed over?"

He nodded. "Yeah, I talked to Beckett last night. He was all ready to hop on a plane and come back. But we came up with a plan while he finishes what he needs to do."

I tilted my head as I tried to figure out what that plan could involve. "A plan?" I asked.

Max filled me in. And while it wasn't the most ideal situation, it was the best we could do since I still wasn't up for going to the cops just yet. Max would basically be my bodyguard until Beckett came back. Max and I would both stay the night at Beckett's place since he had more bedrooms, and we'd ride into work together and ride home together.

I frowned. Max barely knew me and yet he was uprooting his life for a few days to watch out for me. "Thanks, Max. I'm sorry about all of this."

"There's nothing to apologize for." He smiled at me. "You're my best friend's girlfriend, so that makes us friends too. I've got his back and yours." He stood up and placed a hand on my shoulder. "Go pack a bag, and we can stop by Beckett's house before work."

☾

MAX and I fell into a routine over the few days while the plan was put to the test.

And it worked.

We traveled into work together, and whenever I'd close Starlight Books, I'd walk over to Remnant Hearts bar and eat dinner with Max while he worked behind the bar. When it was time for him to head out, we'd ride back to Beckett's house together and just hang out until one of us got tired.

Max became a fast friend as he told me stories of his childhood with Beckett here in Quimby Grove and how he took over his dad's bar after he passed away. When his dad had died, a huge piece of Max's heart went with him. What was left, Max had poured into renovating the bar and making sure his father's legacy live on. The bar had been named after the remaining pieces of his heart.

The pieces that went into making the bar something that his dad would be proud of.

The pieces that made Max into the man he was today.

The pieces that brought a new friend into my life.

CHAPTER 18
Beckett

I'd been working around the clock at Walden Advertising these past few days so I could get back to Quimby Grove as soon as possible. Everyone at my company had sprung into action to make it happen, especially Mrs. Lively, who had single-handedly rescheduled all my meetings so they'd be done in a day or two instead of spreading them out over the course of the week. And the few that she couldn't get rescheduled with me had been rescheduled with Kennon instead.

After the most recent note, everything had been going according to plan. Ellawyn and Max had been glued to each other when possible. Pops had started his treatment a few days ago, and that had gone well. The only thing out of place back home was me.

Home. I wasn't sure when Quimby Grove had become home again, but it had. Being back in Boston felt foreign to me, like I didn't quite belong here anymore. Each night after work, I'd gone straight home instead of going out and catching up with friends and coworkers, and I'd talk to Pops, Ellawyn, and Max. They had become my priority.

A knock sounded on my office door. "Come in."

Kennon entered, closing the door behind him. "Morning, boss. Today is the day, isn't it?"

I smirked. "You know it is."

He took a seat across from me at my desk, dropping a stack of papers on its surface. "You sure this is what you want?"

I could understand where Kennon was coming from. Walden Advertising had been my whole life for quite some time. Kennon's, too. And while it would continue to play a huge role, it was no longer the only thing that was important to me. "I'm sure. Pops comes first during this time, and along with that comes running Starlight Books. There's Ellawyn to consider as well."

"You're serious about her?" He watched me carefully. "That girl is worth it?"

My gaze narrowed as I leaned further onto my desk. "Ellawyn is very important to me. Remember your place, Kennon."

His facial expression remained unbothered as he gave me a curt nod. "I've never seen you so affected by a woman before."

"And I've never seen you act like such a dick toward your superior before either, but here we are."

☾

WHEN I FINALLY MADE IT back to Quimby Grove, my driver dropped me off about a block away from Starlight Books so Ellawyn wouldn't see me just yet. I stopped by Remnant Hearts, pulling my luggage in behind me and placing it in the corner so it'd be out of the way. When I turned to the bar, Max was behind it, wiping the counters. "Hey, Max," I greeted as I pulled out a barstool.

"Hey, man." He grabbed a glass from beneath the bar and filled it with beer before sliding it over to me. "Was Ellawyn stoked to see you?" He filled another glass for himself and took a drink.

"I haven't seen her yet, actually," I said as I took a drink. "I wanted to see if I could stash my suitcase here for a little bit until I take her home?"

Max walked around the bar and joined me on the barstool next to me. "Yeah, no problem." He took a drink of his beer and finished it off. "She's really great, you know. She and I have become fast friends these past few days. She's even designing me a new logo for the bar, and she's excited about it." He chuckled to himself. "I'm glad she's around."

Hearing my best friend speak so highly of Ellawyn made me realize how lucky I was to have them both in my life. I had no doubts that their friendship would be long lasting and exactly what they both needed.

When I left the bar, I walked a few shops down to our local floral shop, Fairytale Blooms, and picked up some flowers for Ellawyn. When I entered Starlight Books, the shop was quiet, and no one was around. Maneuvering around the tables within the shop, I heard a laugh coming from between the bookshelves on the other side of the room. Following the beautiful melodies of laughter, I was led straight to my girl.

Ellawyn was reading the inside of a book and laughing. She smiled down and lightly ran her fingers over the printed text inside as if she'd been trying to pick up the book's essence just by sheer touch. I cleared my throat, hoping to get her attention.

She turned around, and as soon as she saw me, the book dropped to the floor as Ellawyn lunged herself into my arms. I picked her up and swung her around as our lips found each other in a duel for control while we claimed each other. I bit her lower lip, causing her to let out a whimper. When her mouth opened with a gasp, I slid my tongue inside, tilting her head as I deepened the kiss.

"Mine," I claimed. Her body melded with mine as I wrapped my arms around her waist and held her up.

She pulled back, gasping for air. "Beckett! You're home." She beamed.

I picked up the flowers I had deposited onto a table and handed them to her. "I'm glad to be home, baby."

Ellawyn brought the flowers to her nose and inhaled their scent. "Sunflowers and poppies." She smiled down at the bouquet. "My favorites." She leaned in, pressing her lips to my cheek. "Thank you for coming back to me."

The sound of her voice caused a pang in my chest. Holding her hand, I gently squeezed three times before I pulled her back toward the counter. "Come on, let's close up early tonight."

We locked up the shop with the promise of coming in early tomorrow to clean up and complete prep work. After getting my luggage from the bar, we walked back to Ellawyn's apartment and ended up getting cozy on the couch while we watched a movie together.

Except halfway into the movie, my leading lady fell asleep with her head resting on my lap. Moving the strands of hair that had fallen onto her face, I took a moment to admire her.

My Ellawyn. My fearless, strong, intelligent, ambitious, and beautiful Ellawyn. I was lucky that she had chosen me as the one she wanted to be with. The one she wanted to trust. The one to break down those walls she had so carefully erected.

And I'd spend all my days proving to her that she had made the right choice.

Grabbing the pillow I'd been lying on, I eased myself out from underneath her and placed the pillow under her head. When she stayed asleep, I grabbed the blanket from above the couch and covered her up. I leaned down, placed a kiss to her forehead, and went into her bedroom to make a phone call. I tapped Rhiannon's contact number and checked in on Pops to see how his treatment was going.

We ended up talking on the phone longer than I had anticipated. She filled me in on Pops's reaction to the treatments and how hard those side effects had hit him. Extreme nausea had been the main culprit, along with fatigue. Despite anticipating those potential side effects, the news was hard to hear.

After I hung up with Rhiannon, I sat on Ellawyn's bed in the dark and completely zoned out. There were too many problems circling the drain within my circle of family and friends but no solutions to those problems.

Pops's treatment was out of my hands. And while I never really had a hold of it to begin with, knowing there was nothing I could do was a fucking disappointment. I'd always been a man that had been in complete control over most of the things in my life. If I didn't have control, I'd figure out a way to get it. But now, there was nothing I could do to get the upper hand here.

The diagnosis was destroying me.

Destroying my family.

I wasn't going to go down without a fight, but for once in my life, I didn't have the upper hand anymore.

CHAPTER 19

Ellawyn

Since Beckett had returned home six weeks ago, life had been busy and uneventful—a nice change of pace. Beckett and I had been working together and sharing responsibilities at Starlight Books. When we weren't there, we were spending time with Benji, or Beckett was working remotely for his advertising job.

Benji's initial round of radiation and chemotherapy had come to an end and left Benji feeling weak and nauseous, along with taking his hair. He tried to laugh it off, but I could tell the treatment and the effects had been wearing him down. Despite all of that, he remained optimistic about his overall treatment and never once complained. The time spent with him was always precious and something I'd always cherish.

And the best part of these last six weeks? My stalker had finally moved on. I hadn't received any more notes since that last one at Illusion. And with the new security system Beckett had installed at my apartment, I felt comfortable in my space again.

I was finally beginning to feel safe. Like I could breathe and not have to be on alert twenty-four seven. It was as if all the moving pieces in my life had finally come together and allowed me to escape the burdens of everything I'd been feeling. Allowing me to spread my wings so I could fly, so I could be free. I felt empowered and ready to take control of my life and *really* begin living here in Quimby Grove.

It was time to take full advantage of the town I'd grown to love.

A ringing sounded from the shop's landline. Picking up the receiver, I answered the call. "Starlight Books, Ellawyn speaking." I paused, waiting for the person on the other end of the phone to speak. When they didn't, I tried again. "Hello," I said. "Hello? This is Starlight Books. How can I help you?"

Silence.

I hung up the receiver and waited to see if it would ring again. The sense of empowerment I'd felt just moments ago had vanished.

All because of a phone call.

Needing to calm my nerves, I meandered into the kitchen, grabbed a bucket, and filled it with hot soapy water. The bucket was filled about halfway when I turned the water off. I carried it out into the shop and placed it by the counter before stepping back to evaluate what needed to be done.

Did I just want to spot clean the counter, only focusing on the areas with visible grime, or did I want to do a deep clean?

Deep clean.

I snagged an apron and wasted no time removing everything in sight from the counter.

Cash register? Gone.

Napkin and utensil holders? Gone.

Cups? Gone.

The cycle continued until I was left staring at an empty countertop. The bell above the door rang just as I hoisted the bucket up onto the counter. I felt the shift of energy in the air before I saw him. Blowing a strand of hair out of my face, I wiped my forehead with the back of my hand. "Hey, Beck," I called out.

He came around the counter and wrapped his arms around my waist as he plastered kisses down my neck and to my collarbone. "Mm, I've missed you," he said in a hushed timbre that was full of lust. He pushed his erection into my backside. Instinctively, I pushed back against him, egging him on. "Don't make me take you over this counter."

"Don't threaten me with a good time," I clipped.

Beckett laughed and tapped my ass before he stepped back out of the way.

"You're back earlier than I thought," I pointed out.

Beckett had gone with Benji to his MRI appointment. Turned out, that Benji's neuro-oncologist had a last-minute appointment and could fit him in.

"Yeah, it went well," he replied. "Pops wants us both there whenever he gets the results. The radiologist is going to try to review them tonight so we can get the results tomorrow."

"Sounds good." I turned my focus back to what I had been doing and dipped my rag into the scalding hot sudsy water and rang out the excess. My hands stung from the heat, but I shoved the pain aside and began wiping down the counter. After I had the counter wet, I grabbed the heavy-duty cleaning spray and sprayed the counter. I could feel Beckett's gaze on me the entire time.

"Quit staring at me," I quipped before I pivoted to meet his gaze.

As he folded his arms across his chest, one of his eyebrows edged toward his hairline. "Why are you deep cleaning the counter on a Monday evening?"

Stepping toward him, I sighed. "Because sometimes things just get messy. Even in the deepest crevices, where no one sees, things get messy," I ranted as I grabbed my sponge and went back to the counter and scrubbed until my knuckles turned white. "And if no one looks... If no one looks for the debris, then it'll never get any better. It will just build and build, until one day, it's beyond repair and the damage is done."

As my words sunk in, the weight of everything suddenly became too much. I slammed the sponge down on the counter and stripped off my apron. Without looking in his direction when he called my name, I grabbed my bag and walked out of Starlight Books. I took off running down the block until I got to the square. I stood still, getting lost in a sea of people. People who knew where they were going, who they were going to go be with, and where they belonged. Suddenly, I felt small.

Trudging forward, I lowered myself onto one of the benches placed along the Square. Bringing my knees to my chest, I wrapped my arms around my legs and laid my head down as I blocked out the rest of the world.

When I opened my eyes again, my legs and arms felt heavy. I must have been in that position longer than I had realized. To alleviate the stiffness, I stretched my legs out and sat up straight. When I looked to my left, I jumped. There was someone sitting next to me.

"Sorry about that," I offered. It wasn't until I turned my head in the opposite direction that the person next to me spoke up.

"Ellawyn," the voice acknowledged. "I didn't realize that was you sitting here when I grabbed a seat."

A feeling of disgust crept up as I turned my head to face him.

Dr. Reinhart.

"Small world," I responded as I forced a smile. I made a point to look around the Square. When I noticed that the crowd of people had diminished, I couldn't help shifting in my seat as I pulled my bag tighter across my chest. Recrossing my legs, I waited to see if he would get up to leave or say something else. But he didn't.

My phone dinged. When I pulled it from my bag, I was relieved to see I had a message from Beckett. I responded to him, letting him know I just needed to clear my head and was going to head home. Figuring this was as good a time as any to leave, I stood up from my spot on the bench. "Got to go." I took a few steps forward. "Have a nice day," I called over my shoulder as I took off toward my apartment and didn't stop until I was safely inside.

Once I settled into the comfort of my couch with a glass of wine in hand and my favorite book on my lap, I felt a sense of calm again. As soon as I settled into my book, a knock on the door startled me, which caused my wine to spill onto my shirt.

I exhaled as I set my wineglass onto the coffee table. "One second," I called. As I made my way to the door, I glanced down at my wine-stained shirt. Feeling annoyed, I whipped open the door and stepped back as I swung my arm out as an invitation inside. "Hey," I mumbled.

Beckett stepped inside, pushing the door closed behind him. He peered over his shoulder at me as he slid the deadbolt into place. "So…"

Suddenly, I felt even more annoyed than I already was. I stepped around him as I whipped off my stained shirt so I could put on a clean one.

"What are you doing?" he called from the living room.

"You spilled wine on my shirt," I huffed. "I need to change."

Despite knowing I shouldn't be annoyed with Beckett, I couldn't help it. I was just agitated at how the day had gone and even more agitated by how I'd handled it. A sigh escaped as I removed my bra. The tension lessened a fraction. Plucking a long sleeve thermal shirt from my closet, I tugged it over my head and returned to the living room.

Beckett was sitting on the couch, reading the back of my book. I stood there, crossing my arms over my chest, and stared at him. He started speaking without even looking up from the book. "Care to fill me in on what caused you to be so upset today?"

I raised my eyebrows at him. "Seriously?" I turned and went into the kitchen to grab another glass of wine because I didn't want to walk over to the couch for the first glass. "Well, for starters, you spilled wine on me." My hands flew to my hips.

He chuckled as he rose from the couch.

I turned my back for a moment to put the wine away, and when I turned around, he was right in front of me, our chests practically touching. He reached under my chin and lifted my head to meet his gaze. "I did not spill wine on you."

When I went to respond, he interjected by smashing his mouth on mine. A sudden entanglement of limbs and a collision of tongues were the culprit of the pile of clothes that ended up on the floor right before his body became one with mine.

When we finished, we were left breathless and sweaty while we laid on my living room floor. I rolled onto my side, propping my head up with my hand, and watched the rise and fall of Beckett's chest as the glistening beads of sweat rolled off his body.

It was hard to imagine him looking any more handsome than he normally did, but right now, naked on my living room floor, he was the most handsome man I had ever laid eyes on.

And he was all mine.

I'd treated him poorly earlier. "I'm sorry," I said in a hushed tone. I was embarrassed.

"What was that?" He rolled over to face me, mimicking my position. His lips tipped up in a smile.

"I'm sorry," I repeated. "I just had a rough day and a bit of a freak-out." I couldn't adequately put into words how I'd felt today. How I'd gone from feeling empowered to feeling overwhelmed. No words would be enough to quantify this feeling, but I knew I'd have to try.

Beckett leaned over and pressed his lips to mine, then to my forehead, and lastly, the tip of my nose. "Does that mean I'm forgiven?" I giggled.

Beckett stood and gathered his clothes from the floor. "There's nothing to forgive," he said. He slung the clothes over his shoulders as he sauntered back over to me and extended his hand to help me up. "I do want to understand, though."

After we were both dressed, we decided to order dinner in. Since we couldn't agree on what to eat, I introduced Beckett to my family's favorite tradition—an à la carte night, where we ordered food from multiple places so we could get a little bit of everything that we wanted.

While Beckett hadn't heard of the concept before, he was all for it. We ended up ordering pizza, pasta, wings, fries, and Chinese food. I wanted to order more, but Beckett decided to be an amateur and cut me off.

When the food arrived, we spread it out on the kitchen table, along with the different drink options I'd ordered, and we dug in.

Our dinner was a bright spot on an otherwise cloudy-feeling day.

After we ate, Beckett and I worked together to pack up the leftovers and store them in the fridge. "Talk to me," he said as turned on the faucet at the kitchen sink. He placed the sink stopper into the drain before he squeezed some apple-scented dish soap into the sink with the hot water.

Since Beckett was doing the dishes, I hopped up onto the countertop and let my feet dangle above the floor. "Fine," I relented. "But you need to let me get this out all at once before interrupting."

"Sure," he said with a wink.

After taking a deep breath in and letting it out, I explained to Beckett how I had felt earlier today. I had finally felt as though everything was finally coming together. I felt free and ready to take back my freedom here in Quimby Grove. When I first came to town, I'd been running from my past life. And even after I'd escaped, I still had that mentality of needing to hide myself away.

I was simply tired of running and hiding.

Picking up a hand towel, Beckett dried off his hands before grabbing one of mine and leading me to the couch. "I admire you for refusing to run and hide," he said while he laced our fingers together. "I didn't realize that hiding could stir up old feelings. I'm sorry if I set you back by encouraging you to stay close when you were receiving those notes."

"It's not your fault. It was you who gave me the courage to stay and live."

Our conversation lasted late into the night. Whatever had been holding me back had loosened its grip, and I was finally able to tell Beckett what had truly bothered me today—that leaving Moon Harbor the way that I did meant leaving things unfinished. Leaving things like that had felt messy. And fixing it would be impossible to do from Quimby Grove.

"When I realized I needed to go back home, I panicked." I rubbed his leg in a silent apology. "I lashed out at you when I should have just talked to you."

He pulled me onto his lap, settling his arms around my waist. "Thank you for sharing everything with me tonight, for trusting me."

A tinge of shame came over me. "I can't wrap my brain around someone wanting me and caring about me." I tried to pull away, to get off his lap.

He let me stand, but he didn't let go of my hand. "I want everything that you'll give me, Ellawyn." He moved to stand next to me. "You're the greatest thing I've ever encountered, even on bad days."

Standing on my tiptoes, I reached for Beckett's lips and gave him a kiss. "I want all of your days, too." I grabbed his hand, dragging him to my room. "And your nights."

☾

THE CLOCK on the wall ticked. From my chair, I watched as the pendulum swung back and forth. My heart rate increased as my eyes darted from one part of the clock to another.

Tick-tock. Tick-tock. Tick-tock. Tick-tock.

Silence filled the room as the clock's ticking seemed to grow louder. I rose from my chair to rip it from the wall right as the door swung open and the doctor emerged from the hallway.

Feigning a stretch, I sat back down.

"Sorry for the wait." The doctor walked into the room and sat down behind his desk. "I'm Dr. Fisher. Nice to meet you."

Dr. Fisher didn't waste any time after introductions were made. Turning his computer screen toward us, he cut to the chase. "Do you see this small white spot on the image of your brain, Benji?"

Benji leaned forward, staring at the screen, and nodded.

My gaze flickered between Benji and Dr. Fisher. The energy in the room had shifted, and I felt as if the room was getting smaller, like there wasn't enough air or space in here for everyone.

"Benji, you have a tumor reoccurrence. Meaning the tumor has regrown."

A silence spread across the room, the tension radiating from the walls. Beckett was the first to speak.

"What does that mean in terms of treatment?" Beckett questioned. "Would another surgery be in order?"

My focus bounced between Dr. Fisher and Benji. Something wasn't quite right, but I couldn't pinpoint exactly what was happening. Dr. Fisher hesitated to answer Beckett's question and watched Benji carefully until Benji gave a slight head shake.

Dr. Fisher cleared his throat and answered. "Yes, that's a possibility, along with additional radiation and chemotherapy treatments."

It grew quiet again—not even the clock made a noise. Benji looked almost at peace, while Beckett was upset but trying to keep it together. Unable to stand the silence any longer, I decided to ask my own question. "If Benji were to get another surgery and continue with treatment, what are the chances of the tumor regrowing again?"

Dr. Fisher gave a sad smile. "The chances of regrowth are high."

Benji slumped down into his chair, disengaging even further from the conversation. After a few moments, Benji commented, his voice flat. "A vicious cycle."

Reaching out, I took Benji's hand. "It does seem like a lot," I agreed. I knew Benji wasn't thrilled about the idea of repeat surgeries.

Beckett scoffed. "It's a cycle we will endure in order to keep Pops around as long as possible."

His comment caught everyone off guard. The room went silent until Dr. Fisher wrapped up the conversation by letting Benji know he'd be in touch with treatment options.

The walk back to the car was brimming with tension. The closer we got, the more amplified the feeling was.

"I think I'm going to get out of town for a bit," Benji blurted out.

Beckett whipped around to face Benji. His brows furrowed together. "What do you mean you're going out of town?"

When we reached the car, Beckett opened my door while he waited for Benji's answer. Benji hopped into the passenger seat while Beckett got inside the driver's side. When Benji didn't answer, Beckett pushed again.

"You can't just go out of town," he said. "You need to get another surgery and get treatment."

"All the more reason to go now," Benji countered.

The conversation continued in the same pattern—Beckett wanting to keep Benji here and in treatment; Benji wanting to spread his wings before he no longer could. Right before we dropped Benji off, he made it perfectly clear that the decision was his and his alone and that he'd see Beckett in a few weeks.

When we returned to my apartment, Beckett remained silent as he tossed his keys onto the table and laid down on the couch.

"It's understandable, you know," I said as I sat down on the floor next to the couch.

His brows furrowed together. "It's understandable to delay treatment and go gallivanting around the country?" he questioned.

I laid my head on his shoulder as I considered how to respond. "He was just told that, no matter what, he'll spend the rest of his life having surgeries, radiation, and chemotherapy," I explained. "No matter what he does, tumor regrowth will likely happen. He will be poked and prodded while he completes various treatments indefinitely."

He nudged my head and then sat up, planting his feet on the floor. "So, you support him putting off treatment?"

This conversation wasn't going the way I had hoped. "I support Benji enjoying his life without worrying about the side effects of treatment for a while."

He jumped up from his spot on the couch and paced the living room floor. "How could you say that?" He threw his arms into the air. "He could die, Ellawyn."

"He could die either way," I said while I stood up. "If there are things he wants to do in life, he needs to do them now before continuing this journey, no matter which route he chooses."

His hands went to his hips. "What do you mean by that?"

I went into the kitchen and poured a glass of wine. I'd need a drink if I were going to answer Beckett's question honestly. "I mean that I'm not so sure that Benji wants to pursue treatment at all." I brought the glass to my lips and took a big gulp from my glass. "I think he wants to take control of his life."

"By going on a road trip and refusing treatment?" Beckett snapped.

I topped off my wineglass. "I don't know if he'll choose to refuse treatment, but based off the vibe that I picked up on in Dr. Fisher's office, I think it's a possibility."

Beckett sat down at the kitchen table and buried his face in his hands. "I don't agree with this."

Sitting down next to him, I rubbed a hand up and down his back. "I know."

We stayed like that for a while—Beckett trying to process all of this while I rubbed his back and offered the only thing that I could think of: comfort.

Beckett lifted his head from his hands and looked at me with tear-filled eyes. "Will you go with him?"

CHAPTER 20

Beckett

ELLAWYN'S MOUTH hung open in shock. "You want me to go on a road trip with Benji?" she questioned.

Pacing the kitchen, I started putting a plan together in my head. "It's perfect, actually," I said out loud, though mostly to myself. If Ellawyn went with Pops on his road trip, I wouldn't worry so much. She could be there for him, and she would be able to get away for a little bit herself.

Ellawyn went into her bedroom and sat on the edge of her bed. "What if he doesn't want me to go with him?" she whispered.

She'd said it so low that I barely heard her. I took out my phone and sent a quick text to Pops to see if he would be up for some company on his road trip. I also may have let it slip to him that I thought it'd be good for Ellawyn, too.

Pocketing my phone, I went into her bedroom and sat down next to her. "I think it'd be good for you, too, you know."

She arched her eyebrow and gave me a disbelieving face.

I chuckled. "You were just talking about wanting to get out there and live your life," I wrapped an arm around her shoulder, pulling her close. "This could be your chance."

She studied me while she pulled her bottom lip in between

her teeth. In a split second, she abruptly stood up and went to her dresser and started rummaging through it as she tossed pairs of socks on the floor in every direction. "What are you doing?" I asked with a laugh.

"Yes!" she shouted as she turned around holding a pair of black socks with sunflowers on them. "This is my savings." She returned to the bed and pulled a wad of cash out of the socks. "I have a few grand left that should cover my cost of lodging, food, and whatever else I'd need for a little bit."

She shrugged and shoved the money back into her socks before she disappeared into her closet. When she returned, she pushed out a wheeled luggage set. Tilting her head, she evaluated the condition of the suitcase. "This should work right?" She kicked one of the wheels of the suitcase. It popped off and went flying across the floor. Her mouth fell open before she laughed. "Guess not."

Watching her like this made me realize how much I cherished this woman. "Come here, Ellie," I said as I patted the bed beside me.

Ellawyn dragged the suitcase over and lugged it up and onto the bed. She unzipped the suitcase and opened it up. "What's up?" she asked as she unhooked the buckles on the one side.

"Come sit, please."

She smiled and sat down next to me. Her arm looped through mine and our fingers laced together. "I'm ready now," she said.

"I appreciate you being willing to do this for me," I started. "But you are not spending a penny of your savings on this trip. I'm paying for it for both you and Pops. If Pops is adamant about this, I want it to be the best trip possible."

"You don't have to do that, Beckett," she cut in. "I can pay my own way."

"I know you can," I responded. "But you don't have to. I just have one condition."

"Anything."

"Just promise to come back to me."

Her tears broke free and streamed down her face. She leaned in and gave me a kiss before pressing her forehead to mine. "I'll miss you," I whispered against her lips.

She rubbed her nose against mine, giving me an Eskimo kiss. "I'll miss you more. Now help me pack."

The rest of the evening was spent packing for Ellawyn and Pops's trip, making sure she had everything that she would need. When she wasn't looking, I stuck her sock full of money back into her sock drawer and buried it under everything else.

There was no way I'd be letting her spend her savings—not when she didn't have to.

Eventually, Pops called me about Ellawyn joining him, and he was thrilled with the idea. He was actually kind of bitter he hadn't thought of it first. After I finished on the phone with Pops, I noticed that Ellawyn wasn't in her bedroom or bathroom.

When she wasn't in the living room, I continued down the hall to the spare bedroom. I found her in her art studio, sitting on the floor across from a blank canvas. She was staring at it, paintbrush in hand, lips pursed together.

I sat down next to her. "You sure you're okay with leaving tomorrow?"

She lowered her shoulders and smiled over at me. "Absolutely," she said as she picked up her paintbrush. She dipped the tip into the black paint and then took it to the canvas. She looked over at me out of the corner of her eye. "Mind if I paint a bit before bed?"

I pressed a kiss to the top of her hair and then stood. "Of course," I said as I walked to the door and gently closed it behind me.

After fixing the wheel on her suitcase, I rolled it out to the living room and placed it by the door. Then I threw a sweatshirt on top, just in case she hadn't packed one.

Hours passed by, and Ellawyn still hadn't come out of her studio. Deciding not to bother her, I headed into her bedroom and got ready for bed. I sent her a text, letting her know I was going to bed, and she responded a few moments later with a heart.

I fell asleep as my thoughts drifted to Ellawyn and how much I'd miss this girl while she was gone.

☾

I ROLLED over in bed with the need of wanting Ellawyn near. I reached out to her side of the bed, hoping for the warm body I longed for, but instead, I was met with an uncomfortable coldness. The alarm clock read two in the morning. Sitting up in bed, I wiped the sleep from my eyes and got up so I could go check on my girl.

Figuring she must be in her studio still, I slowly opened the door and stepped inside. Ellawyn was lying next to her canvas with her paintbrush still in her hand. She was wearing an oversized old T-shirt, forgoing pants, and her long brown hair had been thrown messily on top of her head. There were streaks of paint on her arms, legs, and even her face.

She was a rare find, a true work of art.

I closed the distance between us and crouched down next to her, then took the paintbrush from her hands and gave her a kiss on the lips. Her eyelids fluttered open as she began to wake. She rolled onto her back and stretched out her body. "What time is it?" she said, her voice groggy.

"Two in the morning," I replied as I rubbed my fingers up and down the length of her arm.

She pushed herself off the floor and moved for the door. When she entered her room, she went straight to her side of the bed and pulled the covers down.

"Do you want to shower first?" I asked before she could climb into bed.

She looked down at herself and burst out laughing. "Yeah." She buried her head in her hands. "I guess I do."

She went to shower while I fell back to sleep, dreaming of her once more.

☾

WAKING up the following morning was damn near impossible. I didn't want to let her go, despite this being my idea. But knowing how much this trip meant to both of them made the departure a little more bearable.

"Ellawyn," I called out as I grabbed her suitcase, purse, sweatshirt, and sketch pad. "Come on, babe, I've got to drop you off at Pops's place in ten minutes."

I looked up right as she came up next to me and I was at a loss for words. She was dressed simply, wearing black pants, a key necklace, and a white oversized sweater that went down to her thighs, but she had never looked more beautiful to me. "You look stunning, Ellie."

Her cheeks flamed as she gave me a kiss. "Thank you, Beck."

"Have I told you how much I love it when you call me Beck? Because I like it."

She laughed as she pulled her purse from my shoulder and took her sweatshirt from me. "I'm glad. I wasn't going to stop even if you hated it."

We loaded up the car and headed to Pops's place. Ellawyn's hand was in mine the entire drive over. Neither of us made a move to break the connection.

After we arrived, I loaded up the rental car with her luggage while she went to grab Pops and his belongings. They both walked down the sidewalk together, laughing, with big smiles plastered on their faces.

When they reached the car, Pops pulled me in for a big hug. "I love ya, boy," he said. "I'll miss you the most. Promise me you'll be good. Always remain good."

I laughed and hugged him harder. "I'm always good." We pulled apart and he stood there with tears in his eyes as he looked into mine. "I love you too, Pops. Go enjoy this trip. Make the most out of it." His gaze on my face never wavered. "Everything okay? You're acting like you won't ever see me again. I'll be here when you get back."

"Yes, I suppose you're right." He chuckled as he pulled me in for one last hug.

Ellawyn cleared her throat before she pulled me toward her and pressed her lips to mine. Her tongue darted into my mouth, taking what she wanted. We broke apart, our foreheads pressed together. "I'll miss you," she whispered.

After a few more hugs from Pops, they drove off into the distance with both of their arms hanging out of the window as they waved goodbye. With a sense of finality lingering over my head, I waited until I could no longer see the car before I decided to head into Starlight Books.

☪

THE HOURS FLEW by after Pops and Ellawyn had embarked on their road trip, and I hadn't heard from them since. It had been radio silence.

I pulled out my phone, ready to text Ellawyn, as the bell above the shop's door chimed. "Oh, Beckett," a familiar voice called out in a singsong tune.

I shook my head. "Hey, asshole."

Max walked up to the counter with a cocky grin as he glanced around the shop. He jerked his head toward the kitchen door. "Ellawyn back there?"

"Nah, she went on a road trip with Pops."

Max looked at me bewildered. "A road trip," he repeated. "With Benji?"

"Yeah, come on, let's go catch up." After I locked up the shop, Max and I went back to his bar to have a drink and shoot the shit.

Max had been stunned to hear about Pops's tumor regrowth and how he had suddenly decided to go on a road trip. He was even more amused that I managed to convince Ellawyn to go along with him.

"It was good for her to go, too, though," I added.

Max nodded along as he poured us two more drinks before he walked back around the bar to sit next to me. As soon as he sat down, he threw a shot back before he grabbed his beer.

I took a drink of what Max poured for me and sat it back down. "What's with all the drinking tonight?" I gestured to the collection of glasses in front of him.

As he rubbed his face, I noticed how he really looked. His clothes were disheveled, dark circles formed under his eyes, and his hair looked as though he'd been tugging on it way too much. His gaze drifted as he looked anywhere but at me.

"Max," I barked. "What's going on?"

I'd never seen him like this—even when his dad had passed away. Guilt worked its way through my head as I realized that I'd been so caught up in my own life, I hadn't even noticed that my best friend might have been going through hell.

He groaned. "Remnant Hearts has been having some financial trouble," he admitted. "And it's stressing me out."

He filled me in on the new establishments around town. A lot of them were attracting more customers, which took away from his business. He'd been working on doing a whole new rebranding and trying to use different ideas to market the bar.

"That's where Ellawyn came in." He took a drink of water this time. "She knew about my problems and offered to help with the rebranding."

I nodded along as I vaguely remembered one of them mentioning a logo. "I had no idea it was this bad for you, man."

"I asked Ellawyn not to say anything. I knew you'd want to fix it." He chugged the rest of his water. "Anyway, she emailed me over some files this afternoon and they are badass. I wanted to thank her in person." Max pulled out his phone and showed me the logo designs Ellawyn had sent over.

It suddenly dawned on me that this was what Ellawyn had

been painting last night. She nailed it. The logo was shaped like a shield almost, with two hands coming into the middle on both sides, each one holding a beer. The bottles crossed at the top, and below the image was the business name along with two sets of leaves.

"She did an excellent job, man," I said. "This could draw in the younger crowd for sure. Make up some T-shirts with the design," I suggested. "Oh, and maybe a koozie, too. Sell those here."

As Max pondered the idea, a slow smile pulled at his face. "You're right. People will love merch that goes with their favorite bar in town."

After a brainstorming session on ways to draw in the crowd, Max had left with the promise of getting a full night's sleep, and I had left with a promise of visiting Remnant Hearts Bar tomorrow for dinner.

When I got home, I slid off my shoes and sunk onto the couch. I reached for my phone and dialed Ellawyn's number.

She answered immediately. "Beckett," she exclaimed with laughter.

Her laughter had a ripple effect that made me laugh into the phone with her. "What are you guys up to?"

Her excitement was palpable. She filled me in on how they ended up in New York City, went to a Broadway musical, and even had their auras read. She also had her picture taken with a naked cowboy in Times Square while Pops had his picture taken with a princess.

I laughed along with her as I enjoyed this side of her. The fun, carefree Ellawyn, who I hadn't seen until now. "It sounds like you had an eventful day," I said as I yawned into the phone.

"Beckett, you sound tired. Fill me in on your day," she said. "Benji says hello, by the way."

I told her about Max and our plans for getting the bar back on track. She sounded relieved when she heard that Max's mood was improving.

A loud applause came through on the line. I pulled the phone from my ear as I waited for the noise to pass. "What's going on?" I asked.

"Sorry, Beckett. Benji took us to a comedy show tonight. Apparently, it's on his bucket list, and it's getting loud. Can I call you tomorrow?" she asked.

After we said our goodbyes, the line went dead. I was left alone within the silence of my own home while I wished for my people to return to me as soon as possible.

CHAPTER 21
Ellawyn

THESE LAST FEW weeks on the road with Benji had turned into quite the journey. We had been to New York, Ohio, Vermont, Maryland, and Rhode Island so far.

We vowed to only purchase souvenirs that held meaning, or in my case, weren't complete pieces of junk. I opted to collect keychains and magnets during our adventure, while Benji had chosen to purchase two postcards from each state.

Our next stop was Maine.

The closer we got, the more my stomach twisted into knots. The feeling was so deep in the pit of my stomach that I was afraid I could physically become ill. Instead, I found myself constantly rubbing my palms against the legs of my pants.

Benji caught my movement as he drove down the highway. "What's going on with you?"

I babbled about how everything was fine and decided to change the subject. "So, what's in Maine that's on your bucket list?" I asked as I pulled a map out of the glove compartment of the car.

He twitched in his seat, not responding to my question.

Thankful for the reprieve, I let it go and continued staring out the window until I was jerked forward by a sudden movement.

When I looked around, Benji had pulled off into a rest stop and was parking the car. He hopped out of the car and motioned for me to do the same. When I got out, I followed him through a grassy area surrounding the rest stop until we reached a pair of picnic tables. When I sat down across from him, he was looking at me with such kindness and patience. "What's wrong, Benji?"

"There's something I need to tell you," he started. "But I want to know what's gotten you so shaken up about being in Maine?"

My resolve crumbled right then and there as my story spilled out of me, slowly taking over. My body racked with sobs as I told him everything. I confessed about my manipulative, abusive ex-boyfriend and how I had to up and leave my parents and friends behind without a proper goodbye. I told him how I lost myself during those dark times, and how I didn't know who I was anymore back then, that I'd never felt so ashamed in my life. Shame for becoming someone's puppet for so long—not living my own life and playing the role I had been cast in. Benji's hand had been on top of mine the entire time I spoke. The silent support spoke volumes.

I sniffled. "So coming back here brings back a lot of bad memories."

"We don't have to stay here, Ellawyn," he offered. "We could go somewhere else."

I shook my head as I pulled a tissue out of my purse and pressed it against my eyes. "Maybe it would be good for me to see my parents while we're here. It's just hard, that's all. I was just telling Beckett how I needed to take control of my life again. This seems like... fate or something."

Benji's face paled as he jerked his hand away from mine. A lone tear slid down his cheek. "It's ironic that you should mention wanting to take control of your life again."

I couldn't put the pieces together. I thought that this trip *was* him taking control of his life. He put off treatment to have the trip of a lifetime.

"You don't have to talk about it if you don't want to."

His voice shook. "I don't want to be a victim of this brain tumor any longer than I already have been. Beckett... Well, Beckett wants me to fight this tumor and keep up with more surgeries, radiation, and chemo. He wants me to fight until the end of my time." He paused and wiped his eyes with the sleeve of his shirt. "But I can't fight anymore. I don't have it in me to keep going like that."

I knew from the doctor's visit that he hadn't wanted to continue with treatments like that. I just thought that after this road trip, maybe he'd reconsider. "So you want to just forgo treatment, then?" I asked.

Benji looked away and stared out at the highway, watching as cars flew by. "No, I don't want to leave the world that way either."

He leveled me with a single look, and I could feel my whole world suddenly being pulled out from under me. "What are you saying?" My breath quickened, and tears rolled down my face as I waited for Benji to confirm what I was hearing.

"I'm going to start the process of becoming a resident of Maine while we're here. I'm going to take matters into my own hands. I don't have a lot of tomorrows left in my life. I don't have the promise of a future anymore. I need this." He gripped my hand. "In another life, I'd have fought harder. In another life, there'd be no stopping me. But now? At this point in my life? It's all I've got, and I don't have it in me to keep fighting and being miserable."

The tears rolled down my face faster now. I was unable to contain the wreckage that was happening. I shook my head, silently protesting his decision, while he came over to my side of the table and pulled me into a hug.

We stayed like that for what felt like hours, sobbing together as we tried to make sense of this life.

"You can't control the hand that life deals you, Ellawyn." He sighed. "But you can choose to keep playing. You mustn't fold. And as far as this life goes, I'm thankful to have played with you for as long as I did."

"This feels an awful lot like folding," I whispered.

"That's because, for me, it is."

⸻

THE NEXT FEW days in Maine were difficult. Things had shifted between Benji and me. I could feel him start to drift away, but I couldn't quite tell if it was intentional or if it was just a side effect of the heaviness that lingered before us.

But he kept reassuring me that this was what he wanted to do. Even when I protested, he remained firm in his decision.

But the worst part was that he had made me promise not to tell Beckett. He was adamant that he be the one to break the news to him. And while I understood his request, this secret had already started to cause a shift between Beckett and me. Our phone calls that had once been long and frequent had shortened drastically due to the stress. I couldn't stand lying to him, but I knew that if I talked to him for long, I'd slip up and spill the secret.

I'd been put in an impossible situation.

And it was about to become much more difficult.

Today was going to be a big day for Benji, as we scheduled an appointment to view a studio apartment that was for rent in Maine. As we pulled up to the apartment complex, my stomach dropped.

The building was run-down and ragged. It didn't look like anyone cared for the property at all. When we exited the car, my feet remained planted next to it, unmoving.

"Ellawyn," Benji scolded. "Let's go."

I followed him through the grassy front yard to the broken steps that lead up to the front door. When I went to grab the railing for support, I practically fell forward as it became unattached and fell to the ground.

When we entered the building, there was a piece of paper duct taped to the wall that had an arrow drawn on it in sharpie, pointing out which way to go for the leasing office. Outside the office door, Benji tapped on the frame.

A grunt came from inside, followed by the sounds of a squeaky chair. The door whipped open, and an older man appeared. He greeted us with another grunt. "What do you want?" he grumbled.

Benji and I both stepped back.

Where the hell were we and why would Benji want to rent a place here? This couldn't be right. This wasn't at all where Benji belonged.

"Hi, I'm Benji Walden and we're here to view the open studio apartment." Benji held out his hand.

The man stared at his hand but kept his arms at his side. Suddenly, he pushed past us, leaving us behind without so much as a word.

Unsure of what to do, Benji and I shared a glance as he lowered his hand.

Shrugging, we took off after the disgruntled man and caught up to him at the elevator. He eyed me up and down, remaining silent in his evaluation of me.

Ignoring him, I refocused on the elevator. It was making a hell of a noise. If I had to guess, I'd say it was on its last leg. When the doors opened, we were met with the sound of metal scraping metal.

I stared at the man. "When was the last time this was inspected?"

He crossed his arms over his chest. "Does this look like a place that follows inspection protocols?"

My mouth dropped open in disbelief.

Benji entered the elevator first, followed by the man. They both stared at me, waiting for me to enter. I sighed as Benji gave me a pleading look, and I entered the elevator. The door closed in front of me, and I held my breath, hoping I wouldn't plummet to my death in this deathtrap.

The elevator creeped and crawled slowly as we ascended

toward the top of the building. Out of the corner of my eye, I watched as Benji looked completely neutral. There wasn't a hint of fear or anything on his face. I forced my focus back to the doors in front of me as the elevator sounded a pathetic ding before opening.

I practically flew out of that damn thing. When I turned around to make sure Benji had gotten out okay, the creepy man pushed ahead and walked down the hallway. Benji fell in line, and I stayed standing outside the elevator as I stared at his back while he walked away.

Finally, I followed him down the hallway. When we stopped outside of the room, I noted the unit number: 21. I'm not sure why it seemed important right now, but I snapped a picture of the crooked rusty numbers that hung on the door.

The man pushed the door open and stepped out of the way.

The first thing I noticed when we entered was the foul odor that occupied the room. The chipped yellow paint complemented the wallpaper that was torn and hanging off parts of the wall. The kitchen area was much worse. The sink was rusted, and the cabinet doors were falling off the hinges. The refrigerator, once white, was now a dark shade of gray. The curtains were covered with cigarette burns all throughout. And there was a single chair sitting in the middle of the space.

When I zeroed in on the bed, I almost lost my shit. I felt sick to my stomach. I couldn't imagine Benji living in this space, spending money on this horrible apartment.

Unable to keep my mouth shut, I took a step toward the man and crossed my arms over my chest. "Is this what you meant by fully furnished?"

Benji's head whipped toward me. "Not now, Ellawyn," he hissed.

I turned to face him and dug in a little more. "You can't possibly be considering wasting money on this dump." I waved my arms in the air toward the mess of an apartment. "Literally anywhere else would be better."

Benji let out a breath and turned back to address the landlord. "I'll take it." He went into the kitchen area, inspecting the place. "Do you mind if we have a moment to chat, and we can meet you down in your office in a few?"

The landlord nodded and threw me a dirty look while he pulled the door closed behind him. The door slowly opened back up, with both Benji and I staring at it.

I stretched out my arm, gesturing to the open door. "See what I mean?" I walked over to it and secured it with a deadbolt. "You can't live in this death trap, Benji."

His face softened. "This place is my death trap, Ellawyn. I would never truly live here. It's simply a means to an end. This place represents the ending to my story. The end of me."

A tear broke free and slid down my cheek. Now it was making sense. "It doesn't have to be, though." I took a few steps toward him, pulling him into a hug. "Your story could end differently, you know."

He didn't respond. He simply unlocked the door and left, leaving me alone in apartment 21, where the story was supposed to end.

I found Benji inside the leasing office, filling out rental paperwork with the landlord. I stepped just inside the door and stood off to the side and out of the way.

The room we were crammed into was no bigger than a generous walk-in closet. There was a desk cramped up next to the wall, messy and overflowing with bills and paperwork, along with about a dozen or so beer cans in the trash can next to the desk and on the floor nearby.

"Thank you for your time today," Benji addressed the landlord. "I'll be back soon with the security deposit in cash, as requested."

I found it hard to imagine this place needing a security deposit. But I kept my thoughts to myself this time.

Once we left the apartment complex, we were back to a tension-filled car ride, both of us silent as we drove back to the hotel where we were staying. When we missed our exit for the hotel, I became unsure of where we were going. "Benji, I think we missed our exit back there." I turned in my seat, looking out the back window.

"We're not going back to the hotel yet," he answered.

"Oh." I turned back around in my seat, confused. "Okay." I almost wanted to ask where we were going, but I realized I didn't quite care. If Benji wanted to drive around Maine, then so be it.

My phone vibrated in my pocket. I pulled it out, expecting it to be Becket, but saw a notification from an unknown number.

Unknown: It's time for you to come back to Quimby Grove. You've been gone far too long, and I can't come see you when you're all the way in Maine.

I froze as I read the text message, my free hand covered my mouth as I tried not to scream.

Benji glanced over as he drove. "What is it, dear?"

"I... He..." I tried to speak, but the words wouldn't come out. "Found... Watching..." I couldn't even form a coherent thought.

Benji pulled over on the side of the road and reached to turn on his hazard lights. I handed him my phone, figuring it'd be much easier to have him read it than for me to read it out loud.

When he finished, he glanced at me and then back down toward the phone. His mouth spread into a grim line. "How long has this been going on?"

Letting out a breath, I sank further into my seat. "A couple months, I guess. But the encounters have been infrequent. Mostly it was a letter or two delivered at Starlight or stuck to my door. One time, though, the person was at Illusion, and they paid for my food. But this is the first text I've received."

Benji handed me back my phone. I grasped it, hands shaking, and placed it inside my purse. Unsure of what to say, I decided to offer up the only thing I could think of. "Beckett knows."

"And the authorities?"

I shook my head no. "We installed security systems at both of our places, and then the activity stopped." I tucked a piece of hair behind my ear. "I figured the person had moved on."

Benji looked at me with the saddest face I'd ever seen. "They know your cell phone number and where you are geographically."

I stayed silent, not knowing what to say.

Benji started the car back up. "Well, let's deal with this another day. I was about to drive us to your parents' house. How does that sound?"

My mood instantly improved at the mention of my parents. "That sounds amazing." I grinned as I pointed him toward the highway.

Benji merged back onto the highway while I cranked up the radio, feeling excited about seeing my parents, and allowed myself to truly feel happy in this moment. My arm was hanging out of the open window, feeling the air from the drive. I glanced over at Benji, seeing him smiling at me, his arm out his window too.

All of a sudden, the sky began to darken as the trees rocked back and forth swiftly. We saw a flash of lightning in the distance up ahead. "Looks like we're about to drive into a storm."

"Looks like a rough one," he added.

We both rolled up our windows just as the rain began to fall. It was slow at first, and then a fast downpour took over. I glanced at Benji, just to make sure he was okay to drive, and I suddenly had the urge to talk to him out of nowhere. "Hey, Benji."

"Yeah?"

"I just wanted you to know that I respect how you want your story to end. It's just that, well, you don't have to end your story alone."

He turned his head just slightly so he could look at me. "I know."

As we continued our drive on the highway, the weather became more intense and aggressive. The rain was coming down harder, and it was getting more difficult to see the road ahead of us.

Benji slowed down as he tried to navigate the road while other cars seemed to fly by him without much of an issue. "These cars that are flying past us are just reckless."

"Seriously. They could kill themselves," I added.

I stared out of the windshield, watching as the wipers flicked back and forth at warp speed. For a moment, it was almost as if my mind was playing a trick on me. The wipers appeared to be going more slowly now, despite the speed not being changed.

"Are you sure you don't want to pull over?" I asked Benji as I leaned forward and turned on the defrosters to clear up the windshield a bit. "It's not letting up at all."

"No, we're almost to our exit, and then we'll be okay."

I nodded and looked back out the window again. When I glanced behind us, I saw that a car was coming up on our rear quickly. I continued to watch, hoping they'd slow down or get in the left lane.

"The car behind us isn't slowing down." I turned on our hazard lights in hopes it would draw attention to our car. "We may want to pull over so they can pass."

Turning back around, I looked at Benji while he tried to pull off onto the shoulder of the highway.

But we were too late.

In an instant, everything changed. I felt the impact of the collision as my body jerked around in the car, followed by a feeling of dizziness. Time stilled as we spun in circles, unable to tell which way was up. Broken glass shattered and flew toward me as I raised my arms to cover my face. The sound of metal scraping against metal filled the air, and as the roof of the car caved, I heard a scream.

Suddenly, everything went quiet as I succumbed to the darkness.

CHAPTER 22
Beckett

There had never been a moment where I could say that my entire world came crashing down before my very eyes.

Until now.

The moment I saw a Maine telephone number flash across my screen, I knew something was wrong. Even moments before the phone rang, something hadn't felt right.

The call had come from a nurse at Northern Memorial Hospital. The words still replayed in my head on repeat.

"Sir, there's been an accident."

I hadn't heard anything else after that beyond the nurse saying to get there as soon as possible. The rug had been pulled out from underneath me. The room had started to spin. Everything moved in slow motion, just slightly out of my grasp.

I had been at Remnant Hearts when the call came through. Max saw the look of panic that had flashed across my face. Taking the phone from me, he wrote down all the pertinent information from the nurse. He closed his bar early and drove me all the way to the hospital in Maine.

We had been waiting for four hours in the waiting room and still didn't have answers. Max had been a godsend, taking over for me when we first arrived at the hospital. I'd been completely out of touch with reality. It was as if I was watching the situation play out in front of me instead of living it.

I was there. But I wasn't

I felt my leg shake as my name was called.

It happened again. "Beckett." The voice was louder this time, along with more aggressive shaking.

I felt the fog within my head clear as my vision refocused on who was standing in front of me—Max and a man dressed in white scrubs. I gulped through a dry throat. "Sorry, I'm here."

The man in the white scrubs stepped toward me. "Hello, I'm Dr. Ward. I've been treating both Benjamin Walden and Ellawyn Calloway. They were brought in due to a car crash on the interstate."

"Okay." I closed my eyes and took a breath. "How are they?"

Dr. Ward's face was unreadable. I couldn't tell if I was about to be given good news or bad news. "Ellawyn has sustained a broken arm on the left side, a sprained ankle, a few minor lacerations across her face and chest, and some bumps and bruises."

I nodded. "So, she will make a full recovery?"

"Yes, she'll be fine. But she's in a lot of pain."

Max clapped me on the back as we shared a look of relief. He turned back to the doctor. "What about Benji?" Max questioned.

"Mr. Walden sustained life-threatening injuries. We did everything we could but..."

My chest tightened and burned a trail to my heart as it cracked from the inside out. All the feelings I'd had before this moment vanished as a heaviness settled in.

"I never should have let him go on this trip," I whispered. "Excuse me."

I turned around, leaving Max and the doctor standing there while I went back to my seat in the waiting room. I lowered myself into the chair and leaned forward onto my knees as my hands cradled my head. My eyes drifted closed as I imagined Pops standing in front of me, a smile on his face and his arms opened wide.

I stood up, reaching for his warm embrace, but when I stepped into his arms and opened my eyes, he was gone.

And I was alone.

My eyes began to burn, and I opened and shut them again as I willed the tears to fall, like a desert begging for rainfall in a drought. But the well had dried up, and there was nothing I could do to fix it.

When I looked back over to where the doctor had been, Max was walking toward me. "Hey, man," he said as he reached my side. "Dr. Ward said they're keeping Benji in his room for a bit so that you can say goodbye." He pulled me in for a hug. "You go be with Benji, and I'll go check on Ellawyn."

When I didn't respond, Max took off toward the elevator bank with me tailing him. We took the elevator ride in silence, and when he got off, I continued to follow him down a long corridor until he stopped in front of a room with the door pulled closed. When he turned to me, his eyes were bloodshot, and tears were sliding down his face.

"I'll be with Ellawyn," he said as he jerked his head toward the far end of the hallway. "Take your time here."

He walked away without another word, his stride easy as he navigated the hallway. I stayed in place until he disappeared into a room at the very end.

Glancing down at the doorknob of the closed-off room, I paused before placing my hand on the clean stainless steel. Closing my eyes, I grabbed the doorknob. I drew in a sharp breath as the coldness of the doorknob pierced my skin.

No one must have been inside for a while.

I eased the door open and stepped inside a semidark room.

It was silent.

There were no beeping machines, no monitors to capture the vitals of the person residing within the hospital bed. Just a deafening silence that filled the room.

With heavy steps, I slowly walked toward the center of the room, stopping when I reached the foot of the bed. My gaze drew from the end of the bed to the top. He looked so peaceful in this moment, like his body and soul were finally at rest from the raging war within him. I took a few more steps toward him and stopped when I reached his bedside. I placed one of his hands in between mine. He was so cold. I rubbed his hand with mine as I tried to warm him up.

"We were supposed to have more time." I squeezed his hand, hoping he felt it somehow. "You weren't supposed to leave, not like this," I whispered.

A single tear slid down my cheek.

Needing a moment, I stepped out into the hallway and went in the direction of Ellawyn's room. When I reached the room I saw Max go into, I paused and shifted closer toward the door while I listened for sounds of life. Machines beeped and whispers sounded through the door.

My heart clenched as I repeated the motions I'd done just a little bit ago. Bracing myself, I put my hand on the doorknob.

This time, it was warm.

Walking into the room felt like déjà vu. When I looked toward the hospital bed, I saw Max sitting in a chair next to Ellawyn's bedside while he held her hand and laid his head on their conjoined hands.

She was wrapped in bandages, with tubes and IVs connected to her. Her face was covered in cuts and bruises, her skin pale.

She didn't look at peace.

I watched for the rise and fall of her chest before moving further into the room. When I got to her bedside, I bent down and placed a kiss to her forehead. "Ellawyn. I'm here, babe," I whispered into her hair. "Please wake up." Grabbing her other free hand, I gave it a squeeze before sitting down next to her.

Max lifted his head and looked over at me with a frown. "She hasn't woken up yet," he said.

Taking a deep breath, my senses filled with the aromas of

flowers that I hadn't noticed when I first walked in. I stood up and surveyed the room. There were about half a dozen bouquets of flowers lining the windowsill.

"What's the matter?" Max questioned as he stood up and looked toward the window.

Turning back around to face him, I pointed behind me. "There's a lot of flowers over there, and no one knew about the accident but us." I took off toward the flowers and looked at the arrangements with narrowed eyes.

Poppies and sunflowers—Ellawyn's favorites. Each arrangement had a card attached. Plucking the card from the first arrangement, I opened it to a single typed word. I threw it down and opened the remaining five cards. All had a single word. Lying them all down on the windowsill, I moved the cards around until the message appeared.

"Do not ignore me again, Ellawyn."

A taunt. It had to be from her stalker back in Quimby Grove. "Each card had a word written on it and it spelled out a message to Ellawyn," I called over my shoulder. "It said to not ignore them again."

"Wait, are they from the stalker?" Max questioned.

The tiny cards crumbled in my fist before I dropped them into the small wastebasket in the corner of the room. "Must be," I said as I took my seat next to Ellawyn.

I just didn't have it in me to care about those cards right now. I wanted to, but I couldn't. All I could think about was Pops. My mind couldn't handle any more.

It refused to.

A faint whisper caught my attention as I was dozing off in the chair next to Ellawyn. Assuming it was Max, I tried to ignore it, turning my head away from the hospital bed.

"Benji," the faint whisper came again.

My eyes popped open at Pops's name, my head whipping around to see Max standing up and looking down at Ellawyn.

"Hey, Ellie." Max's voice was low and gentle. "It's Max."

She tried to open her eyes as I gripped her hand. "I'm here, too, babe."

Her eyes sprang open, and she scanned the room. "Where's Benji?" She looked from me to Max and then back to me again. "Is he in another room? Can I go see him?"

Max and I shared a look while I silently pleaded with him to tell her the news.

He slid to the edge of his seat. "Ellawyn," he said. When she turned her head toward him, he continued. "I'm sorry, but he didn't make it."

Tears tracked down her cheeks. "You're lying," she pleaded. She tried to push herself up in bed, wincing at the pain. "He was just here. I just saw him."

Her body shook as she broke down and sobbed. I'd give anything to hold her, to comfort her and let her know that everything was going to be okay.

But I didn't feel that way, and I wouldn't lie to her.

Shoving myself upright, I took a few steps backward as I watched Ellawyn try to pull off the cords that tied her to the bed. Pausing by the door, I looked over my shoulder just as she collapsed into Max's arms. "He was just here," she wailed.

That was the last thing I heard before I pulled the door closed and walked away.

The sound of her sobs echoed throughout the hallway. I picked up my pace to escape the heartache and practically jogged until the sounds of her cries were no longer following me.

Running away from her heartache did nothing to ease mine. I kept walking until I was at the opposite end of the hallway. I leaned against the wall and slid down until I was seated on the floor.

Time had gotten lost, and the sun had started to come up. I had no desire to move from my spot on the floor. I remained rooted in my spot overnight, and no one bothered me. It was as if I'd just been accepted as a permanent fixture.

Glancing up, I stared down toward the other end of the hallway. Down that way were three people who meant the world to me.

But one of them was dead.

My gaze remained focused. A figure appeared out of nowhere, and I watched as it got closer and closer. Eventually, Max's face appeared.

My chest tightened. I tried to rub the pain out, but nothing helped.

Max slid down and sat next to me.

I didn't look at him. I didn't acknowledge him. I just sat, staring toward the end of the hallway.

"Ellawyn has calmed down a bit. She's not screaming and crying anymore. She's ready to say goodbye to Benji. Do you want to take her?"

Looking straight ahead, I said nothing. I wanted to say something, but the words wouldn't come. Everything just seemed so surreal. There were moments of clarity, but they were outnumbered by the moments of complete despair.

Max bumped his shoulder against mine.

I couldn't bring myself to look at him. My focus stayed glued to the room that Pops was in. I imagined his door opening. He'd walk out into the hallway with a big grin on his face. He'd laugh and say, "I gotcha, boy" before pulling me into one of his hugs.

I blinked, my gaze refocusing down the hallway. It was empty.

Max stood up and came around to face me, holding out his hand. "She's hurting, too." He pushed his hand out closer toward me. "She needs to say goodbye, and you need to come with us."

I placed my hand in his and he pulled me up off the floor and urged me back down the hallway. When we got to Pops's room, he paused. "I'll go get her." He nodded toward the door. "We'll meet you inside."

He walked away without waiting for me to respond. He probably figured I wouldn't give him one.

He was right.

When I gripped the doorknob this time around, the coldness didn't bother me. It matched how I felt: cold, numb, distant, unbothered. I entered his room, going straight to the windows, and whipped the blinds open for some light. Turning around, I looked at the bed again. He looked so frail. He didn't even look like Pops. I looked away, not wanting to remember him like this.

The door opened as Max pushed Ellawyn inside. She was in a wheelchair, not looking like herself at all.

I felt like I'd lost a piece of her, too.

She looked down at her hands for a moment before taking a breath and looking at Pops. I could see it on her face the moment she realized Pops was truly gone. She swallowed a knot of emotion before she stood from her wheelchair and hobbled from the chair to Pops's bedside. Grabbing his hand, she held on tight while her tears stained her cheeks with silent cries.

"This isn't how your story was supposed to end," she whispered. "This isn't how it was supposed to go. Your story should have been different. We had more pages to write, more chapters to enjoy together." She leaned down and gave him a quick kiss on the cheek. "You were supposed to see me through the hardest part of our journey." She sniffled as she wiped her eyes. "I'm so sorry that our adventure was cut short, Benji."

Silence washed over the room. Max stood staring out the window, Ellawyn stayed next to Pops, and I was as far away as possible. The last few weeks replayed in my head. The doctor's appointments. Pops's sudden road trip and how I made Ellawyn go with him. It dawned on me that I'd lost so much time with him in his final days. He hadn't been with me. He'd been with her. She had received those final days, not me.

And it fucking stung.

The anger began to stir within me. "I can't believe you were the one to spend his final days with him. It's not fucking fair."

Ellawyn looked over her shoulder at me. "I know. I'm sorry."

"You're sorry?" I scoffed and stepped toward her. "You're fucking sorry? He was the only family I had left, and now he's fucking gone," I screamed. When she didn't answer, I kept going. "I bet you two wouldn't have even gone to Maine if it weren't for you."

Max came up and stood in front of me. "Beckett," he warned.

I stepped closer, getting in his face. "It's her fucking fault that he's dead."

Ellawyn looked at me as if she'd been slapped, and a fresh batch of tears ran down her face. Max moved to stand next to her.

"Knock it the fuck off, Beckett." He helped Ellawyn into her wheelchair and held onto her as she lowered herself down. He turned the wheelchair around, facing away from me. "It's not her fault. I get that you're hurting, but you can't blame her."

"Get out," I demanded.

☾

MY ANGER KEPT me company as I dealt with the hospital staff and the planning of the funeral. It kept a fire lit within me, keeping me warm as it pushed me forward with the arrangements. If I stayed mad, I didn't have time to feel any other emotion surrounding Pops's death.

I hadn't heard from Ellawyn since Max had wheeled her out of Pops's room the other day. Max had been in touch, but he'd been distant since the hospital. I knew he'd been taking care of Ellawyn—making sure she had her medication, helping her around the apartment, and just being there for her.

I wanted to tell him that I appreciated it. But I just didn't have it in me right now. But more than that, I wanted to go back in time and take away her pain and stop Pops's death from happening. I'd give anything to spend an evening with them, laughing and enjoying one another's company like everything was right in the world.

While they returned home to Quimby Grove, I stayed behind in Maine for a multitude of reasons. I didn't want to go back home where everything reminded me of Pops, and I also needed to collect Ellawyn's and Pops's belongings from the hotel and the car.

But mostly, I just wanted to be alone in the last place where Pops was alive. I wished I'd known what was so special about him coming here. There had to have been more to it than Ellawyn's parents being here.

A ringing from the backseat of the car pulled me out of my head. Reaching back, I grabbed the duffle bag of Pops's belongings and dug through it until I found his cell phone. The number that flashed across the screen wasn't one I was familiar with. "Benjamin Walden's phone," I answered.

A disgusting wet cough came through the line before a male's voice broke through. "Yeah, uh, it's the landlord." He coughed a few more times. "Calling to see if you've got my money."

What the hell?

I cleared my throat. "This is his grandson, Beckett, and I have no clue what you're talking about, but he's gone."

He groaned into the phone line. "Sucks for me. Does the chick he was with still want the place?"

"No, I doubt it."

I could hear him shuffling papers around in the background, along with the sound of a lighter being flicked. With a sharp inhale, he finally responded. "Why don't you come see it for yourself. Maybe you want it?"

I almost told him to fuck off. But I was curious. I wanted to know who this asshole was and why Pops and Ellawyn would ever visit a place where this dude works. Then realization hit. Pops was going to rent an apartment here. In Maine.

"You know what?" I said as I turned the ignition. "I'd like to see it."

Thirty minutes later, I found myself parked in front of a rundown, condemned-looking apartment complex. There was no way Pops would have wanted to live here. Hoping to get some answers from the landlord, I headed inside to the leasing office. The man sitting behind a very tiny desk shouldn't have surprised me, but he did.

I wrapped my knuckles against the doorframe. "Hello, I'm Benji Walden's grandson." I took a few tentative steps inside the threshold of the office. "We spoke on the phone a little while ago."

He took a puff from his cigarette and coughed.

Such a charmer, this one.

"Yeah." He coughed again. "He was gonna rent a unit from me." He wiped his hands on his pants and stood to face me. He looked me up and down. "He was gonna pay cash, too."

"Well, considering he's dead, I don't foresee that happening." I looked around the leasing office. "Mind if I see which unit he was looking at?"

"I guess." He pushed past me and entered the hallway outside of his office.

Following him down the hallway, I took in the building. The wallpaper was yellowing and peeling off the walls. The pictures that adorned the walls were crooked, with broken glass accompanying the photos.

Broken glass for a broken home.

When we arrived outside of the unit, he kicked the door on the bottom left side, causing it to pop open for us. When I entered, I realized how much this didn't make sense. I couldn't imagine Pops and Ellawyn standing in his very room just days ago.

I turned to the landlord. "I don't understand why they would want this place."

He huffed. "The girl was against it."

That made sense at least. "Do you know why he wanted it?" I asked.

"Why the hell would I care? Money is money."

Of course he only cared about the money. "Yeah, I get it. Just weird is all."

The landlord shook his head as we left the room, and he

kicked the door shut again. He stopped for a moment and stared at me. "I do remember her sayin' somethin' about how a story didn't need to end here or something." He shrugged before continuing down the hallway.

When I didn't answer, he piped up again. "Whatever the hell that means."

CHAPTER 23

Ellawyn

I FELT like I was mourning the loss of two people instead of just one. One person had left the world physically, whereas the other loss was ambiguous. I'd lost Benji due to a horrific car accident that had claimed his life, but I'd lost Beckett, too.

The only difference was that Beckett was still alive.

It had been days since I'd heard from him and even longer since I had seen him. Max and I returned to Quimby Grove while Beckett stayed behind. The pain he had caused in the hospital was still raw, and while I didn't have the strongest desire to see him yet, I hoped he was doing okay.

Max had been a great source of company, though. Ever since we'd returned home, we stayed at my apartment while I hid away from the world—him on the couch while I stayed in my own room.

I didn't know what I would have done if I had to return home alone. Max had been my rock. He knew the perfect balance of how to be there for me without pushing me to talk about something I wasn't ready for. But at the same time, he knew when to push just enough.

I heard popcorn being cooked in the kitchen, followed by the smell of butter and salt permeating the air. A smile shone through as he yelled from the kitchen. "Get your ass out here. The movie is about to start."

Tugging on my most comfortable hoodie, I headed out to the living room. Plopping down beside him on the couch, I snagged the bowl of popcorn and placed it between my legs.

"You thief," he teased as he pressed play on the remote app on his phone.

I frowned at him. "How come you get to pick the movie again?"

He laughed as he stole the popcorn out of my grasp. "Because I had to download a damn remote app because you keep losing the real remote."

I yanked the popcorn back. "Whatever," I said as I popped a piece into my mouth while the movie started.

My mind kept wandering back to Benji, like it had ever since we were in the hospital. A heaviness had taken over, and I didn't have room for much else. I barely left my apartment. I haven't worked on any art or visited Starlight Books, and eating and sleeping had taken a backseat.

There would be moments of time, though, where everything stood still. I felt normal. Like when I teased Max as we settled in for a movie. It was a moment caught in time, right before reality came crashing to the forefront of my mind, reminding me of the loss we'd suffered.

With a sigh, I sat up straighter on the couch and pulled my legs to my chest.

Max paused the movie as he cast a worrisome glance my way. "What's wrong?" he questioned.

"I need to finish what I started in Maine," I answered as I stood and went into the kitchen. I pulled my favorite mug from the cupboard and started a pot of coffee. As the coffee brewed, I stared at my mug and felt the comfort of the familiarity. It was a white mug with gold stars, along with the phrase 'chase the light.' My mother had given it to me a few years ago, and it had become my favorite mug.

"I'm going back," I told Max.

He joined me in the kitchen, pulling a mug down from the cupboard and placing it on the counter. "Alright, what do you have to do?" Once my mug was full, he removed it from the base of the coffee maker and replaced it with his own.

The warmth of the coffee tickled my nose as I inhaled the strong scent. I took a seat at the kitchen table and prepared for the conversation that was brewing between us. The conversation I really didn't want to have.

"I want to visit my parents," I offered.

Max's brows furrowed as he shot me a perplexed look and joined me at the table. "I'm not following. What's the big deal?"

I hesitated and wondered if I should tell him about my past. It wasn't that I didn't trust Max, but my story wasn't a happy one. It was one laced with shame and filled with secrets I'd tried to bury. With a sigh, I filled him in on the details of my past and why I hadn't seen my parents in a while.

"Let's go." Max stood from his seat and went back into the living room and put his shoes on. After shoving his wallet into his back pocket, he grabbed his car keys and shoved them into his hoodie. "We're going to go see your parents in Maine," he declared.

He disappeared into my room and came back out with my sneakers. After he placed the sneakers on the floor next to me, he went back into my room, shut off the lights, and pulled the door closed.

After shoving my feet into my shoes and yanking the sweat-shirt over my head, I turned to Max. "Should we text Beckett?"

He nodded. "I talked to him earlier, to see if he'd be home today or tomorrow," he explained as he led me into the hallway. "He said he probably won't be home until Friday." He turned, locking the door behind us, and then walked toward the stairwell.

My mind wandered back to Beckett and how annoyed I was that he hadn't returned to Quimby Grove yet. I missed him. Despite all the horrible things he'd said in the hospital, I missed him. I knew he was going through a hard time, but so was I. I just wished he'd talk to me so we could clear the air and work through the heartache we had both endured.

When we left my apartment building, Max's car was parked right outside. He drove a Jeep Grand Cherokee and it was very sleek. The exterior color was black, which matched the nice black leather interior. I ran my hand over the hood as I walked around to the passenger side. "I love this car."

He laughed and shook his head. "Yeah, yeah," he mumbled. "Now she needs a bath because of your grimy fingerprints."

I shrugged as I buckled up. "Don't be so dramatic." Pulling down the visor, I checked my hair and smoothed it into a pony-tail. "I bet you wouldn't even let me eat in here."

He scoffed as he rolled down both of our windows and adjusted his mirrors. "You're damn right I wouldn't. No food, no open containers, and clear liquids only."

Laughter escaped and I couldn't control it. "You're telling me I can't eat in this car, *and* I can only drink water?"

He threw a hand over the back of my headrest and backed out of our spot. "Yep," he said.

"I don't think I've ever met someone that was on the same level as you when it came to car care."

He nodded. "Probably not," he said as he shifted in his seat. "I care a lot about two things and two things only."

I quirked an eyebrow. "Oh yeah? What two things?"

"My bar and my car," he answered. "That's it."

Studying him, I wondered if he was joking. But he must be serious. It dawned on me that I didn't know a ton about Max. I knew surface-level things—he was Beckett's best friend, his dad had died, and he loved his bar. I knew he was sweet, quiet, serious, and a great friend. But that was it.

"You know I respect the love of your bar, and now your car. But, uh, what if a nice girl comes along and wants to drink coffee in your precious Jeep?"

He side-eyed me as he merged onto the highway. "Are you asking what happens when I get a girlfriend?"

My gaze narrowed. "Basically," I answered with a shrug.

"I doubt that will ever happen," he said as he let out a breath. "No one ever wants to date the local bartender."

Saddened by his answer, I defended him. "Max, that's not true. You're a catch."

"There was one girl, though," he offered. "I met her like four years ago at the beach. I'd been playing the guitar on the boardwalk, alone, when she showed up wearing some long gown and holding a bottle of champagne. She was maid of honor at some wedding, I guess, but she was fucking beautiful." He smiled over at me as he recounted the memory. "She was playful and full of sass. You could tell she wouldn't take anyone's bullshit. She was perfect."

"What happened?"

"We hooked up, and that decision has affected me ever since. I think she could have been my person. We never got each other's names or anything. But every year, I go back to that very boardwalk and hope like hell I'll see her again. I'd do anything to go back and get her name or her number." He reached for the knob and turned the volume up on the radio. "What I'd give to just go back and change what went down."

"I hope you find her," I whispered, but I wasn't sure he'd heard me.

I felt like shit that I'd stumbled upon a sensitive subject for him and caused him to shut down. I just wanted him to be happy.

We rode in silence for the duration of the trip as I leaned my head up against the cold glass of the window and watched the trees pass by my line of vision. Before I knew it, the navigation system said we'd reached our destination as Max turned into my parents' driveway.

My head felt heavy as I sat up and took in my surroundings. In a moment, I'd been transported back in time. Back to a time where I felt small, safe, and protected. A few tears broke free, and I wiped them away.

"I didn't think I'd feel like this," I admitted.

Max turned the key in the ignition and shut off the car before he leaned back into the seat. "What do you mean?"

"I... I'm not sure how to describe it." I sniffled. "But I thought I'd feel a sense of peace coming back here—back to a place that had once held the key to fixing all of my problems." I turned to face Max. "But all I feel right now is a longing for my parents. To feel that protection from them."

"Go on in, and take your time. I'll wait here."

"Okay, yeah." I opened the car door and looked back at him before getting out. "You don't want to come in?"

He shook his head. "This is something you have to do on your own. But I know you can do it."

I didn't bother responding, because I knew he was right. I closed the car door behind me and made my way to the front porch. Before I could step up to the door, I waited and admired the front of my childhood home. The porch was my favorite thing about it. The house had this beautiful porch that wrapped around the entire home. When I was younger, I'd come out here with my favorite pillow, blanket, and book, and I'd lay down on the porch and read.

They'd had to drag me back inside at bedtime.

I smiled as I took the four steps to reach the top of the porch and rang the doorbell. I could hear footsteps approaching the door, and I knew right away that my mom was on the other side. My gaze was glued to the doorknob as I watched it turn before the door opened slowly. When my mom realized it was me, she burst into tears and pulled me into a hug.

"I love you, Mom," I said into her hair as I squeezed her tightly.

"Oh, I love you, too, sweet girl." She pulled back and assessed me. "You look good. Healthy, even with a cast." She stepped back into the house, pulling me in with her, and closed the door behind us.

☾

AFTER SPENDING three hours with my mom and dad, I was ready to head back to Quimby Grove with the promise to visit more frequently. I stepped out onto the porch and went back to Max's car. Before getting in, I turned around and waved at my parents, who were watching from the window.

"Hey," I said as I slid into the passenger side and buckled up. "Sorry for the long visit."

He smiled at me as he backed out of the driveway. "It's no problem."

Silence washed over the car again as we merged onto the highway to head back home. I couldn't tell if Max was upset with me about earlier or if it was something else. "Earth to Max," I called as I crossed my arms over my chest.

"Huh?"

"You've been distant ever since we left town and talked about you finding love someday."

He exhaled. "Sorry. How was your visit with your parents?"

Deciding to let it go, I answered his question. "It was amazing," I explained as the tension left my body. "And guess what? They told me that my ex-boyfriend landed himself in jail for abuse. I feel like I can breathe again."

Max whipped his head toward me, looking between me and the road ahead of us. "What does that mean for you?"

It meant that I was finally free. That I no longer needed to run and hide. It meant I could breathe again without worrying about someone watching my every move and judging me or questioning every decision I made.

A weight had been lifted.

Turning back to Max, I said, "It means I'm free to live my life in Quimby Grove without watching over my shoulder constantly."

A grin spread across his face. "Good."

The rest of the car ride home was spent chatting and listening to music. Well, he listened while I sang along to every song that I knew. Max even caved and let us stop for snacks and a drink on the way home.

Today was my first good day in a while.

"I feel bad," I confessed as I took a bite out of my licorice.

He looked over at me, confused. "Why?"

"Because Benji is gone, and I just had a good day." I pulled my hoodie over my head as a chill seeped in. "I miss him a lot, but I was so relieved to have seen my parents and have some closure in that part of my life." I sighed. "Am I a bad person?"

He shook his head. "Not at all."

Once we arrived back in Quimby Grove, Max pulled up in front of my apartment complex. After unbuckling my seat belt, I reached for the handle of the door, but a hand on my arm stopped me. "Wait," Max said. "You know you aren't truly a bad person, right?"

"Maybe not," I mumbled with a shrug. I shrunk deeper into my seat. "I just feel like I don't deserve to be happy when we're all mourning the loss of Benji."

"Listen to me, Ellawyn, and listen closely. Benji passing away was tragic and devastating for us all. We're all trying to adjust to that loss and the pain that comes along with it. I've been watching you these past few days, and you've barely eaten or slept. I'm not sure how you're functioning. But today, when you visited your parents—that was the first I've seen the light in your eyes in days."

I wiped the tears that fogged my vision. "Yeah."

"There's no set timeline for grief or any rules that need to be followed. You can be happy that you've fixed your relationship with your parents while also missing Benji. You can live, Ellie. Benji would have wanted you to."

I was full-on crying at this point. "Thanks, Max."

He leaned over, giving me a hug. "You're welcome. Now let's go to bed. I'm exhausted from driving your ass around all day."

We both laughed as we walked back to my apartment. Once we got inside, I tossed my purse onto the dining room table before grabbing a bottle of water from the fridge. I turned around and faced the living room, practically jumping out of my skin when I found someone sitting on my couch.

"Beckett, you're back."

CHAPTER 24

Beckett

SHE LOOKED DIFFERENT. It had only been about a week or so since I'd seen her, but she looked different. The lack of food and sleep was evident, but there was also relief swimming in those beautiful brown eyes. My girl had the weight of the world on her shoulders and it showed.

And the last time I'd seen her, I'd been a complete dick.

She tilted her head while glancing down toward my hands, which hung by my sides. "What do you have there?"

Glancing down at my hand, I was reminded of the card I'd just pulled off her door. I extended it toward her. "There was a card taped to the door."

She took the card and flipped it over in her hands, eyeing it suspiciously. "Thanks."

A throat cleared behind Ellawyn as Max walked up to us. "Hey, Beckett," he said as he pulled me into a hug. "Glad you're back in town."

He turned his attention to Ellawyn. "Careful, Ellie, it could be from the stalker."

Oh, fuck. I hadn't even considered that it could be from the stalker. I reached to take it, but Ellawyn turned her back to me as she slid her finger under the seal.

She kept her facial expression neutral as she read the card. Clearing her throat, she tucked it inside her kitchen cookbook. "I'm tired from our adventure today. I'm going to bed." She turned to Max and gave him a hug. "Thanks for the ride."

Max and I both watched as she walked into her room and closed the door behind her. As soon as the light in her room went out, we both headed to the kitchen. Max grabbed the cookbook and flipped it open to the page where the card was.

You'll be mine soon.

The words were scrawled across the middle of the card in black marker. Something about the handwriting was familiar, but I couldn't place it.

"Do you think he'll make a move?" Max asked.

Closing the cookbook, I pushed it away before running my hands through my hair. "Honestly?" I turned to face him. "Yeah, I do."

"Me too." He jerked his head toward Ellawyn's room. "You cool if I head out since you're back? I should check in on the bar."

"Yeah, man. Thanks again for looking after her these past few days. I just needed to get my head on straight."

"I get that." He grabbed his keys and walked to the door. "Lock up after me."

Once he was gone, I locked the door and went back into the living room to shut off the lights. Curious if she'd fallen asleep yet, I stood outside her door to see if I could hear anything. The sound of her crying pierced through the door and straight to my heart.

Nudging the door open, I poked my head inside. "Ellie, are you okay?"

"No," she mumbled as I heard the shuffling of her grabbing a tissue.

Instead of waiting for an invitation, I stepped inside and closed the door behind me. One look at my girl and I wished I could have bandaged up all the pain she'd been feeling. She was curled up in bed, lying in the fetal position while clutching a box of tissues to her chest. Her hair was sprawled out all over the bed. I pushed it aside, then sat down beside her and stroked her back.

After a few minutes, she stopped trembling and pushed herself up to a seated position. She looked at me, and silent tears rolled down her face. Her skin was pale, with blotches of red on her cheeks and chest.

"I just want it to end," she sobbed.

Tucking a piece of hair behind her ears, I pressed my lips to her forehead. "How about we go to the cops and file a report tomorrow?"

"Okay." She looked down and away. "I just want to feel safe."

The woman in front of me had gone through hell for as long as I had known her. She deserved to be cut a break for once. I pulled back the comforter on her bed, and we slid underneath. Pulling her into my chest, I made her a promise that I hoped I could keep.

"I'll keep you safe. No matter what."

THE POLICE STATION turned out to be a bust.

We knew it would be, but it still sucked to be told there wasn't much they could do right now considering we didn't know who the perpetrator was. We did what we could, though. Ellawyn provided copies of the notes, cards, and text messages, while I told them about the flower arrangements at the hospital and the message that the note cards spelled out. We figured out that the stalker had been using a disposable phone to contact Ellawyn, though that wasn't a shock. The police couldn't track the number, which left us with a dead end.

Ellawyn looked defeated as we left the station. I pulled her close and tucked her under my arm. "How about we head to Remnant Hearts and grab some lunch?" I suggested.

She didn't answer. Instead, she led the way as we walked down the block toward the bar. When we walked inside, we were met with an empty space. Ellawyn pulled out a barstool and sat down.

"Be right there," Max's voice carried from the back of the bar.

When I glanced at Ellawyn, she'd been staring out the window in the direction of Starlight Books. Neither of us had been back since Pops's death. It was just too hard right now.

Sliding a menu her way, I snapped her out of her daze. "I have to meet with the funeral director after lunch to discuss the services for Pops." I read over the menu in front of me. "Do you want to come along?"

She shook her head. "When is the funeral?"

"Friday," I answered.

Max came out of the kitchen with a faint smile on his face when he spotted us. "Hey. What have you two been up to today?"

When Ellawyn didn't answer, I took the lead. "We just came from the police station. We filed a report on the stalker."

"I think that's a good idea." He looked to Ellawyn when she still didn't speak. "Hey." He tapped her on the hand.

She turned to face him and gave him a soft smile. "Hi, Max," she said as she looked at his shirt. It had the new logo she'd designed for him. "I like the shirt."

"Thanks, my best friend designed it for me." He winked at her.

Ellawyn laughed and I scoffed. "I thought I was your best friend."

"It's almost a tie. But she's leading by a little," he said. After Max brought our drinks and took our orders, he left to go work on the food in the kitchen.

For the first time, I was nervous to be alone with Ellawyn. There was so much hanging over us right now, and I didn't know what to do or say. We hadn't yet discussed what was said in the hospital. I owed her an apology, but the timing hadn't been right. I hadn't meant what I'd said. I could never blame Ellawyn for Pops's death. Deep down, I knew that. But at the time, she'd been the closest target for my rage.

It wasn't an excuse. Just the shitty truth.

But now she was as closed off as ever, and I couldn't blame her for it. I just wish she'd open up to me. Come out of her shell and talk to me. Yell at me. Whatever she needed to do, I wish she'd do it.

But until then, I was left trying to get us back to where we had been before the accident. "Hey, babe, can you look here for a moment?" When she turned around but didn't say anything, I continued. "I heard from Pops's lawyer yesterday. Pops had requested that you give the eulogy at his funeral on Friday."

"Me? I can't."

"He chose you. He made the change a few days before he passed away." I could see in her eyes that she was terrified. "If you don't want to do it, you don't have to."

She swallowed and nodded her head. "I'm sorry. It's not that I don't want to do it." She lifted her glass to take a drink of water. "It's just... What if I'm not strong enough? What if whatever I say isn't good enough?"

I pulled her barstool closer to mine and wrapped my arm around her shoulder. "You are good enough. You're the best that there is. Pops would love anything that you say."

The conversation came to a halt as Max brought our food out. He joined us for lunch, and conversation moved to lighter topics and how he was doing with the bar.

"The bar is doing better than ever." His smile was contagious. "I'm even planning a vacation to the beach in a week or two."

I was happy for my friend. He hadn't had a vacation longer than a day or two since before we'd graduated high school. "That's great, man. Well deserved."

"Thanks," he said. "My dad always loved this one beach up north, so I want to check it out."

"That's sweet, Max," Ellawyn chimed in as she slid off the barstool. "I'm going to skip the funeral home and instead spend some time at Starlight Books and work on Benji's eulogy." She walked around the bar and gave Max a hug before giving me a hug and a kiss on her way out. "See ya later."

Max and I both kept an eye out as she crossed the street. We agreed that we'd have to be more vigilant these next few days and hope for the best. But constantly waiting for the other shoe to drop was exhausting.

☾

AFTER I'D MET with the funeral director, I went back to my place to wait for my girl to come over. I'd thought about joining her at the shop, but I wasn't ready to go inside there just yet. I also figured that Ellawyn needed some alone time, so I stayed away.

Turned out that I needed some space to decompress as well. Today had been harder than I'd thought it would be. When the funeral director had asked me which outfit I planned to have Pops buried in, I'd almost lost my shit. Thankfully, Rhiannon was willing to go through Pops's closet for me and drop off a suit to the funeral home. Thank fuck, because I wouldn't have been able to handle that today.

Settling further into my couch, I pulled out my phone to see a missed text.

Ellawyn: I decided to stay at my place tonight and tomorrow to prepare for the funeral. I'm sorry. I just need some space to sort through this.

As disappointed as I was, I got where she was coming from.

Me: It's all good. Just keep your door locked and call if you need anything. I'll pick you up for the funeral on Friday.

I let out a breath as I put my phone down on the coffee table. The next few days without her would undoubtedly be difficult, but I had a sick feeling that lingered in the pit of the stomach that told me that Friday would hold the worst.

CHAPTER 25

Ellawyn

I had just gained a smidge of happiness back in my life. I'd felt that tiny bit of joy for a moment. But then Beckett returned home, came to my apartment, found a card from the stalker, and now I had to eulogize Benji.

It was too much all at once. Before all of this, I'd thought I was on the mend. Now I was even more of a wreck over Benji, and I couldn't string two sentences together when it came to writing this damn eulogy. I'd never even attended a funeral before. I didn't want to be alone, but I also needed to get my shit together before Friday.

I spent all night writing nice thoughts about Benji onto a bunch of note cards. For every note card that I wrote, I crumbled one up and tossed it aside. By sunrise the following morning, I'd written a few semi-decent things down, and I was satisfied enough to call it a day. I hoped what I had to say would be enough for Benji, and for Beckett. I hoped that I would measure up and make them proud.

When I finally made it back to my apartment, I decided to stay in until the funeral. The only downside was that I was low on food. Peeking into the fridge, I saw about seven bottles of water, a few Pepsi Zeros, and some Jell-O. That wasn't sustenance—it was pathetic.

Delivery would have to do.

After writing down a list of things to get done today, I started the first task: pick out an appropriate funeral outfit. In my closet, I went directly to the section of black clothes. After flicking through the hangers, I plucked two dresses and laid them out on the bed.

There was clearly only one winner here.

The dress was short-sleeved. The top had elegant pieces of lace around the neckline and also had lace outlining the bottom of the dress. The other option was a little black dress that cut down the front to my belly button, which would cover very little of my chest.

Definitely not funeral material. I hung the winning dress in my bathroom and snagged a black wristlet for my phone and my black flats.

Everything was ready to go for tomorrow.

I plopped down on the couch and got comfortable, my phone in hand. Since picking out an outfit didn't take long, I decided to place an order for lunch through a food delivery app. I scrolled through the possibilities and landed on a local hotdog joint called The Hamilton. I'd never been there, but I'd heard great things from everyone in town. I placed an order for one of their special "hotchee" dogs and an order of fries.

With a rumbling stomach, I headed into my art studio to kill some time.

A blank canvas stared back at me. It felt like ages since I had last created something. With everything going on in my life, art had taken the backseat. After pulling my hair into a messy bun, I went to my paint supply and pulled out a few shades of blue and green paint, along with some white.

I tied the apron around my waist and found myself staring at the canvas with the paintbrush poking out of my mouth as I contemplated what I'd create. Remembering that Max had mentioned the beach earlier, I gravitated toward that image like a wave would gravitate toward the beach as it crashed against the shoreline.

By the time the doorbell rang with my food delivery, I'd managed to get quite a bit painted. I threw my paintbrush on my palette and picked up my order from the delivery guy. I returned to the studio with my food and an ice-cold Pepsi and sat across from my painting.

I'd always done that sort of thing whenever I created. I liked to look at my art during the process so I could think about what moves I wanted to do before touching the brush again.

When I popped open the Styrofoam container, the aromas of hotdogs and French fries took over my senses. I salivated at the mere sight of the meal.

No wonder it was so popular.

I devoured my food and made myself a promise to check out the physical location in person next time. Maybe I could even take Beckett and Max.

After lunch, I dove back into my artwork and ended up spending the rest of the evening painting. I'd been so in the zone that I hadn't come up for air until my phone vibrated in my pocket.

I had texts from Beckett and Max. They were checking up on me to see if I was okay. I sent them each a quick response before putting my phone away and stepping back from my canvas. My mouth dropped open at what I saw.

A beach scene filled the canvas with its rough waves crashing into the shore. But the surprising part was that off to the right-hand side of the canvas, I'd painted a man holding onto a woman in an emerald green dress, with long blonde hair.

I painted Max finding love at the beach.

☾

WHEN I WOKE up the next morning, I went through the motions of the day—showering, dressing, curling my hair, applying makeup. It was almost robotic. The doorbell rang just as I finished packing up my wristlet.

"Come in," I called from my bedroom.

The sound of my door opening and closing almost sent a chill up my spine as I panicked about the stalker just being able to walk in. I hadn't thought about that.

"You need to keep your door locked," Beckett growled as he crossed into my room.

"I don't think my stalker would have announced himself and knocked," I retorted.

"Sorry." His shoulders relaxed a fraction. "I'm just all worked up today."

My reflection found his in the mirror I'd been looking into. "I get that."

Beckett helped me into a light sweater and even complimented me on how nice I looked, but the words fell flat.

I didn't want to look nice.

I didn't want attention.

I just wanted to crawl into a hole and hide for the rest of the day.

When we arrived at the funeral parlor, the place was packed with people who had shown up to honor Benji and support Beckett. The outpouring of love was sweet but slightly overwhelming. I didn't know any of these people.

Beckett must have read my mind. He leaned in and lowered his voice. "I don't know half of these people. Holy shit."

"Benji was well loved. This is a testament to that."

He squeezed my hand three times as he led us through the crowd and to the front row. After making sure I was seated, he went to stand by the casket and started greeting the visitors. The long line of people paying their respects seemed to last forever. I found myself staring straight ahead, right at Benji's casket, and debating on when to pay my own.

"Hey, Ellie."

I looked up to see Max standing above me. "Hi, Max. Care to join me?"

He sat down beside me and bumped my shoulder with his. "How about we pay our respects together at the end of the service?"

"Absolutely." I was relieved to be able to wait until the end. And even more relieved that I wouldn't have to say goodbye alone.

As the line shortened, Beckett joined us in the front row. A member of Benji's church led the service, and many sniffles filled the space. It was a beautiful moment.

And then I was asked to come up and deliver the eulogy.

A wave of nausea washed over me as I stood from my seat and walked over toward the podium. I played with the stack of note cards I'd pulled from my purse, but when I went to look down at the words I'd planned, I couldn't see them. My vision was glossy with unshed tears, clouding the handwriting on the cards.

I cleared my throat and took a deep breath. "I don't know why Benji requested that I speak at his funeral service." I picked up the cards and placed them down again.

"My relationship with Benji had only recently begun. When I first arrived in Quimby Grove, I went straight to Starlight Books. I was drawn to the little bookshop, but I couldn't pinpoint exactly why. The first day I was there, Benji came and sat down with me, and we ended up talking. Our friendship was like diving into a brand-new book where you find a deep connection with the main character. It may have been new, but it was special. It was like a book that became a favorite. The one you kept in a special place on the shelf, adorned with special mementos."

I turned around, glancing at Benji's casket. "He was one of my favorite characters." The tears spilled down my face, and I let them fall freely as I turned my attention back to the living. "Benji would have done anything for anyone. He took in strays right off the street, including me, and he'd been so proud of his family." I turned to Beckett. "He loved you so much," I said through watery eyes.

"I was fortunate enough to spend the last few weeks of his life with him. We traveled around with no real destination in sight. We laughed. We cried. We faced our hard truths." My voice cracked. "And he knew how he wanted to pass."

Beckett came to stand by my side and rubbed a hand up and down my back as I continued. "Benji didn't want his story to end at the hands of his brain tumor. And in his final days, he had been adamant about that. He was determined to rewrite his ending."

I took a deep breath. "And while a car accident wasn't what he had outlined for his ending, I know he would have preferred to go this way. Since coming to Quimby Grove, I've learned a valuable lesson, and it's that some people are only meant to be in your life for a short time. But that doesn't make the loss any easier to handle. I'll forever remember one of the last things Benji said to me before he passed. He reminded me that we only get one life to live, and now I've got to continue on and live it."

I turned to Beckett and took his hands in mine. "Each state that we traveled to, Benji would buy two postcards—one to keep as a souvenir and one to write a note to you, as a goodbye. I have your copies back at my apartment, and the blank copies will be buried with Benji."

Beckett wiped his face as his tears broke free.

The service continued as other people shared their memories of Benji. I didn't think I'd ever felt so happy and so empty at the same time. I was happy to hear how Benji had touched the lives of others. It was such a bittersweet moment—learning more about Benji from others, but also longing for him to come back to this earth.

As the service concluded, everyone filtered out of the funeral home while saying their goodbyes. Benji had opted for a private burial instead of a public one. I thought it was the right call and would give Beckett the space to mourn without a full audience.

A hand landed on my shoulder. When I turned around, I saw

Max with a little smile on his face. "Benji would be proud," he said.

"Thanks." I nodded my head toward Benji's casket. "Ready?"

He grabbed my hand and walked us toward the deserted casket. The closer we got to the casket, the more my nerves came out. I began to shake as we came up next to where Benji laid. He looked peaceful. I couldn't quite grasp how he could look the way he did while I felt so much pain. I dropped Max's hand and reached for Benji's. Giving it a few squeezes, I whispered a message that was only for him. "I miss you, Benji. I love you."

After we said our goodbyes, Beckett joined us and pulled me in for a hug. "Ready to go to the cemetery?"

Taking a step away, I looked over my shoulder at Benji. "Do you mind if I go home for a bit instead?" When I returned my gaze to Beckett, I almost expected him to be angry. But instead, I was met with compassion and understanding.

"Of course." He rubbed my arms with his hands. "I know today hasn't been easy."

Beckett and Max walked me back to Beckett's car before they left for the burial. Beckett opened the driver's-side door for me. "Everyone is coming to Starlight for food and to celebrate Pops after I'm done with the burial."

"Oh. I forgot." I hesitated and debated on whether I felt like being around people today. "You two go, and I'll go straight home. I just want to be by myself for a while."

"Okay," he said as he pulled me into his arms and pressed his lips against mine. "Call us if you need anything or want us to pick you up."

The drive back home was quick, and I drove it on autopilot. I couldn't remember the drive back at all. Shaking my head, I tried to get rid of the fog that was clouding my mind. When I got to my apartment, I noticed that my door was slightly ajar.

Weird. I could have sworn I'd shut it this morning when we left. I stayed standing just outside of my apartment as I debated what to do. Feeling silly, I pulled out my cell phone and dialed a neighbor who lived on the floor below me and asked if he could come up and do a walk-through of my apartment for me.

He came right away. I explained the weird situation I was in, and he went inside and looked around each room for me. After a few minutes, he met me back in the hallway and told me that no one was inside and I was good to go in.

After we chatted for a few minutes, I went inside and shut the door behind me. I hung up my sweater and wristlet on the coat rack and went straight for the fridge.

I needed a drink—preferably something alcoholic.

When I pulled open the fridge, I was sent flying back into reality as I realized that I had literally nothing to take the edge off today. I opted for a glass of water instead and decided that a nice, warm bubble bath would be a close second.

I grabbed some clean pajamas, my robe, and my small Bluetooth speaker in my room. When I entered the bathroom, a chill crept down my spine as the hairs on the back of my neck stood up. Flicking on the lights, I looked around and tried to ease my apprehension.

There was nothing there.

Convinced that today's events had caught up to me, I placed my clothes and robe on the bathroom counter. I gathered my hair and secured it into a messy bun and then queued up my playlist for my bath. Just as I placed my phone down on the counter, I looked into the mirror and noticed that the shower curtain was pulled across the bathtub.

I froze.

I never pulled the shower curtain across the bathtub, because I'd always been afraid of something lurking behind it. Taking a breath, I turned around and stepped in front of the bathtub, then slowly pulled the shower curtain back a little bit at a time.

There was nothing there. A sigh of relief escaped as I turned back toward the mirror and bent down to wash my face. When I stood up from rinsing my face, I glanced in the mirror as I reached for my glass of water.

This time, when I saw my reflection, it wasn't the only one staring back at me.

The glass I was holding fell to the floor and shattered at my feet. Then everything went dark as I succumbed to excruciating pain.

CHAPTER 26
Beckett

Except for the fundraiser for Pops, I hadn't ever seen Starlight Books packed with so many people. From family friends and friends who felt like family to the people around town to the doctors that cared for Benji, everyone was here.

The tables throughout the shop had been pushed as close together as possible to allow everyone to be closer together. All the seats had been filled, and those without seats stood behind those who sat. Everyone took turns speaking and sharing their stories about Pops and Starlight Books. There were those who cried at the memories and those who laughed through them.

I stood back by the entrance of the shop and greeted people as they came in, then gave them my gratitude as they left. I had the best seat in the house. I was able to watch the love and admiration for Pops unfold before my very eyes. It sunk in that this was the first new memory within Starlight Books without Pops.

"Oh, Beckett. There's my dear, dear boy."

Turning my head toward the door, I watched as Mrs. Lively and Kennon entered the shop and headed my way. Mrs. Lively shoved Kennon aside and reached me first. "Mrs. Lively." I chuckled. "Thank you so much for coming."

She pulled me in for a hug. "Of course. We're family." She

pulled away and looked around the shop. "Which one is Ellawyn? She's the one bright spot on this otherwise devastating trip."

"Yeah," Kennon chimed in. "I assume the security alert was a false alarm."

I shot him a narrow look. "Let's chat," I said as I nodded for him to go toward the couch in the corner of the shop where Max was.

He nodded and went to join Max.

Turning my attention back to Mrs. Lively, I smiled. "Ellawyn had a rough time at the viewing and wanted to go home and rest."

"Oh my, the poor thing. Oh!" She let out a small gasp. "I think I see some old friends. I'm going to go make the rounds."

She took off and joined the crowd of people that mingled within the center of the shop. When she was settled, I turned around and joined Max and Kennon in the corner. "Hey," I sat down in the chair across from them. "What security alert?"

Kennon arched an eyebrow. "You didn't get a notification on your phone?"

Reaching into my pocket, I grabbed my phone and sure enough, there was a notification indicating that the alarm had been triggered and then disarmed less than a minute later. "Okay, so it was triggered and then disarmed. Not a big deal."

"Hey, hand me your phone," Max added as he reached for it. "Huh, that's interesting."

"What is it?" I asked.

He rubbed the back of his neck. "The notification indicated that the alarm had been triggered at a quarter to eleven this morning."

"Yeah," I said. "So?"

He sighed. "We were still at the viewing well after that time. Ellawyn wasn't home yet. She was with us."

Oh, fuck.

"Someone triggered her security system and disarmed it. Someone could have been inside her apartment when she got home," Max continued as he stood up.

My heart rate increased as I stood up and paced the length of the couch.

"Have either of you heard from her since she left to go home?" Kennon questioned.

I snatched my phone back from Max as I rushed to check my notifications. "I don't have anything from her." I raked my hands through my hair. "Max, do you?"

He shook his head. "No. I even texted her an hour or so ago, and I haven't heard back yet."

"Fuck," I growled "If someone broke into her apartment, they've been there with her for about four hours." I turned to Kennon. "Can you stay here and keep things going for Pops's memorial?"

His response was automatic. "Of course, go. But call the cops on the way."

We left Starlight Books as fast as we could. She was all I had left. I couldn't lose her.

CHAPTER 27

Ellawyn

The throbbing pain in my head was the first thing I noticed, followed by an overwhelming feeling of nausea.

This couldn't be good.

I slowly tried to open my eyes, but they were too heavy, and each movement caused the pain in my head to radiate throughout my entire body. The pain was unlike anything I'd ever experienced.

Keeping my eyes closed, I focused on remembering what had happened and tried to replay the events before now. Beckett had picked me up for Benji's funeral. We'd had the service, and I'd given my eulogy for Benji. And then I'd driven home.

The moments were hazier after that. All I could focus on right now was the pain. Taking in a deep breath, I forced my eyes open and tried to get a good look at my surroundings.

I was in my room... and in my bed. My body was so stiff, and I couldn't move my arms or my legs. It felt as if a weight had been placed on my limbs. I craned my neck, searching for whatever had caused me to be this uncomfortable. My arms had been spread out on either side of my body. My eyes drifted up the length of my arms until I found a thick rope wrapped around my wrists, tying me to the headboard of my bed.

Instinctively, I tried to kick my legs, but I was met with a searing pain around my ankles as the rope dug into my skin. I squeezed my eyes shut.

Think, Ellawyn, think. What the hell happened?

Panic set in. I was tied up in my own fucking house. The ache in my head was unbearable; my legs and arms felt weak. I couldn't move or focus on anything besides the pain.

Suddenly, it hit me. When I had returned home, the door had been open slightly, which meant someone was inside my home the entire time. I'd been alone with whoever had done this ever since I got home.

My heart was racing, and my body shook all while I choked on my breaths. I felt like there was nothing left of me. My body thrashed around on the bed, the ropes digging into my skin as the pain coursed through my body and radiated up to my head.

"I never had the pleasure of watching you squirm until now," a voice taunted. "I quite like it."

I froze, and a chill ran through my body. I knew that voice... but I couldn't place it. I squeezed my eyes shut as I begged my body to stay still, to cooperate long enough to hopefully get out of here.

Footsteps sounded closer and closer as my heartbeat thrashed in my ears. My breathing was nonexistent as the footsteps halted next to where my head was lying.

"Open your eyes," he bellowed.

The harshness of his voice caused me to flinch. Turning my head away from him, I kept my eyes closed and held my breath for what was to come.

"Now," he growled. "You don't want what will happen if you don't comply, Ellie."

My eyes flew open, and I whipped my head to face him. "Dr. Reinhart." My voice cracked at the revelation. I felt like I was going to throw up. My stalker was Benji's doctor? I had no idea... I never would have guessed... I didn't know...

"Oh, now you notice me. Took you fucking long enough," he

said as he stomped off and grabbed the chair from next to my window. He dragged it until it was positioned right next to me before he lowered himself down.

"W-why... Why are y-you doing this?" I hated myself for my shaking voice. I knew I had to be strong, that I shouldn't show fear, but I just couldn't help it.

"I told you we'd be together soon," he answered as he trailed a finger down my arm. "I sent you notes, flowers, cards, and bought you dinner. I've taken care of you."

Fresh tears rolled down my cheeks. "Why am I tied up?"

"Because..." He stood from the chair and leaned over me as he raised his arm and backhanded me across the face. "You never fucking listen."

I cried out in pain as I turned my face away from him. Without thinking, I tried to cover my face, but the pull of the rope burned my skin as I groaned in pain.

"Look at me," he demanded.

I can't move.

"LOOK AT ME," he roared.

I can't breathe.

His fingers dug into my skin as he gripped my face and whipped it toward him. The sudden movement coupled with the slap and my already pounding headache caused me to be dizzy and overwhelmed with nausea. My eyes fluttered open and shut as I tried to look at him, but the room was spinning and out of control. Choking down the nausea, I opened my eyes again and held them open as I spoke.

"I don't understand," I whimpered. "Why?" I cried repeatedly as my body trembled.

He scoffed. "Because I'm tired of you leading me on." He ran his hand down the left side of my face and then trailed it down my body. Down my neck, over the swells of my breasts, and over my stomach. When he got to my waist, he hesitated. "You were a slut and slept with Beckett when you belonged to me, and now you'll be punished."

My eyes slammed shut right before I took another blow to the face.

☾

I FELT like I'd been hit by a truck.

Everything felt still. Black spots clouded my vision as I tried to open my eyes. The pain was unreal. My eyelids grew heavier as I tried to remain conscious and listen for any sounds within the room or the apartment. Everything was quiet.

Closing my eyes again, I allowed myself to rest for a moment while I tried to figure out how the hell to get out of here. I couldn't get over the fact that my stalker had been Dr. Reinhart this whole time. I couldn't reconcile it in my mind. I had rejected him for a date, but I never would have anticipated this happening.

I never realized that I'd caused this much damage.

But none of that mattered now. The only thing that mattered was survival. I had to fight and try to get out of here somehow. Forcing my eyes open, I scanned the areas of the room that I could see. There was no sight of him. My bathroom door was wide open, so I knew he wasn't in there. Closing my eyes again, I slowly turned my head in the other direction, careful to not cause any more pain, and pushed through the wave of nausea that threatened to take over.

When I opened my eyes, I screamed. I was lying face to face with Dr. Reinhart. He was in bed with me.

"Don't scream, darling," he whispered as he brushed my hair out of my face and tucked a strand behind my ear. "You're mine now." He leaned down and pressed a kiss to my forehead as I tried to move my head away. "We'll be sleeping together from here on out."

The intimate behavior made me feel even more ill. I couldn't hold it in any longer—I started sobbing. "Please just tell me why you're doing this," I cried out. "Why are you hurting me?"

He exhaled as he shoved himself up from the bed. "It's Jace."

"It doesn't have to be like this, J-Jace." I choked on his name. "Just let me go."

In an instant, he launched himself on top of me, straddling my waist while he looked down at me. "We'll be together forever. I know you want me. You don't have to deny it anymore."

Shaking my head, I avoided his gaze.

"I know you were only with Beckett to appease that old fuck Benji. Now that I've gotten him out of the way, we can be together."

Did he just admit to what I think he did? "Y-you... You caused the car accident?" I questioned.

He yanked my face toward his as he lowered himself until his lips were practically touching mine. "I ran that fucker off the road," he hissed. "You looked so beautiful unconscious, you know that?" His lips pressed onto mine and he forced his tongue into my mouth as I gasped from the shock of the contact.

Rocking my head back and forth, desperate to create distance, I bit his lower hip, hard. He let out a scream as he grabbed me by the throat and squeezed.

"You'll pay for that, you bitch."

Releasing my throat, he lifted himself off my pelvis and unhooked his belt buckle while I gasped for air. He pulled his belt from his pants and gave me a smirk. "Ready for your punishment?"

As I turned my head away from him, I cried out for help, hoping someone would save me from this nightmare, but nothing came out.

He lowered himself back down and yanked me up by the collar of my dress, the lace ripping at the seams as he gripped it in his fist. He wrapped his belt around my head and shoved the leather into my mouth before pulling the belt through the metal loop and tightening it as far as it would go.

I gagged as I tried to push the thick leather out of my mouth. I couldn't speak. I couldn't breathe. I was running out of air.

He lifted off me again and slid further down my legs. His

hands gripped my dress as he shoved it up around my waist. I could feel his length harden on my leg as he ripped my panties off my body. "You're bare for me—like smooth, fragile porcelain I'm going to demolish."

I flinched and knew he was about to take something that wasn't his.

He crawled up the length of my body and hovered over me, his face above mine. The evil in his eyes was intense and terrifying. They were dark, black even, and looked as though they were bottomless. Desperation started to kick in as I did the only thing I could think of. Using all my strength, I bent my legs at the knees as best I could, and I brought them up to his body as fast and hard as I could.

He grunted as he fell off me. "You little bitch," he seethed. "You'll pay for that."

My breath was ragged as I pulled on the restraints. The rope burned into my skin as I thrashed my body against the tension. Blood started to pool at my wrists.

He stood over the bed, staring down at me with a look so vile that I could have sworn he was about to kill me. His chest rose and fell in fast successions as he lifted his fist and connected it to my head over and over again.

At that moment, all I could think about was how badly I wanted this to end. For the pain to go away and for the heartache to heal. I didn't care how anymore. I'd spent a lot of time regaining control of my life lately, but here I was, at the hands of another man, losing it all over again.

CHAPTER 28

Beckett

I DON'T THINK I'd ever run so fast in my life. My body ached, my breaths were coming in short spurts, and I was ready to kick anyone's ass who dared to cross me.

Beside me, Max was on the phone calling the police as we ran down the Square. "Yes, I think my friend is in danger," I overheard him tell the dispatcher.

I ran faster as the crowd parted on the sidewalk. "Move," I shouted as I weaved through the people, pushing them out of the way.

Max caught up, falling in step beside me. "Police are on their way."

We rounded the corner of the block where Ellawyn lived and pushed ourselves into a full-on sprint. I whipped the door open and raced up the stairs of her apartment building until we made it to her floor.

Max's arm shot out, grabbing mine, and he pulled me away from Ellawyn's door. "Hey, wait."

"What?" I growled. "We have to get in here. Now."

Max placed his hands on my shoulders and pulled me further down the hall. "We need to think about this for a moment. Whoever is in there could be armed. If we rush in like we're about to rip his dick off, he could hurt Ellawyn before we even get to her."

That made sense. "Okay." I nodded. "What's our plan?"

He hesitated while he worked through some ideas. When he started talking, his voice was lowered. "We'll disable the alarm on your phone, and I'll go in first and try to figure out where in the apartment they are without being detected. Once I have eyes on him, I'll see if I can apprehend him, and then you can focus on Ellawyn."

I tilted my head. "Not the greatest plan, but it's all we've got." Pulling out my phone, I disabled the alarm. "Okay, go."

Max carefully opened the apartment door. An inch at first, and then two, as he listened for any sounds coming from inside. He pushed it open further and took a few steps inside. He turned and lifted a hand to have me wait. After a moment, he waved me in while he continued further into the apartment.

We cleared the living room and the kitchen. Next up was Ellawyn's room. Max carefully made his way outside of her bedroom door. Leaning against the wall, he strained to see if he could hear anything in her bedroom. He placed his index finger over his lips while he listened to whatever was going on in the bedroom.

His facial expression alone made me want to charge into that room and beat the shit out of whoever was inside. I stepped toward the door, but a hand flew out and pulled me back toward the wall. "Knock it off," he warned. "Do you want us to get caught?"

Her bedroom door was open enough for us to slip through. Max slid through the opening first, staying close to the wall and hopefully out of sight. He stayed where he was, watching whatever was happening for a moment. The color drained from his face for a millisecond before it was replaced with a dark hue as the anger radiated off him and a glare took shape. We locked eyes and he gave me a slight nod while he mouthed the words "Count of three." We silently mouthed the countdown together.

Three.

Two.

One.

Max ran further into the room as he shouted, "Back the fuck off" before his body collided with another.

I bypassed the scene on the floor of the bedroom and rushed to Ellawyn's side. She was lying unconscious, her lower half exposed with a belt wrapped around her head and in her mouth. Placing two fingers at her neck, I checked for a pulse. When I found one, the breath I'd been holding rushed out.

Grabbing a blanket from the bottom of Ellawyn's bed, I carefully covered her lower half and unhooked the belt from around her head and eased it out of her mouth. After she was taken care of, I looked for Max to make sure he was all right.

Max had the man pinned to the floor with his arms behind his back, and Max's knee was applying pressure to his lower back.

"Who the fuck is it?" I barked.

Max yanked the man up by his scalp and turned his head to face me. The man staring back at me was Jace Reinhart.

That motherfucking prick.

My hands balled into fists as I tried to keep my composure. But the smug look that flashed across his face is what sealed the deal. "Let him up," I ordered.

Max stood and yanked Reinhart up while keeping a firm grasp on his arms, which were still behind his back. I looked him in the eye. "What's to stop me from fucking killing you right now?"

Reinhart sneered. "You don't have it in you." He looked over toward Ellawyn. "She'll never be the same after this. I've tainted her. I took your pretty girl, whole and pure, and made her dirty."

I drew my arm back and threw a hook straight to his fucking jaw. Reinhart's head spun around, and he collapsed on the floor. "Fucking asshole," I spat. "You're lucky the cops just showed up."

When I returned to Ellawyn's bedside, I stared at her and wondered how anybody could do such things to another person.

How could someone do this to Ellawyn? Her face was bruised and beaten. Scratches ran down her arms and legs. There was a hand-print on her throat. If we hadn't arrived when we did, there was no telling what he might have had planned for her. I laid my hand onto one of hers and squeezed.

When the cops arrived, they dragged Jace out of Ellawyn's apartment in handcuffs and called an ambulance to transport her to Pennsylvania Memorial Hospital. Before they wheeled her out on the stretcher, I carefully kissed her forehead and whispered into her ear that I'd meet her at the hospital.

She may not be able to respond, but I knew she could hear me. I needed her to know she wasn't alone and that I'd always be by her side.

I couldn't lose Ellawyn, too.

☾

THERE WEREN'T a lot of things I hated more than hospital waiting rooms. It was the unknown that really did me in. The not knowing the extent of injuries, or what might have happened to her. It killed me to know I wasn't there to protect her when she needed me the most.

I spent hours trying to comprehend that Dr. Reinhart was Ellawyn's stalker. The *doctor* that worked on Pops, to save his life, was also the man who tried to take Ellawyn's away from her. I wished I'd known his motives. Was it simply to be with her, or did he want to hurt her? Neither of those seemed to matter as much now that she was alive and he was behind bars, but her life would be forever altered.

The automatic doors to the hospital parted as Mrs. Lively and Kennon entered and joined us in the waiting room. "Any updates?" asked Mrs. Lively.

"Not a one," I muttered.

Max shifted in his seat next to me. "We've been here for hours, and no one has come out to give us any information. It's pissing me off."

Mrs. Lively reached over and patted his knee. "We'll know more soon," she offered.

After we sat for another hour, a nurse entered the waiting area and scanned the crowds of people. The moment I saw who it was, I knew the update would be for us. Standing up, I met her in the middle of the waiting area with the three others hot on my tail.

"Lucy," I called.

Her brown eyes flooded with tears when she spotted me. "Is it true?" she asked. "Did Dr. Reinhart do that to Ellawyn?"

I nodded solemnly. "Yeah. That fucker did a number on her, unfortunately."

Lucy's tears chased one another down her cheeks. "I'm so sorry. I should have known."

That caught my attention. "What do you mean you should have known?"

Max stepped forward. "Not now, Beckett," he said as he grabbed my arm. Stepping forward, I shook Max's hold off me and had been about to step forward when Mrs. Lively pulled me back again. Max turned to Lucy and smiled at her. "Lucy, how is Ellawyn?"

"Um. There's bruising, of course, and her face is swollen. But there's no long-term physical damage."

"Did he...did he rape her?" The words burned as they left my mouth. If she had to endure that, I might lose my shit and go to the county prison to deal out some justice myself.

Lucy crossed her arms over her chest. "No, he didn't. We performed a rape kit on her. That's what took so long."

"Thanks for telling me." I stepped toward the doors behind Lucy, which led to the hospital wing.

Lucy raised her hands. "You can't go back there."

My jaw ticked. "Why not?"

Her shoulders slumped down. "She doesn't want visitors right now."

My temper flared, and I took a few steps back from Lucy. "Why the hell not? I'm her boyfriend. Max is her friend," I pointed out. "She'll want to see us."

A gentle hand touched my shoulder and pulled me back. Turning around, I saw Mrs. Lively. "You both are males, dear."

I stood and stared at her. "What the fuck does that have to do with anything?"

She sighed. "Ellawyn was just attacked by a male and went through a traumatic experience. I imagine she may be going through some PTSD or could be frightened. If she were to wake up and find a male in her room, it could trigger an emotional reaction."

"Is that what's going on here?" I asked as I turned back to face Lucy.

"It is," she confirmed.

The five of us continued to stand in the waiting room in silence while we stood at an impasse. I didn't want Ellawyn to be alone, but I also didn't want to upset her. An idea came to me, and while it would be risky, it was all I could think of. "Mrs. Lively, would you go sit with Ellawyn? She's heard stories about you from me, so it may be okay."

"Oh, dear." Her face twisted with concern. "Are you sure?"

"Yeah, if you don't mind."

"Of course not," she replied with a hug.

Mrs. Lively followed Lucy through the double doors and into the hospital wing for the emergency room unit. When the doors closed behind them, Max led me back to where we had sat previously. At some point, sleep claimed me as I dreamed about my girl and getting to hold her again.

The only problem was, I knew that when I woke up, it would be to a real-life nightmare.

CHAPTER 29

Ellawyn

IF I COULD GO BACK and redo today, I would. I'd give anything to not be sitting in a cold hospital room by myself. Even more than that, I'd give anything to not have been assaulted in the one place where I should have felt safe.

I did everything I could to be safe. I installed a security system, I had people in my life that looked out for me, and I reported the behavior to the police. I knew I waited a while to formally file a complaint, but I'd thought the situation had resolved itself.

But I was wrong.

And because of that, I ended up being attacked inside my own home. One of the worst parts, though, was that I had been attacked by someone who was publicly respected simply because of their job title. Doctors were supposed to be trustworthy. Had I known that Dr. Reinhart was my stalker, would I have been taken seriously? Or would they have taken his side simply due to his title?

The icing on the cake was that, despite me being the one who was admitted to the hospital, I felt like I was to blame. Had I led him on? Did I give off a vibe that would have made him think I was interested? I tried to replay the memories, but I couldn't see things clearly. I barely paid him any attention. All I could remember was having a bad feeling about him.

Something wet dripped onto my chest. I glanced down as more droplets ran down my face. The tears were falling quickly, but this time, I didn't give a fuck.

A gentle tap rapped on the door. I pulled the covers over my chest, shielding myself from whoever was outside. "Who's there?" I whispered, my voice cracking.

"Ellawyn, it's Lucy. The nurse."

Lucy. I remembered Lucy from when Benji was here. Her voice was soft and gentle. "Come in," I answered.

Lucy entered the room and sanitized her hands with the antiseptic that hung on the wall. I noticed a figure behind her but couldn't tell who it was. "Who... Who is with you?"

Lucy faced me with a smile. "This is Mrs. Lively. She's..." Lucy's face contorted with confusion before she turned around to address the woman. "I'm sorry, but who are you again?"

The older woman laughed before she opened her mouth to answer.

But I beat her to the punch. "She's Beckett's assistant from back in Boston."

Mrs. Lively stepped around Lucy and came over to my bedside. She took my hand in hers. "Yes, dear. Mind if I visit for a little?"

Reluctantly, I shook my head.

Mrs. Lively pulled up a chair and sat down beside me. Feeling anxious, I glanced over at Lucy. She smiled at me and jerked her chin toward Mrs. Lively before she slipped back out of my room.

Silence took over the room. I kept my head down and my gaze locked on my hands as I wished that Mrs. Lively would just leave. I didn't want anyone to see me like this. Shame and embarrassment lingered in the air so thick that I could practically see it.

Exhaustion soon took over. My eyes would drift closed before my head fell to my chest. Then I'd be jolted awake. The cycle repeated itself every few minutes. I knew that I should cave and let myself drift off to sleep, but I was too afraid. What if Dr. Reinhart somehow found me? What if someone else came in to hurt me?

I felt as if I was alone in this. Like I couldn't trust anybody.

"You can sleep, dear," Mrs. Lively said. "I promise to stay with you until you wake up."

With her promise echoing in my head, I drifted off to sleep, the feeling of safety comforting me like a worn, warm blanket.

MRS. LIVELY WAS asleep in her chair when I woke up. Glancing at the clock on the wall, I noticed it was morning already. I'd slept all night while this poor woman was stuck in a hospital room chair.

I felt terrible.

Lifting my hand, I reached over and nudged her arm. "Mrs. Lively," I whispered as I nudged her a second time. "Mrs. Lively?"

A moment or two later, she stirred in her chair and opened her eyes. Her face lit up once she saw I was awake. "Did you sleep well, dear?" She asked as she sat up straight in her chair.

"I did, thanks to you," I answered with a smile.

"I was worried that you may have been afraid to fall asleep alone, and I didn't want to put you through that." She paused and tilted her head. "How are you holding up? I don't know what you went through, and I'm not asking that you tell me, but I just wanted to say that I'm here for you if you do wish to chat. I know it may be too soon, but you mustn't hold anything inside." She pointed to my chest, where my heart resided. "Once you are ready, talk and begin to heal."

Her words brought tears to my eyes, reminding me of something my own mother would say during a time like this. "Thank you." I sniffled.

"Of course." She glanced at the door. "Beckett is in the waiting room, you know."

"Yeah, Lucy told me." I pulled the blanket up a bit higher.

"But I don't want him to see me like this." I gestured to my face and throat. "Who would want to deal with this?"

"Someone who loves you would," she offered.

I scoffed. "I don't think Beckett feels that way about me yet."

"I wouldn't be so sure." She chuckled as she leaned forward and patted my hand.

We ended up drifting back into the quiet of the hospital. It wasn't horrible, and I preferred it to talking about what happened. I just wasn't ready to cross that bridge yet. I couldn't go through it again with Beckett, or Max, or even Mrs. Lively.

Going through the details with the police was mortifying enough; it felt like I'd been violated all over again.

While I relished the solitude of the quiet, but also not being alone, I'd put my energy into devising a plan for when I would be released from the hospital later today. After going back and forth, I'd come to the realization that I couldn't be on my own yet, but I also couldn't be alone with a man yet.

Even if that man was Beckett and it meant hurting him in the process of trying to get better.

A hard knock on the door pulled me out of my thoughts. Mrs. Lively and I both watched as the door was pushed open, and Beckett stepped into the doorway. Mrs. Lively stood and gave him a hug.

I tore my eyes away. I didn't want them to see my tears as I choked back a cry. When I turned my head back, my gaze caught on Beckett's. His eyes darted across my face and then down to my neck and chest before snapping back up. He looked away, and I could tell that he was seeing me exactly how I didn't want to be seen. Like a victim.

His footsteps got louder as he made his way into the room and stopped at my bedrail. "They said you could come home today."

When I didn't respond, he reached out and cupped my chin. I flinched, transported back to my apartment and what had happened last night. I swatted his hand away. "Don't," I yelled.

"I... I mean," I muttered, feeling embarrassed. "Please don't touch me right now."

"Ellawyn." He faltered. "I just wanted to look at you while we spoke."

I closed my eyes and let out a breath before I turned my head to meet his gaze. Deciding to rip off the Band-Aid, I cut right to the chase. "I think I'm going to go to my parents' house for a bit."

He frowned. "You don't want to come home to Quimby Grove?"

"Not right now, no."

He searched my face for an explanation. When he didn't find what he was looking for, he pushed for more. "I don't understand."

"What happened last night was bad, Beckett. I want to talk about it with you, but I'm not ready yet. It's too much. I think I need to go be with my family while I work through what happened and start the healing process."

He crossed his arms over his chest. "So you're leaving just like that?" he snapped defensively.

"I won't be gone forever. I want to come back home to Quimby Grove as soon as I can. But I need to be strong enough to do that. I can't step foot in my apartment right now. I'm not ready."

He rubbed his hands over his face as he sat down in the other chair beside Mrs. Lively. "I'm sorry. I understand what you're saying, I do, but why won't you let me help you?"

"Because right now, I'm broken, Beckett. I feel like I've been shattered into a million pieces, and I don't even know where to begin to piece it all back together again. I need to help myself before I can let you back in." I looked from Beckett to the window. It was a dark, stormy day here. It fit. "This is just what I need to do for me," I said, turning my gaze back to his. "I won't feel safe in Quimby Grove, or in my apartment, for a while. I need to work through it first."

Mrs. Lively stood from her chair and leaned over my bedside

for a hug. "Take care of yourself, girl. I think you're doing the right thing," she whispered in my ear before leaving the room.

Beckett stood next and leaned down to press a kiss to my forehead. "I won't leave you, Ellawyn. I promise that I'll be here waiting for you when you're ready," he whispered.

Little did he know, everyone eventually leaves.

And I just watched him do it.

CHAPTER 30

Beckett

A MONTH HAD PASSED since I'd walked out of Ellawyn's hospital room.

Thirty days since I'd seen her beautiful face and heard her melodic voice.

I hadn't realized how much of an important role she had played in my life since returning to Quimby Grove. She was everywhere I looked, and yet she was nowhere at the same time. Every laugh I heard made me search her out in a crowd, desperately seeking the soundtrack of my life for the past year. But each time, she was nowhere to be found.

The past few weeks had been spent mourning the loss of Pops, but also the time I'd lost with Ellawyn. She'd been radio silent since we parted ways at the hospital. It had taken everything in me to not reach out to her. Instead, I opted for silent support. Max and I had gone over to her apartment and rid all the things that could remind her of the incident with Reinhart. Her apartment had been cleaned, things put away, and we'd changed the security system.

With her apartment in order, my focus had shifted back to Starlight Books. Pops had left me part of the store in his will, which I had suspected he would do, so I'd poured even more of my heart and soul into it these past few weeks.

The biggest project I had taken on was to reorganize the book stock and sort and label by genre. Pops had always just left it in pure chaos. I remembered him telling me that he wanted people to really search for a book to make it their own. He believed that people shouldn't be limited based on genre. I thought back to my childhood, when he'd always said to me that people needed to open their minds to all books and allow their hearts to love various types of stories, because that was what life was—a myriad of different stories that all deserved love and respect.

Pop was right in his logic; we all had different stories that needed to be told. If we were so focused on one type of story, we'd miss the beauty that others had put out into the world.

Because of Pops's passion, I made an entire corner of the shop dedicated to him and his love of all books. A wooden sign hung over top that read Pops's Corner with a smaller sign to the side that explained that this corner was a place to find a book worthy of loving regardless of genre. All the books in Pops's Corner were wrapped in newspaper with a large sticker on the front with a bit of info about the book and the price. The wrapped book had a piece of twine around it, tied in a bow. If Ellawyn were here to see it, she'd be proud with how well those books were packaged.

She was a sucker for good packaging.

Another part of the shop had been dedicated to local artists and their artwork. The art corner was placed in the same area where we had the cozy couches and chairs. I wanted people to be able to relax and take in the artwork as they enjoyed their drinks, food, or even a good book. Ellawyn's marionette piece was still on display, with a little gold marker underneath that read SOLD.

With Starlight Books thriving, I'd begun to get back into my role within Walden Advertising. The familiarity of the work felt nice, and I'd missed it. It felt great to be back at the helm, working alongside my employees again. I had officially announced that my work within the company would continue remotely with plans to expand Walden Advertising within Central Pennsylvania, with my VP Kennon heading up the project.

Quimby Grove was where I belonged. Starlight Books was a childhood dream come true. And Ellawyn... Ellawyn was my person—my heart and soul that was walking around this earth. When she did come back to Quimby Grove, I planned to make her mine forever.

If she would have me.

The bell above the door chimed, and Max walked in. "Hey, man," he greeted with a wave.

"Hey," I said as I wiped down the counter. "How's Remnant Hearts today?"

Thankfully, with the help of Ellawyn's rebranding and working to incorporate some new trends, the bar had been on the mend.

"Business has been great. I'm going on vacation to the beach here soon, and I think I'll end up staying more than a day or two this time around." Max joined me behind the counter, making himself at home, and poured a cup of coffee.

"That's awesome. You deserve the break."

He took a drink of his coffee and eyed the display case full of desserts. "So do you, you know," he said as he slid the door open and grabbed a cookie.

I shook my head and laughed. "Yeah, I do." I let my mind drift back to Ellawyn, and my smile was replaced by a frown. "I just need to get a few things in order before I can catch that break."

Fuck, I miss that woman.

Max eyed me over his coffee mug. "She'll be back soon."

"It's just the not knowing that drives me nuts."

"Trust me, I know about that all too well." He nodded toward his bar across the street. "Let's go to the bar for a drink and have a good time."

Closing early seemed like a no-brainer. The shop had been dead as hell today because of the car show in town. I flipped the OPEN sign over and locked up, ready for an evening of drinks.

The moment I entered Remnant Hearts Bar, I immediately relaxed. The familiar scent of beer, fried food, and the lingering smell of smoke from way back when overwhelmed my senses.

Remnant Hearts was home, too.

Max went behind the bar while I snagged a seat. He grabbed two glasses from beneath the counter and poured us each a drink. I took a big swig and relaxed into the sigh of contentment that escaped. "You know, you should start brewing your own beer and shit."

A small smirk appeared at the corner of his mouth. "Actually" —he grabbed a basket of fries from the kitchen window—"it's on the horizon." He slid the fries down to where I was sitting before grabbing another one and returning to his seat. "I've been looking into it, and I think that may be my next project once I'm back from vacation."

A grin spread across my face. "I think that would put this bar on the map, even more than it already is."

We each threw back a few more beers as we remembered stories from our childhood and reminisced about the past. The buzz took over, and I was feeling pretty good. "If Ellawyn comes back, I'm going to propose," I blurted out.

Max froze, his arm midair, holding a beer. "Wait, what?"

"I'm going to propose," I repeated as I took a drink of my beer. "Maybe not the exact instant she comes back to Quimby Grove, but soon after. She's it for me. I just need her to come back to me first."

Max smacked me on the back of the head. "Be patient, asshole," he growled. "She's been through a lot."

My hands went up in surrender. "I know she has, and I want her to take her time working through those things and finding herself again. I'd wait forever for her."

Max and I hung around the bar until it closed and then we closed the place down together. I took on the tasks like bussing tables, stacking chairs, and cleaning floors, while Max did a quick inventory, cleaned the kitchen, and closed out the cash register for the night. By the time we were both done with our work, we'd been drenched in sweat. "You do that whole process each night by yourself?" I asked as I wiped my brow.

He laughed. "Hell no. Usually, I have some other asshole guy here, but my closers called in sick today."

I shot him a glare. "So inviting me here to hang out was a ploy to help you close the bar?" I arched an eyebrow at him.

He burst out in a full-on laugh. "Guilty," he joked. "But now we're even." He flicked off the lights and led us outside. "I've had to deal with your mopey ass for over a month now."

We both laughed and started walking down the block toward our homes. I'd forgotten how peaceful Quimby Grove was in the early morning hours. The streets were bare and the lights that lined the sidewalk led us outside of the main square. I think I preferred this version of Quimby Grove—the quiet, peaceful, and safe version. After a few minutes, Max and I parted ways. He turned down one block toward his apartment, and I kept trekking on toward my house.

Without realizing it, I found myself standing in front of Ellawyn's apartment building. All the lights in the building were out except for one. I did a double take when I realized it was the fourth floor that was lit up—Ellawyn's floor.

She was back. And I knew now that she was what I spent my entire life searching for, like buried treasure that ached to be uncovered and discovered.

And I was going to fight like hell to make her mine.

CHAPTER 31
Ellawyn

After leaving Quimby Grove for a while, I finally felt ready to return and start the healing process back home.

Home.

When I went back to Moon Harbor to heal, I'd become homesick for Quimby Grove. I couldn't pinpoint exactly when Quimby Grove became home for me, but it smacked me right in the face as soon as I stepped into my old childhood bedroom.

I firmly believed that staying with my parents was the best choice for me. Going back to my apartment wouldn't have worked, and staying with Beckett would likely have started our demise. Moon Harbor had been the answer. I'd mostly gotten my shit together, started therapy, and bought a new car.

After everything I'd been through, I came to the realization that I needed to be back with Beckett and Starlight Books. I needed to go back to work, create art, and start living my life again.

When I finally made it back to Quimby Grove, it was close to two in the morning. I turned the key to cut the ignition as I gazed up toward my dark apartment windows. Swallowing down my nerves, I grabbed my purse and exited my car.

The walk up to the entrance seemed longer than it ever had.

When I reached the double doors, I hesitated and looked around. The beautiful bushes and flowers still lined the walkway to the entrance. The vines that wrapped up the side of the building were as beautiful as ever. More flowers and miniature pumpkins lined the steps into the building for decoration. The door was still a wonderful, welcoming shade of emerald.

Gathering all my strength, I pushed the door open and stepped inside. Relief washed over me like a wave crashing into the shore. It pulled me in and drew me back out as fear settled into its place—a constant tug and pull of emotions.

Hesitantly, I climbed the stairs one at a time until I stood outside my apartment door. I squared my shoulders and unlocked the door. Stepping inside, I disarmed the alarm system and placed my purse on my dining room table. I flipped on the lights and scanned the room for any potential threats.

My apartment had been cleaned. Things that were a mess had now been put away in their proper spot.

Beckett.

A smile spread across my face as I checked my entire apartment for an intruder. I started in the kitchen and the living room by looking in closet doors, under the table, and anywhere that someone could hide. Once I cleared those two rooms, I went back into the kitchen and grabbed my butcher knife before heading into my art studio. I flicked on the lights and stepped inside. I instantly felt peace now that I'd been able to see my safe space. This room was so special. I stepped inside and went to my latest piece—the painting of the beach with Max and a mysterious blonde woman. It was left untouched, thankfully. I made a mental note to deliver the painting to Max tomorrow.

The last rooms to check were my bedroom and bathroom.

The door to my bedroom was wide open. I wondered if Beckett had done that on purpose in an effort to make my transition back home easier. As I stepped up to the open doorway, I pretended that Beckett did this for me and leaned in and flicked the light on.

Beckett had cleaned up my room, too.

To see my room like it had been before the incident was both nice and confusing. My mind almost believed that nothing had happened. But I knew better.

With a deep breath, I crossed the threshold into my room and headed straight for the bathroom. When I entered, the first thing I saw was my Bluetooth speaker sitting exactly where I'd left it. When I glanced up and caught my reflection in the mirror, the panic set in as I was transported back in time.

I whipped around and faced the bathtub so I could avoid being attacked behind my back. My heart was racing as my body trembled with fear. My mind flashed back to Reinhart appearing in the mirror behind me as tears slid down my cheeks. Without a second thought, I yanked the shower curtain down and the rod came crashing down with it.

The bathroom was empty.

When I turned and left the bathroom, I came face to face with my bed. The memories flooded in as I was taken back to the moment when he had straddled me and gripped his hands around my throat. Instinctively, my hands rushed up to my neck to protect myself, but when I didn't feel another set of hands on my neck, I was slammed back into reality.

Now to check under the bed. I dropped down onto the floor to lay on my stomach and yanked the duvet cover up.

Nothing there.

Last up, the closet. I walked to the corner of my room and picked up my baseball bat before I whipped the door open and jumped into the middle of my closet, swinging the bat in all direc-tions. By the time I'd finished swinging, most of my clothes were on the floor.

I dropped the bat to the floor and went back into the living room and threw myself onto the couch. A sense of pride bubbled through me as I realized I'd checked the apartment all by myself. I'd considered calling Beckett or Max to help, but I knew I needed to do this on my own.

To take back control.

The rest of the night, or morning, was spent getting things ready in my apartment. I knew I could never sleep here again, so my plan had been to pack up most of my belongings and then go see Beckett at Starlight Books before they closed in the evening.

I almost considered going to see him first thing in the morning, but I didn't want an audience when we spoke again. Not talking to or seeing him was one of the hardest things that I'd had to do.

All I dreamed of was one of his big hugs with his strong arms wrapped tightly around me. I'd drifted off into fantasy land as I remembered our first night together. It had been such a magical evening. He'd made it so special.

I couldn't wait to be with him again.

Mind. Body. Soul.

☾

I **SURPRISED** myself and ended up packing well into the evening. I'd officially been awake for over twenty-four hours. When I glanced around my apartment, I knew it had been worth it. Most of my bedroom, closet, kitchen items, and living room had been packed away.

I had about an hour until Starlight Books closed for the night, so I snagged my clothes and rushed into the bathroom to change and do my hair and makeup.

Before I left the house, I gave myself a once-over in the mirror. When I saw my reflection, the woman staring back at me was smiling. I hadn't smiled like that in so long that I'd almost forgotten what it felt like.

I twisted and turned in front of the mirror as I looked at my outfit. I'd chosen a long black maxi dress and curled my hair in loose curls and pinned up the top. I found some hoop earrings and paired the look with my favorite key necklace.

After grabbing Max's painting and my gift for Beckett, I left my apartment and started the walk to the shop. There was something extra special about walking the streets of Quimby Grove this evening. Maybe it was because I knew I was here to stay or because I was on my way to see Beckett and lay my cards out on the table for him. Either way, it had never felt so right. As I turned the corner onto High Street, I was stunned at the sight before me. The Quimby Grove Theatre was all lit up. The lights flashed on the marquee and illuminated the message: 'Welcome back, Ellawyn.'

My eyes welled with happy tears. Beckett knew I was back in town. I snagged a picture of the marquee with my phone and picked up my pace so I could cross the street and get closer to Beckett. When I was finally close enough to see inside the shop, I stole glimpses of Beckett as he worked on closing.

He was more handsome than I had remembered. His face was full of scruff, his broad shoulders were covered in a black V-neck T-shirt, and a pair of jeans molded to his body. The man looked good in the simplest of things.

When I opened the door to the shop, the bell chimed above me, and I stepped inside. Standing in the entryway, I waited for my man to notice me.

And it didn't take him long.

He looked up at me with the biggest grin spread across his face. He dropped the broom he was holding and rushed for me.

I placed the painting down and dropped Beckett's gift before I took off and ran into his arms. He picked me up and swirled me around as his mouth devoured mine. Our spin slowed as I slid down his body, gripping the back of his head and deepening the kiss. He succumbed to me as he gave back just as much as I took.

When we finally pulled apart, I looked up into his stormy eyes and felt like I'd just returned home to where I belong. "You knew I was back," I whispered.

He ran a finger down the side of my face. "I did."

I shook my head and laughed while I pulled him over toward

the couches. I sat down and dragged him down with me. "How did you know?"

"Well, last night when I was walking home at three in the morning, I found myself standing in front of your place instead of mine." He laced his fingers with mine as he looked down at me. "I happened to look up at the fourth floor and saw that all your lights were on in your apartment."

Heat hit my cheeks. "Yeah, I'd just gotten in a little bit before that. Listen, Beckett—"

"Ellawyn—"

We both laughed as we cut each other off. "You can go first," I offered.

He let out a breath. "The last month has been so hard without you"—he squeezed my hand three times—"and it made me realize just how perfect you and I fit together."

Squeezing his hand back, I nodded for him to go on.

"I know you've been through something horrific recently, but I don't want you to have to go through that alone anymore." He hesitated for a beat. "I want to be with you every day for the rest of my life."

I managed to hold back the tears as I choked out a response. "Good"—I laughed—"because I already packed up most of my apartment."

"You did?"

"Yeah, big time." I shifted on the couch so I could face him and swung my legs onto his lap. "I never wanted you to leave when we were in the hospital, but I also couldn't face you or my apartment right away. I needed to start the healing process on my own, and while I still have a long way to go, I feel better equipped to handle it back here in Quimby Grove now."

He rubbed his hands up and down my legs. "I'm proud of you for taking care of yourself. And now I want to help take care of you, too." He smiled at me. "I love you, Ellawyn."

My heart skipped a beat at the three-word declaration that

had come out of Beckett's mouth. My world stopped for a moment as it sunk in.

Beckett loved me.

He had shown me since day one that I was worthy of love. That I was enough, just the way that I was. That even though I'd been hurt in the past, and treated like I didn't matter, I was deserving of being someone's whole entire world in the most pure, healthy way imaginable.

I needed to show Beckett how I felt. Swinging my legs from his lap, I stood and went back over toward the door where I'd dropped his gift.

"I bought something for you back in Moon Harbor," I said. "And I knew from the moment I saw it that I just had to get it for you." I dragged the wrapped gift back toward the couches and pushed it in front of him. "Open it," I gushed as I sat down beside him again.

He pushed himself to the edge of the couch and unwrapped his gift. He looked up at me with glossy eyes. "You got me a beanbag chair?"

"Kind of." I took his hands in mine. "I got you the exact same beanbag chair that Benji had given you when you were a kid. He told me where to find it when we were traveling together."

Beckett looked back down at the beanbag chair in awe. He ran a hand over the chair as he let the memory of Benji soak in. "Thank you, Ellawyn," he said, returning his gaze to mine. "You have no idea how much this means to me. How much you mean to me. I'm so lucky to have you."

"No, I'm the lucky one."

"Ella—"

I cut him off. "No, let me finish." I stood and faced him. "I came to Quimby Grove in hopes of finding myself. Little did I know that all I really needed was to find Starlight."

I wiped the tears from my eyes. "Finding Starlight changed my life. Finding you, though, made my life so much better. You've helped me grow while also helping me heal. You encouraged me. You supported me. I've given you my love for a long time, but I hadn't realized it. You're everything and I'm so glad I found someone to love, someone who loves me back. I love you, Beckett."

THE END.

Epilogue

Ellawyn

Six months later

Twinkle lights shimmered throughout the square as they lined the streets and wrapped around the trees and lampposts. Icicles hung on the storefront windows, adding a little extra beauty for the annual Ice Fest.

The Ice Fest was an annual tradition here in Quimby Grove, the event lasting all weekend long. Local businesses displayed an ice sculpture outside of their business for the whole town to admire while food carts set up in the Square. Businesses would also give out free samples of their products. There was plenty of hot chocolate and coffee to go around to ensure that you always had a hot beverage in your hand as you wandered around town.

This year was Ellawyn's first time at Ice Fest, and I intended to make it a night to remember.

"Oh, Beckett," she gushed as she led me across the street by the courthouse. "Look"—she pointed toward the alley next to the courthouse—"they have horse and carriage rides." She looked over at me and beamed. "Can we go on a ride?"

In the alley was a beautiful white horse pulling a white

carriage with red velvet seats that held a stack of blankets for the guests to use to cover their legs.

"Of course, baby," I said as I leaned in and gave her a kiss.

"Do you think we should head back to the shop and interact with the folks who are looking at our sculpture?" she questioned as she led us over to a hot chocolate stand. She grabbed two cups and handed me one. "I love listening to people talk about our sculpture."

Ellawyn had done a wonderful job at coming up with the design of our sculpture. She had wanted the sculpture to be of an open book with the words "Once upon a time..." written out. Beside the book was a small ice sculpture that looked like a cup of coffee.

It turned out wonderfully.

"How about we do that after the carriage ride?" I offered instead.

She nodded as we walked toward the carriage and were greeted by the coachman. "Hello," Ellawyn said as she took his hand and stepped up into the carriage. "Thank you for the ride," she said after he had taken his seat.

The carriage took off down the back part of the alley. The rhythmic padding of the hooves on the pavement had soothed us both as I pulled Ellawyn into my arms.

The carriage ride had been an unexpected addition to our participation of Ice Fest, and I knew it was perfect for what I was about to do. "Hey, Ellie." I lifted her chin to meet my gaze. "Do you think this night could get any better?"

She smiled up at me, the tip of her nose rosy from the cold. "Anything we do together is perfect to me," she said.

"I'm glad you think so." I slid my arm out from underneath her and kneeled on one knee in front of her. I reached into my jacket pocket and pulled out a black velvet box. Popping it open, I displayed a beautiful cushion cut diamond ring with accent stones down the side of the diamond.

Her mouth dropped open as her hands flew to cover her

mouth. Her eyes glistened with tears as she slid to the edge of her seat. "Beckett..."

"From the day you entered my life, you've made it better. The challenges we've faced, the heartache we've endured, and the laughter we've shared wouldn't have been the same without you at my side. You're everything to me, and I want nothing more than to make you mine. Ellawyn Rose Calloway, will you marry me?"

She nodded through tears as she lowered her left hand. After pulling the ring from the velvet box, I slid it onto her finger. As soon as the ring was settled, she dropped to the floor of the carriage and fell into my arms.

"Yes, Beckett, I'll marry you," she said through tears and kisses. "I can't wait for our forever."

Acknowledgments

Whenever I started this journey, I didn't anticipate making friends right away, let alone finding my soul sister, Kate McWilliams, as quickly as I did. Kate had gone from soul sister to best friend in no time. From talking about shared hobbies and the similarities within our lives, to being with each other every step of the way within our self-publishing journeys, I don't know what I'd do without her. She's been my rock and my sounding board. Finding Starlight wouldn't exist without her support. I'm incredibly grateful to have her in my life.

To my friends, old and new, I appreciate you so much. Miranda Snyder, for always dreaming with me and encouraging me throughout this whole process. I'm so incredibly thankful for your friendship. When we both showed up crazy early on our first day of work all those years ago, I didn't just get a coworker out of it. I got a best friend for life. To Summer, Kathy, and Jaime, your support throughout this journey has been incredible.

To the writing community that welcomed me with open arms, your encouragement and support mean the world to me. I never truly felt alone when I've had all of you in my corner. There's too many to name but you know who you are. It wouldn't have been the same without you.

To my editors, Amanda and Jeanine, I appreciate you both more than you realize. Thank you so much.

To my friend Jonnie Baker of Relic Hearts for allowing me to use a few lines of your lyrics within this book and for always being an inspiration when it comes to chasing dreams. You have an incredible gift when it comes to songwriting. I'm so incredibly proud of you and all you've accomplished.

To my dearest son, Kohler. When I first started this book in 2021, he was ten years old. We sat outside on the swings as I told him that I wanted to write a book. He was so supportive of me as we talked about my ideas for the foundation of the book. Later that evening he came up to me and told me how much he also wanted to write a book. His love and support is everything to me and I cannot wait to continue to support his hopes and dreams throughout his life.

And finally, a huge thank you to anyone who took a chance on reading Finding Starlight. It means more than you know.

Shannon Nikole is a lover of books, art, true crime, ghost hunting and all things Disney. She runs on sarcasm and Pepsi Zero. When she doesn't have her nose in a book, she can be found getting into shenanigans in Pennsylvania with her son.

facebook.com/ShannonNikoleAuthor

instagram.com/ShannonNikoleAuthor

goodreads.com/shannonnikole

tiktok.com/@ShannonNikoleAuthor

bookbub.com/authors/shannon-nikole

amazon.com/author/shannonnikole

www.ingramcontent.com/pod-product-compliance
Lightning Source LLC
Chambersburg PA
CBHW032155190726
48290CB00005BC/1574